RESCUE

RESCUE

a novel

by

MICHAEL HEATH

Designed by: Vince Pannullo

Printed in the United States of America by
One Communications LLC 800-621-2556

ISBN: 978-1-7321478-0-5

Dedicated to every dog in need of a safe and loving home. May you be rescued.

Chapter 1

CAGE 49 was the Chihuahua's home. Not that a cage is ever a home, any more than a prison cell is a home. It is where the ten-week-old puppy lived. Where he resided. The place in which he existed. The Chihuahua paced nervously on a metal-meshed floor that sored growing foot pads while fecal matter mixed with dry food scattered the tight quarters. A wire-held water bottle hung emptied since the morning before as a square of urine-soaked cardboard covered three-quarters of the cage. The Chihuahua's situation was like the other seventy-three puppies being raised at the Tender Love Kennel; a farm sub-operation housed in a windowless metal shed. Cages like the one in which he was held were positioned side by side in a row of nine and stacked four high. Each confinement housed one or two puppies. Across from the block of cages were three larger containments made of wood planks and chicken wire. Crammed into those cells were six to ten bigger dogs that still had not reached maturity. Mature dogs were much harder to sell than puppies. Older dogs were eventually put into the service of breeding or taken to the field where they met death at the end of a rifle. All cages were filled with dirt, neglect, confusion, and fear.

Life did not begin in the cage. The puppy of tan fur with white markings was brought into the world some forty feet away in the breeding room. There, in a filthy makeshift stall, the Chihuahua was born with six siblings to a mother on her unprecedented fourth litter. Knee high walls of two-by-fours and plywood separated four breeding mothers. Floors were nothing more than grimy carpeting laid on bare cement slab. The Chihuahua lived in that cramped place for the first half of his puppyhood. Those days were filled with the warmth of a mother's belly and nourishment from overworked teats. A red motherly tongue cleaned the puppy's eyes and face. Gradually, the Chihuahua played with siblings while watched by a mother who rarely moved from her side-lying position. If the puppy knew any happiness, it was there with his mother, brothers, and sisters. Love was found in the togetherness of a warm maternal tummy.

There came a traumatic day when the calendar reached a full five weeks, the day that the fat man, wearing an everyday attire of overalls and truckers cap, entered the building. He picked up a dingy cardboard box off the floor and walked past the cages into the breeding room. He leaned over, staring down at the Chihuahua and her family. The mother barked distressing yelps, alarming her brood that huddled urgently to her fleshy stomach. The Chihuahua peeked up at the fat man with the ruddy complexion and Coke-bottle glasses. The Chihuahua's mother growled, snapping at the man's hand as it dropped toward the puppies. She sensed the threat. An instinct to protect her brood. The defensive action only caused the fat man to laugh, flashing a mouthful of nicotine-stained teeth. The hand reached down and, one by one, pinched a puppy by the scruff of the neck, snatching each whelp from its mother. Then his turn came and he was lifted toward the box. He looked down at his mother who lay there in a worn, bloated body. She snapped jaws futilely at the thieving hand. The fat man continued laughing. The young Chihuahua wanted to go back. He also wanted his brothers and sister to be back with their mother. Distress. Sorrow. The puppy never knew fear until that very day. He was scared. Very scared. The mother's sad watery eyes connected with the young Chihuahua. The look of sadness. A tearful goodbye.

The Chihuahua frantically crisscrossed the box to find a way back, hearing the motherly cries. Siblings wept. The Chihuahua wanted badly to be back with her. Puppy cries meant nothing to the fat man. The mother was a breeder with nothing left to give. All bred out. Her only hope was adoption. An old friend of the fat man, a lady named Grace, occasionally adopted the birthed-out breeders and kept them on a small farm one town over. There, breeders lived out their retirement in a warm home with plenty of backyard. But to the fat man, the mothers were nothing more than puppy factories. Just a business. Purebred Chihuahua puppies sold to pet stores for six hundred dollars. Direct sales to dog owners brought the illegal kennel upwards to a thousand dollars. Fertility was a ticking time clock. No rest between birthing. Always nursing or pregnant. The more puppies, the more money. The fat man carried the box out to the middle of the warehouse. The Chihuahua was lifted into Cage 49 and kept there for the last five weeks. For the puppy it was a miserable life. Food was inconsistent. Heat was unreliable. Love was non-existent. The Chihuahua wanted to be back next to the warm belly of his mother. There, he could suck the nourishing milk from her ever-ready teats. Next to her he could snuggle in her warmth. Every day the Chihuahua paced the tight quarters of Cage 49. Young eyes focused on the breeding room. Endless back and forth. Non-stop yearning for his mother. Barks. Yelps. They were calls to her. She was in there. The Chihuahua knew it. He missed her.

As deplorable as the conditions were in the small quarters, his housing was a bit better than most. The number four meant that the cage was the fourth, or top stack. Nine was the last of the row. Lower cages were susceptible to urine and excrement that did not stay on the cardboard flooring. Body wastes often rained down on the dogs below, causing eye infections, fur matting, ailments, and discomforts. The end cage also gave the Chihuahua a view of the breeding room.

Yelps and cries echoed throughout the metal shed. The innocents lived in such wretched conditions only because fate was so unfortunate as to bring them into the cruel underbelly of the puppy mill world. There, the mission was breeding in the pursuit of revenue. Breeder mothers were overbred and under tended. No weaning of the newly born. Puppies taken from their mother's teats too early only to be turned over to solid food. Little or no human contact. No affection. No medical attention. Food was a ledger expense, so it was dispensed sparingly in pursuit of low overhead. Water poured into never- cleaned bowls was always contaminated. Urine and fecal matter festered into a poisonous ammonia odor that permeated the entire building.

A portable kerosene heater set at seventy-five degrees kept the New Jersey winter at bay. Chilled air triggered the thermostat, causing a welcome roar. A burner glowed red. Dogs pressed close to the front of cages to get near drifting warm air. At three that morning, the heater began to sputter. Not enough fuel. Then a flame-out. In the remote area on the edge of the New Jersey Pine Barrens, outside temperatures stood in the teens. It did not take long before winter reached its cruel hand inside the uninsulated steel building. A single lightbulb hanging from a ceiling wire was the only source of illumination. The warehouse was nearly dark. Falling temperatures amplified existing misery. Temperatures fell to twenty-seven degrees. Skim ice formed on water bowls. The ten-week-old puppy in Cage 49 shivered uncontrollably. Incessant pacing. The Chihuahua in Cage 49 could no longer rest on the bed of damp cardboard.

He searched the far side of the warehouse to the breeding room. Through the doorless opening the Chihuahua saw the glow of overhead heating lamps that burned twenty-four hours a day. To the owners, the kennel canines were nothing more than livestock. No socialization. No playing. Paws burned from uric acid. Respiratory problems aggravated by lingering ammonia. Rodents competed for the little food rationings. Water dishes floated foreign substances.

Barking distress calls were fruitless. Yelps turned to whimpers. An instinctive quieting to conserve energy. Dogs held in group cages huddled together in shivering mounds. Warehouse silence signaled a death knell. Dogs on the verge of dying, some giving up.

Hours later the Chihuahua in Cage 49 heard something, a familiar crunching noise. Sounds of boots stepping into frozen snow. It meant the ponytail girl was coming. Just her. He recognized those footsteps. More fast-paced than the lumbering, heavy footfalls of the fat man. It was never good when the fat man came. All the puppies feared the fat man. He shouted at the young dogs and banged the cages. Sometimes the ponytail girl would yell at him to stop but often continued the sadistic pleasure it brought him. The meanness. The nastiness. The puppies were afraid of him and would retreat to the farthest corner of their cages when he passed by. The fat man normally came by just to fix something or put dogs in portable cages and load them into the van backed up to an open overhead door. Dogs pulled out of the cages and placed in the van were never seen again. No dog wanted to go with the fat man. They were terrified of him. Some started crying when he took them from their cage. *Hush up!* He yelled at them and that stopped the crying. They would retreat into a shiver of fear.

The sound of walking feet got closer. Some of the other Chihuahuas heard the sound, too. They also knew they were the better footsteps. The Chihuahua yelped and yelped, causing some of the other dogs to yelp. The metal sound of an outside latch. The knob turned and door opened. Winter morning darkness. More frigid air. A flip of the switch. Lights brightened the room. The ponytail girl rubbed hands on the sides of her arms; an attempt to warm herself. She breathed in the cold warehouse air.

"Oh, no," she said to herself.

The ponytail girl ran over to the heater. Twist and turns to the thermostat dial. Quick steps to a kerosene can. She poured fuel into the tank. As she did, the suffering dogs barked for some relief. A couple of puppies laid listless on the bottom of their cages, their bodies unable to withstand hours of low temperatures. A hollow clank of the empty can dropping to the rock-solid floor. The push of a heater button. A welcome roar consumed the warehouse.

The Chihuahua in Cage 49 watched the ponytail girl go to work, hand-shoveling dry food from a feed bin into a scroungy plastic pail. She laid the bucket on a table cart. A turn of a faucet. A garden hose scribbled on the floor. Water spit from an opened nozzle end. The ponytail girl bent and twisted the hose to loosen the ice clogging the passageway. A lift of the curled rubber tubing. A tangled drop. The crack of breaking ice. Water streamed weakly out the end. The ponytail girl filled two one-gallon plastic milk bottles.

The shed warmed. Heated air reached the Chihuahua in Cage 49. Then the reminder of hunger and thirst. Stomach pangs. Sticky mouth. Anxious pacing. Puppy eyes studied every movement of the ponytail girl. He wanted food. He wanted water. A look over to the breeding room. The open entryway. The heating lamps glowing red over makeshift stalls. It was what the Chihuahua did every day, all day long.

The wondering, the searching. There was one thing the Chihuahua in Cage 49 wanted more than food and water.

He wanted his mother.

Chapter 2

ROGER Wilson steered the ten-year-old Subaru Outback down I-195 toward Trenton, a ride consisting of miles of green-needled jack pines, barren trees made naked for winter and dormant farmland. The stretch of east-to-west road connected the Jersey Shore to the New Jersey Turnpike and placed travelers closer to the Garden State's capital. The hour and a half drive was Roger's once-a-month meeting with his parole officer.

Off the Turnpike he took the Route 29N exit that put the car within a couple of miles of the small metropolis's grittier part. Once a bustling manufacturer of most things rubber and ceramics, the urban area experienced the decades-long economic decline as production moved offshore. Good jobs left; people moved away. Lower-paying jobs that remained led to cheap housing. Cramped urban streets became more compact when single-family homes were converted into multiple dwellings. Roofs sported three or four satellite dishes and an equal number of mailboxes. Cars and work vans. More vehicles serving the locals than places to put them. Littered streets. Crime. Murder.

Drugs. People wandering around with faces of hopelessness. Others wore expressions of simple resignation.

The Trenton Lower Bridge displayed neon, stating *Trenton Makes, The World Takes.* The slogan was a relic. A cruel reminder of another time. A bygone era when the city made things, shipping products around the globe. Those days disappeared, with no promise of ever returning. Production that once belonged to Trenton escaped to foreign locales. There was only one shining spot: no toll lanes. Travel on the bridge remained free.

Government was now the business in Trenton. Market Street made up the epicenter for all things state bureaucratic. It was where the state capitol building, with its golden globe, rose above other stone buildings serving as the home of legislative, administrative, divisional, agency and bureau offices. Maybe the most important of the structures was the state courthouse where New Jersey laws were made, interpreted, and enforced. In its halls were the state probation and parole office. Roger was going there. It was time for a monthly drug test and to sit with Jamal, his parole officer. Drugs were not Roger's thing. He never ingested the stuff. Not marijuana or anything else. Not even before the arrest. The drug test was easy. Jamal was another story.

Downtown was a bright spot for Trenton, a zone catering to the government employees with lines of vibrant stores and restaurants. The revitalized area usually bustled anyway, but that day all pay-parking lots were full. Traffic cops fronted barricades, waving cars away from areas normally open to traffic. The detours disrupted Roger's plan. Usually, he went to one of the pay-parking lots, handed an attendant a ten-dollar bill and left the car for a five-minute walk to the office. Now those lots were not accessible, forcing Roger to abort the normal routine. He drove past overflowing parking lots and idling, curb-hugging buses. Then, hurried turns onto side streets. There, Roger found neighborhoods full of cars left by drivers forced into the same circumstance.

A drive down an unfamiliar street. A left and then a left. More cars lining the sides. Another street away. Houses more ramshackle the farther he drove from downtown. A turn onto Liberty Street. More vehicles parked bumper to bumper. A tight spot on the oncoming lane side. A tight K-turn, then a parallel park. Eyes studied the deteriorating surroundings. There was something ominous about the neighborhood; Roger felt it. He did not let himself get too wrapped up in what was there. It was morning, broad daylight. He would only be there a couple of hours, maybe not even. Across the way a shiny black Escalade with tinted windows stood on chrome wheels. Too new and clean for the mixture of tricked-out rides and beat-up autos belonging to the street. Too flashy for the visitor cars that were only borrowing space for a few hours. It lay out front of one of the many once-proud homes whose owners either fell on hard times or simply stopped caring. Faded vinyl siding. Leaning front porch steps. Stained curtains. Barred windows. Roger got out of the car and looked around. Graffiti on road signs. Sneakers dangling overhead on a telephone wire. Not a place Roger wanted to be after dark.

A backseat window was used to check himself out. Combing fingers raked through thinning hair. The beard grown after the prison release was an attempt to compensate for early baldness. Quick fingertip strokes through facial bristles.

He locked up the car. A cell phone glance. It was 10:45 a.m. Fifteen minutes to get to the appointment. Jamal, a former Marine, did not tolerate lateness. He knew it. The edict drilled into Roger at the very first parole meeting. Roger was never late. He was athletic. A surfer. A former high school football player in top shape. Roger was going to need that athleticism to run several blocks. He started. The black Escalade on his left. A driveway filled with an old Mercury Marquis resting on four flat tires. Roger speculated about the broken-down vehicle. It probably belonged to the homeowner. Maybe an ailing grandfather or other aged relative. Roger peeked toward the backyard. There was a Pitbull Terrier chained to a metal stake. Roger stopped to get a better look. The dog shivered. A food dish was tipped over. A water bowl looked empty. A doghouse nothing more than a plastic barrel laying on its side containing a bed of dirty straw. Roger stared at the animal. He thought about canine's suffering. *Poor dog*.

Snow and ice topped most of the sidewalks. Roger chose to run on the streets where tire wear exposed the blacktop. Up to Market Street and then a left. He ran like the marathoner he was before the arrest. Three marathons in three years. No records or ribbons but respectable times. He paced himself and liked the freedom of moving past cars that were stuck in traffic. He made it to the Brendan Byrne building named after a former governor. Then the security drill. Empty pockets. Slow walk through a metal detector. Smiles from uniformed personnel. They recognized him.

Another phone glance: *9:58*. Two minutes to go. People congregated in front of the elevators. No time to wait. Roger opened the steel door to the stairway. He ascended four flights, taking two and three steps at a time. Then quick steps across a lobby to a front desk. The squeaky thump of sneakers on waxed tile. Several people milled around a busy receptionist, each vying for attention. Roger helped himself to a registration book, adding a sloppy signature. He headed toward the offices.

"Hold it," said the receptionist to Roger before turning her head toward the cubicles centering the room. She spoke over her shoulder in a raised voice. "Can someone come up here and give me some help?"

A gray-haired woman meandered to the desk, chewing a mid-morning snack. Eyeglasses hung from a neck chain. She recognized Roger, who stood anxiously.

"Are you here for Jamal?" asked the woman, knowing the answer.

"Yes."

"Jamal!" yelled the woman in the direction of his office.

"Send him in," was the response.

Roger took quick steps into the opened-door office. Jamal was tall, black with a bald head and the serious look of a drill sergeant. He threw a finger at the wall where the hands of the clock said 10:06.

"You're late."

Roger took another look at his phone. He held the screen up to Jamal.

"10:01."

"We go by that clock," said Jamal evenly.

"Sorry, Jamal." Roger detected nervousness in his voice. "I couldn't get to my regular parking lot. I had to park on a street far away. There was no place to go but there. The streets were blocked off."

"No kidding. That happens here in Trenton. The

vice president is coming to town to address a group of mayors, so parking is at a premium. You need to plan for things like this." Jamal's body language relaxed, an encouraging sign that the parole officer was loosening up a bit.

"I parked on Liberty Street and ran all the way here."

"Liberty Street? That's a tough street. Rough area. You got gangbangers and drug dealers over that way. You would never want to be there at night. Maybe not even in the day."

"I'm going back there to get my car and that's it. Next time I come to Trenton I will give myself more time. You know, in case someone big is in town." Roger fell into a metal chair. The squishy exhale of a high green cushion.

A window reflection behind Jamal. A woman standing in the doorway. "Jamal, sorry to interrupt. Can I speak with you a moment? It's about the case you saw earlier."

The parole officer raised his head to stare past Roger. A slight turn back. Apologetic eyes. "Let me take care of this. I won't be long."

Roger lifted shoulders in an unconcerned shrug. He did not care that some of the parole meeting would be taken up by a side conference. He hated the meetings. To him they were unproductive. A waste of time. Just some bureaucratic activity that solved little. Privately he was amused by the term *case*. It sounded so euphemistic. He was not a parolee or a felon; he was a case. Roger dropped a forehead corner into a hand and gently shook it.

Eyes bounced around bland walls decorated with Marine regalia, wood and gold-plated achievement plaques, and a framed associate's degree from the local community college. Several family pictures adorned the government desk. Roger glanced at the window. Not out of it. Just at it. His mind drifted back to what brought him there. A chance encounter with an old high-school acquaintance named Quincy. An offer of cash to drive to West Virginia to pick up bottles of OxyContin pills hidden in an old bedroom chest. He initially dismissed the idea. Roger was not a drug guy. Surfer buddies could not even get him to try pot. Anything criminal was not his thing. It was mostly his upbringing. He grew up in a strict household. Like Jamal, his father was an ex-marine and lived it, never giving up the tell-tale crewcut. The overbearing father wanted Roger to follow in his footsteps. He wanted Roger to join the Marines and then become a professional firefighter. A father who mapped out a life for him.

Roger detested everything Marines. The *Semper Fidelis* mementos hung around the home were a constant reminder of his father's past, his father's identity. The *oo-rah!* shouts. "Outstanding" his favorite Marine word. The discipline thing, being told how to live and what to do. That was Roger's father, not him.

He thought of himself as an entrepreneur. The successful T-shirt company he started from scratch as a teenager in the garage grew into a storefront establishment conducting both retail and wholesale transactions. A business that grew so fast that inventory growth far exceeded the merchandise delivery and receipts for in-house orders. Cash-flow problems worsened in winter months. Money then poured in when spring arrived, as tourists flowed into the area. Roger thrived on the knife's edge, living the action a start-up owner faced. No matter the challenge, he always managed to figure a way to succeed.

Back then, he invested in a new silk-screener that would double production, but the deposit and monthly payments set him back financially. Money was tighter that fourth winter. He was scared. Worried about payroll. Concerned that a layoff could mean losing trained workers. Repossession notices threatened the loss of a work van. Delinquent rent payments could not be covered. Money offered to pick up the haul would not solve all problems but would do a lot to keep creditors happier until Roger could get his hands on spring receipts. Quincy hounded him. *C'mon, I need you to pick up the Oxy, easy money and it's no big deal.*

In desperation he reconsidered the proposition. The old high-school acquaintance told him what to do. An address on an index card led to a West Virginia consignment shop fronting a drug trafficking enterprise. Leave at midnight for the ten-hour drive down. If anyone asked him anything, all he had to say was that he was visiting relatives. Quincy even gave Roger the name of a cousin living in the vicinity. Go to the consignment shop in the morning and get the chest. He recalled the nervousness. It was a big deal. Transporting narcotics over state lines was a crime carrying stiff penalties. He mentioned the concerns. Quincy admitted there was risk but with ten thousand dollars waiting at day's end, he was being compensated for the little gamble he was taking. He added that there were other people who made the trip and wanted to do it again but sending the same people too soon could draw suspicion. No one got caught because couriers were used in wide rotations. Roger wanted to believe Quincy. That it would all be easy. He also needed the money.

Roger drove the work van out of the area on a cool, breezy March midnight. Temperatures hovered in the mid-thirties. He drove the rest of the night and was deep into West Virginia before sunrise. By the time he was an hour away from Williamson, a yellow sun showed through the windshield. Endless blacktop curled through mountain passes as Appalachian morning mist drifted down from higher elevations.

Signs invited tourists to Civil War sites. Trailer homes. Pickup trucks. Junk littered yards. Mud covered roads. Poverty. Unemployment.

Guilt coursed through Roger. He knew then what he was doing was wrong. There was the self talk. Promises that it was a one-time situation. He would never do anything like it again. That day, he was committed. No turning back. Quincy's handlers were real criminals. There could be violent reprisals for a failed operation. Quincy's people were counting on the shipment. They would not take lightly to anyone weak-kneed. A deal was a deal. Roger had to keep going. He needed to complete the assignment.

Roger drove through the town of Williamson, the epicenter of the opiate crisis. A place where pain centers lined the boulevard. Rogue doctors prescribed copious amounts of pain medication. Pill poppers flocked to the municipality. Some were people with real chronic conditions in search of pain relief. Others were recreational users who fell into the dark hole of addiction. The city earned the infamous moniker of Pilliamson. Roger witnessed underdressed drug abusers standing in clinic lines, tolerating cold morning air to get their fix. The more he saw, the greater the remorse. Roger realized the mission was part of something awful. He also knew better than to over think it. Roger was in. Eyes were turned away. No point in staring. A look straight ahead.

The cell phone GPS led the way. It took him to the consignment shop. A twenty-something woman behind the counter. Hair dyed jet black, waif figure, tattooed arm sleeves and lip ring. She gazed at Roger. A nod of the head. The woman knew who he was. The van out front told her as much. Roger milled awkwardly as a faux shopper. Racks and racks of used clothing. A stale, old-closet smell. Store edges cluttered with tacky furniture and used toys. She signaled to a bored teenager distracted by an iPhone. Bad complexion. Rumpled attire. The order was given to load the van. The kid disappeared behind a curtain of stringed beads and returned hand trucking a scratchy particle-board chest of drawers wrapped in clear plastic.

Roger recalled the ride back. Paranoid eyes searched the rearview mirror for a trailing patrol car that never came. Two hours past. Then three and four. Roger relaxed. Easy. Just a ride. No big deal. He was a mule. He reconsidered previous thoughts. Maybe he would do it again. He could rent a van and take the drive. Another ten grand, then another until all the bills were caught up and then he would quit. He got to Quincy's mother's house that evening. That was the drop-off spot. A quiet residential neighborhood. Someplace safe. Quincy climbed into the van. The guy was flustered, stammering. A big blow out fight with his mother. The older woman no longer wanted strange happenings on her property. *Who could blame her?* New plans. He instructed Roger to go to a self-storage facility. Drop the chest there. The money was waiting in the unit. Roger easily recalled the dread he felt. That sinking feeling. A bad omen. An arrangement unraveling. A story plot with an unsettling twist. Roger could sense a bad ending. There was nothing he could do. All he wanted was to get the drugs out of his van. Another reconsideration. *He would never do it again.*

The van rolled into the storage facility. Heart thumping. Adrenaline coursing through every vein. No one around. Clean pavement. Pylon lighting. Empty and barren as an abandoned movie set. Quincy told him where to go. Roger did as he was instructed. One row up and three rows over. A cold Saturday evening. He stopped the vehicle and turned to Quincy. He remembered what he said. *Let's just get this over with.*

Then the sudden appearance of a plain clothed New Jersey state trooper in the passenger side, gun pointed. Then a blue uniform. More law enforcement. Turning his head, Roger saw an officer through the windshield. Doors pulled opened. Orders barked. *Hands up. Exit the vehicle.* A strong grip pulled Roger from the driver's seat. A violent slam to the ground.

In the window reflection, Roger saw Jamal reenter the office. A change in demeanor. He was apologetic for the absence. Jamal explained that the side conference took longer than expected. The allotted one-half hour of time was nearly reached. Jamal tried to salvage some of the meeting. The usual questions about the job at the Amazon warehouse. Some notes taken.

Six months since his release. Six meetings. Roger asked a question. "Can we begin doing this every other month?"

Jamal's expression got serious. "Every other month? No. Not now. But when the year is up, we can consider it. Let me put a note in your file." Jamal typed a message onto the screen and then spoke. "Maybe we can do a phone meeting every other month then. Come in one month, call in one month. We'll talk about it when a year is up."

"Thanks."

"Go up the hall and do the urine test. If you're clean, you can leave."

Roger completed the screening and was given permission by a nurse to go home. He walked back out onto a street dreary with overcast skies and low temperatures. There were regrets for only wearing a zip-up hooded sweatshirt on such a cold day. Ungloved hands were stuffed into pockets. Then a quickened pace.

Roger reached the car. The black Escalade was gone. Keys pulled from a pant pocket. Eyes were drawn past the broken-down Mercury Marquis to the backyard. There was the Pit Bull he noticed earlier. The canine took some sips of water. In the time he was gone someone up righted the bowl and filled it with dog food. That was all the attention the dog was getting, some food and water. The poor dog still looked cold and miserable. The Pit Bull stepped back and forth, imprisoned by a chain anchored to a stake driven into the ground. Roger wondered how people could be so neglectful.

The dog stared at him. Roger stood in the middle of the street staring back. Eyes fixated to one another. A woof-woof. The dog spoke to Roger. He understood what the Pit Bull said.

Help me.

Chapter 3

THE Chihuahua poked his nose at the wire mesh wall of Cage 49. The ponytail girl moved around the corner of the warehouse, adding the bucket of food, water bottles, whisk broom, cardboard squares to the cart. Since the heater was pointed toward the dogs, the warmth had not reached to the corner and the ponytail girl exhaled dragon breaths into the chilly interior air. The Chihuahua searched the limited surroundings for the first hints of warmth to reach him. An awakened stomach also kept the puppy watching the ponytail girl move the shaky, squeaky-wheeled cart. He was hungry.

As the air warmed, anxious Chihuahua puppies thawed from their huddled inactivity. The yips and yelps were not for warmth but for food and water. The Chihuahua in Cage 49 joined in, nervously moving back and forth. Drifts of warm air finally reached his snout. A glance down the aisle. The ponytail girl opened the doors of individual cages. Quick sweeps cleaned fecal matter and bits of dry food onto the floor. Food scooped into empty troughs. Water poured into slimy dishes and dry water bottles. Nourishment was a short respite for the scared animals. Cage 49 was at the end of the aisle; always one of the last to be tended to. The Chihuahua yelped to the ponytail girl. His way of saying he was hungry. A way of saying, *hurry up!*

The ponytail girl pulled a lifeless dog from a cage. It happened sometimes. She shook the flesh and bones like an old rag. A finger flick to the dog's cheek, a mechanical attempt to wake the puppy out of a frozen slumber. No results. No reaction. No waking up from the death sleep. The canine was dead. Unable to survive the conditions. A few steps to the garbage pail. A lift of the lid. The ponytail girl dropped the puppy into the can where it disappeared.

She went back to work. Cold and scared, the little dogs bumped into one another within their cramped spaces. Each poor puppy anticipating the needed breakfast. No human touch. No love or affection. The animals were nothing more than a commodity. Some were diseased. Some eyes swollen red with infection. Hair matted with filth. Sore foot pads. No comfort for the needy creatures.

More warmth reached the Chihuahua in Cage 49. He paced feverishly, anxious for the ponytail girl to bring food and water. A growling stomach. A dry mouth. He looked down at the food dish. All it contained was a dead bug.

The ponytail girl got to Cage 49. She opened the door to the cage and reached a rubber-gloved hand into the Chihuahua's metal-meshed home. A finger pinch to the urine-soaked cardboard floor, nasty with moist fecal matter. It was pulled from the cage as the Chihuahua shook against the back wall. Then the ponytail girl swept the cage while the Chihuahua dodged the hard pointed bristles. Debris fell onto the floor at the ponytail girl's feet. More rained down onto the unfortunate denizens below. She swept the rest of the cages, adding food and water to each. The ponytail girl dragged the garbage can closer. The lid was off. From the Cage 49 vantage point, the Chihuahua peered inside. There lay the deceased puppy dishonored in so much trash. A sibling of the same litter. The Chihuahua was confused. The sight caused fear in the poor dog. Then sadness. Sorrow welled up in the Chihuahua's stomach and into its throat. He did not want to end up in the garbage can. The Chihuahua retreated to the farthest corner of the cage in search of a sanctum. He wept. He shook. He looked toward the breeding room with its glowing heating lamps. A puppy yearning for his mother.

The ponytail girl leaned the broom and went to work on more cages below. She slammed a door. The harsh noise caused a body shake. More food dispensing. More cleaning. The Chihuahua in Cage 49 waited. What else could he do?

Scary thoughts of a deceased dog at the bottom of the garbage pail. Cries of fear from other puppies.

The Chihuahua shook. Not cold shivers, but nervous shivers. Shaking. Uncontrollable shaking. Whole body rattles. Shakes and shakes. The ponytail girl moved away from the front of the cage. He felt slightly better when she was not right there moving about and making noise. A puppy stomach hungering for nourishment. A couple of wobbly steps. Water sips and bites of food.

A hissing sound came from the plastic garbage can as it was dragged across the hard floor. The ponytail girl swung the bin into the corner and grabbed a push broom. Swept to the middle of the aisle was a putrid pile of dog hair, fecal matter, dry food, and soiled cardboard. As the ponytail girl swept the floor there came the sound of heavy footfalls. Dread landed on the cage occupants like a rainstorm. It was the fat man. The dogs knew it. All the Chihuahuas hated the fat man. Sounds of his approaching caused all the puppies to mill around nervously. He tormented the young dogs. Side fist bangs to the cages. Face to cage barking imitations to scare the puppies. Sinister laughing. A mean prison guard who relished the command he held over the helpless subjects.

Crunching sounds of footsteps landing into frozen snow increased. The fat man entered the building. A door left carelessly open as he slammed boot soles on the floor to loosen collected ice and snow. Frigid outside air reached the cages.

"Grandpa, would you shut the door?"

"All right," he said through a gravelly smoker's voice. A door slam. Then more foot stomping. He looked over at his granddaughter. He wore a canvas hat and lumber jacket. A bulbous liquor nose of a heavy drinker hung above his curious smirk.

"It's cold in here. You saving money on kerosene?" said the fat man mischievously.

"Of course, it's cold in here. You must have forgot to add fuel to the heater. It must have been off half the night. I'm just now heating up the dogs."

"They're dogs, Ally. They have fur. They can deal with a little cold."

"No, they can't Grandpa. Not that cold. It must have been twenty-five degrees when I got in here. We lost one. I hope we don't lose any more."

The snarky grin fell away. The fat man started to walk over. "Did you remove the dead one from the cage?"

"Of course, I did," said the ponytail girl evenly. "It's in the garbage can. Make sure you dump the garbage. We don't need a rotting dead dog smelling up the place."

"The live ones stink up the place enough. Throwing a dog in the garbage is like throwing six hundred bucks away."

"I hope you did not expect me to keep it, did you?"

The man looked into the cages but appeared distracted by a thought. Then gave half a laugh. "No, no. I'm just saying that when we lose one, it's money out the window."

"Well, maybe you can remember to keep kerosene in the heater. That's your job."

The man did not respond but instead stood in front of the heater to get warm for a moment. Then lumbered toward the back of the building where the breeding mothers stayed. "No problem with the electric heating, right?"

"No, the back room is warm. But mother number three is not doing anything, now that she is all breeded out. Just sitting there. Thought you were going to get that crazy lady to take her. You know, Grace. The one who takes some of our breeders. May want to move her from the stall and give it to a young one."

"Finally spoke to that do-gooder yesterday. Now she says her husband is sick and can't take any more dogs. She's got seven dogs, you know. Four of them are breeders she took from us. Four that I didn't have to waste a bullet on. But the one back there, I have been feeding her old fat ass for weeks, waiting for Grace to take her. Turns out I did that for no reason. Got to get rid of her. She's worthless and just eating our food."

The fat man spoke as he continued into the breeding room. The Chihuahua in Cage 49 studied the fat man as he walked to the where room his mother was. A mother he yearned for during the past five weeks.

"You can't keep her in there forever if we can't use her."

"I was thinking the same thing," said the fat man, sauntering along without turning around. "Time for her to say good-bye."

The fat man disappeared through the doorless entrance. The Chihuahua in Cage 49 watched the fat man work the stalls, providing food and water to the poor mothers penned up in their cubicles. The ponytail girl moved around sweeping up the floor and finishing up her work. After leaning the broom in the corner, she lifted a backpack onto her shoulders.

"I better get going now, Grandpa, or I'll miss the school bus."

The Chihuahua in Cage 49 looked over toward the back room. The fat man could still be seen passing back and forth. Then a surprising sight. The Chihuahua in Cage 49 saw his mother. She exited slowly from the breeding room. It was a pitiful sight. Years of no exercise took its toll. She could barely walk on atrophied legs. Overworked teats sagged painfully, nothing more than drooping flesh. Fur matted with dirt. A body used as a puppy factory. Tired, resigned eyes. Slow agonizing steps. Rotten teeth. As bad as her condition, it was a welcome sight for the young Chihuahua. He yelped happy yelps. The first happy yelps since he was taken from her. *His mother. Oh, his mother!*

"Get moving, you old bitch." Yelled the fat man as he stood in the doorway, not leaving the room as if completing some unfinished task.

"She gave us four litters, Grandpa. No bitch ever gave us four litters. Three, a lot of times, but never four."

The Chihuahua in Cage 49 yelped for his mother. The other dogs yelped too. Soon there was chorus of dog sounds filling the air. Yelps intended as cheers. They barked and yelped her on. When the old mother reached the middle of the floor she stopped as if resting painful joints. The dogs continued to bark, louder and louder. The Chihuahua in Cage 49 missed his mother badly. He wanted desperately to leap from the cage and greet her. He yelped again and again. He wanted to tell her where he was. She turned to him. And looked up. The mother yelped.

She saw him. This made the Chihuahua in Cage 49 so happy. He was charged with the warm loving that only a mother could give. The Chihuahua paced back and forth. A dog smile. He yelped until he could not yelp any louder.

The fat man spoke over the barking. "Look at her," he said with ridicule in his voice. "She looks like she doesn't know here she is."

"I don't have time to deal with her, Grandpa. I have to go to school."

"You don't have to do anything, Ally." I'll take her outside and shoot her. No point in wasting food on her. She's finished working."

"Take her far away from the building when you shoot her. The dogs don't like gun shots. It makes them shaky. They shake enough as it is. The shops don't want shaky dogs."

The fat man walked toward the Chihuahua's mother. "Get moving, you old bitch," he yelled. The mother sensing the fat man's footsteps took a couple of struggled steps. The fat man neared her. The other dogs yelped warnings.

"Didn't you hear me?" A right leg cocked. Then a football kick. The mother's last breath was a sickening high-pitched cry of pain. She sailed through the air until hitting a wall, landing on the ground as a motionless bag of collapsed flesh. The building erupted into angry barks. The Chihuahua in Cage 49 cried and whimpered by the sight. He strained to see what happened to his mother. No movement. The red tongue used to wash him hung listlessly from her mouth. The ponytail girl stood impassively gripping the straps to her backpack.

"I gotta go, Grandpa."

The fat man reached down and picked up the breeding dog that produced almost two dozen puppies, providing him and his granddaughter thousands of dollars in revenues. A pinch to the scruff of the neck, then a lift to just inches from the fat man's face. Closed eyes. Drooping tongue. Dead legs.

"No need to shoot this mother. She's a goner," said the fat man, as if discussing an old shoe. "Saved me a bullet." The fat man walked over and lifted the top to the garbage can before dropping the deceased mother into the receptacle and closing the lid. The puppies, traumatized by the scene, continued their angry barks. They were mad. Mad at the fat man. Mad at the ponytail girl who barely took care of them. Mad at illnesses inflicting their bodies. Mad at hunger living in every stomach.

"Shut up, you pooches. Mind your own damn business," yelled the fat man.

"You got them all rattled up now, Grandpa." The ponytail girl reached into a pocket and pulled out a phone. She glanced at the screen.

"I'm leaving right now, Grandpa. The school bus will be here any minute."

"Well, then go, Ally. You keep saying your leaving. Just leave."

As the ponytail girl turned to take steps toward the door there was the sound of vehicles approaching the building. Then the squeal of brakes. Doors slammed.

More footsteps. An alarmed expression crossed the face of the fat man. "That better not be who I think it is."

There was a knock on the door. The ponytail girl turned to the fat man with a questioning look.

"Don't let them look in the garbage pail."

The fat man moved faster than the Chihuahua in Cage 49 had ever seen the man move before. He found some scraps of cardboard and threw them into the opened garbage can to hide the dog corpses. He replaced the lid. The fat man turned to the ponytail girl with an expression of dread. He spoke in an even voice.

"You better answer the door, Ally."

Chapter 4

THE ponytail girl stood and stared at her grandfather as if waiting for a different answer. There was another knock. Then the knocks turned to pounds.

"Go ahead, Ally," said the fat man in a voice raised into a command. "Do as I said. You have to answer it."

"Grandpa, what do I say to them?"

"Answer the door," said the fat man impatiently.

The Chihuahua in Cage 49 yelped along with the chorus of other puppies. Someone coming might mean help. Instinctively the young dogs yelped and yelped. Louder and louder.

"Ah, shut up, you damn dogs," said the fat man.

A loud voice from outside. "Open up. Police."

The ponytail girl stepped toward the door, but it opened before she got there. Bits of early morning light streamed inside. A police officer framed by the opening. He wore a blue jacket with faux fur collar and patches on the arm. Aviator glasses wrapped around an angular face. The police officer peeled off the spectacles exposing steely blue eyes. Other uniformed personnel stood outside. He stepped in. A curled nose with a lift of open hands.

"Whoa, the smell. It stinks in here real bad." He spoke to the people behind him without taking eyes off the fat man.

Another police officer walked in and spoke to those still outside. "You may want to use the face masks. This place is a doozy."

They waited. Two of the outside people added face masks. The fat man and the ponytail girl appeared to recognize him. The first police officer spoke.

"Jack, I have a warrant to search the premises." He waved it in the air.

"What for?" asked the fat man.

"You know what for, Jack. Cruelty to animals. One of the stores you sell to reported that the Chihuahuas you are selling are sick and malnourished. Plus, you are operating without a license."

"This started off as a hobby for Ally. Then it became a business. We've been planning on getting a license but just never got to it. We take better care of these dogs than most people take care of dogs in their own homes. And what do they expect? Am I suppose to bring them all to bed with me?"

The police office waved a hand in front of the fat man's face to stop him from talking. He turned to the people outside and waved them in.

"Everyone knows you have been operating for over three years. Hell, you even have a sign out front about buying your dogs. When were you going to get a license? Jack, this place is such a mess you know you would never have passed an inspection."

Puppy yelping got even louder. The officer walked to the fat man and handed him the documents. The fat man looked at the paper for a few seconds before dropping the clutching hand to his side. "This is ridiculous."

"Jack, you and your granddaughter need to step over by the wall." The policeman pointed to the side toward the food barrel and tangled hose. The fat man and ponytail girl followed the order.

The ponytail girl stared up at her grandfather. All the angry confidence the fat man showed just minutes earlier vaporized like cold morning breath. The fat man now held an expression of despair. Tears filled up in the eyes of the ponytail girl. The rescue team of two women and one man entered the warehouse donning green uniforms emblazoned with *County Animal Rescue* patches. Cold air pushed past the trio triggering the butane heater thermostat. A lion's roar of heat.

The yelping was no longer signals of distress. The barking sounds changed. Chihuahua barks sounded like hope.

The fat man did not move. He stood watching the rescuers go to work removing puppies, tagging each and recording their conditions on an electronic device.

"Jack, please move closer to your granddaughter. You won't be asked again," said a police officer evenly.

Dread morphed into anger. The fat man responded, "This is my property, you know. We're farmers. This is what we do. This is our crop, our livestock." Animosity tinged the man's voice.

One of the rescue team women rolled eyes in resignation. Another recorded the activities with a video camera. All three of the rescue workers wore double-filter masks. The cops sans masks complained about the odor.

"How could you people stand the smell in here?" asked the second officer of the fat man and his granddaughter. "Did you just get used to it?" Neither answered the question.

A rescue worker pulled his mask down so he could speak to the cops. "These cages looked like they were just cleaned but they are still a mess. The floors are filthy. The puppies are underweight. Sores and eye infections are rampant. The top cage puppies piss on the ones below. That's why this place smells so bad. That's how you get that terrible ammonia smell. That odor is hell on the dog's respiratory systems."

"I just cleaned their cages this morning," said the ponytail girl defensively.

"They call this clean?" said the rescuer to one of the cops.

The woman with the camera finished videoing the front area and signaled to a police officer that she wanted to go into the breeding room.

"Do you have another mask? I know it's going to be bad back there. Probably worse than here," asked the police officer to the rescuer.

The video woman pointed to a canvas bag that contained supplies including collars, leashes, and high-quality treats. The cops fumbled through the bag and pulled out a painter's dust mask. It was primitive compared to the masks that the rescue team used. He held it in a hand with an inquisitive expression on his face.

The woman with the video camera pulled her respiratory mask down to speak. "We are assigned these masks and we keep them. Those flimsy masks are just for back up. Sorry, but that is what we have. Don't worry, it's new. Never been used."

"It's better than nothing, I suppose."

The cop turned to the fat man and daughter. "Are the breeders back there?"

"What do you think?" said the fat man.

"You are only making your situation worse, Sir."

"What's that suppose to mean?"

"It means your attitude will be a part of my report." The cop turned to the video woman. "Let's see what's back there."

The video woman and police officer walked toward the breeding room. The Chihuahua in Cage 49 paced slowly back and forth. Some of the dogs were being removed and placed in clean portable cages. The thought of leaving the puppy mill brought a sudden hope never felt before.

The yelping in the warehouse subsided. There was a new calm that descended within the building. The dogs all knew that these were good people. That they were there to help them. Their barks were finally answered. The people in the green uniforms cared.

One of the rescue team pulled his mask from his face to speak. "Look at this."

A couple of rows over and down, a long-haired Chihuahua had its matted fur entangled in the cage mesh.

"This poor thing is part of its cage. He is actually stuck to it. He can't even pull away from it."

"Those on the bottom always get the worst of it. They get dumped on, literally."

The other rescue worker grabbed a pair of scissors from the canvas bag and began snipping the dog's hair. Once the Chihuahua was free of the entrapment the man pulled the dog from the cage and lifted it to the other rescue worker. He pulled his mask away to speak. "Poor dog is nothing but a bag of bones. He couldn't get to the little food given to him. Didn't these people see that? Or I guess they didn't care."

"We cared, you know. We cared for our dogs. More than you realize," said the ponytail girl, speaking through sobs. Since the rescue worker was back wearing a mask, she answered with a resigned shrug.

The police officer who was in the breeding room came out and pulled down the flimsy mask. He yelled over to the other officer guarding the fat man and his granddaughter. "Wow, if you think it stinks out here, go in there. That room is a horror. Those poor mothers are all living in their own filth. Even worse than out here. There's sick puppies in there with sick mothers."

"The chief said it was going to be bad. Let me arrest these two. I better have a squad car come down to pick them up."

The police officer spoke into the handset clipped on a shoulder. "Dispatcher, requesting a 10-16 Hathaway Brook Farm."

The ponytail girl burst into a waterfall of tears. She leaned into her grandfather. He held her side stroking an arm. It was the first exhibit of affection that the fat man expressed in the presence of the puppies.

"But I have to go to school!" exclaimed the ponytail girl as tears streamed down her face.

"Can't you just let her go? She had nothing to do with this. She's my granddaughter and just a high school junior. All she does is feed the dogs."

"I have to take her in. I won't handcuff her. But she will be arraigned." He turned to the girl. "How old are you?"

"Sixteen," she said through uncontrolled sobbing.

"I have to take her in. She's part of this. I have no choice."

The police officer read the fat man and ponytail girl their rights. The team continued to remove grateful dogs from their entrapped hell. One rescuer pulled the garbage can over and opened it to throw away debris.

"Oh, no!" was the muffled reaction when she looked inside.

"What?" asked the startled police officer.

She pulled down her mask to speak. "I see a tail."

The police officer walked over and looked in. A reaching hand grabbed some cardboard and other debris. The rubbish was tossed to the ground. He lifted the Chihuahua's mother. Her limp deceased body.

The Chihuahua in Cage 49 barked angry barks. The remaining dogs did the same. Holding the mother by the back of the neck he looked down and then up again. "There is another one in there. A puppy."

"Put her back in the garbage can. The sight of her is upsetting the other dogs," said a rescuer.

"The police officer gently laid the Chihuahua mother back into the garbage can. The police officer went back to work arresting the grandfather-granddaughter team. The Chihuahua in Cage 49 continued to study the rescuers work. He saw how they were gentle and kind. He felt their energy. The Chihuahua was not shaking like he often did. The police officer walked the fat man with hands cuffed behind his back and the crying granddaughter toward the door. The Chihuahua could see through the open door. Another squad car waited to transport the two. When they were gone the room quieted again.

The video woman returned from the breeding room to help take each Chihuahua puppy out of its cages. "That back room is horrible. Those poor mothers. We have some work to do back there."

"We found one of the mothers in the garbage can along with a baby."

"Oh, no."

The Chihuahua in Cage 49 watched the rescuers carefully take each dog from its cage. They held each puppy lovingly. Every young dog was petted and spoken to in a calm, assuring voice. As much as the puppies suffered, they each waited patiently. Yelping became rare and sporadic. Help had arrived. They were there in the uniforms of law enforcement and County Animal Rescue. There was a collective consciousness among the dogs. They all knew their nightmare was ending. The Chihuahua watched as each of his fellow puppies was lifted out of confined misery into the caring arms of a rescuer.

When a female rescuer reached the end of the aisle, she jiggled the latch and pulled back the metal gate.

The Chihuahua shook, a natural reaction whenever a human got so close. A gloved hand reached in. The Chihuahua backed up and fell on its haunches. The hand grabbed the back of his neck and gently pinched the flesh and pulled him out. The woman cradled him. She rocked the Chihuahua by twisting her body back and forth. He felt the delicious tenderness of the rescuer's hold.

"You need to be better fed, sir. But you are in better shape than a lot of your brothers and sisters. Being in a top cage helps. We're going to feed you and give you some shots. You are going to a much better place, my little man," said the woman rescuer in a voice filled with gentleness.

The rescuer with the electronic device recorded information about the Chihuahua, including malnutrition and shakiness. It was also noted that there were no obvious signs of eye infection or other ailments. She handed the Chihuahua from Cage 49 to a male rescuer who covered him in a little blanket. The cloth covering would guard against the cold when taking the short walk to the rescue van. Cradled on the man's arm and warm under the blanket, the Chihuahua was full of hope. He looked back, watching the workers releasing the last of the puppies before going to work rescuing the mothers and newborns from breeder-room captivity.

When they got to the door, the Chihuahua became fixated on the garbage can where his deceased mother lay in an undignified state. The same mother who brought the Chihuahua into the world, nursing and caring for him under horrid conditions. The Chihuahua recalled how a red tongue cleaned him, a warm belly napped him, succulent teats nourished him. A mother who never knew human affection. The only love she knew was the love she gave. Nothing more to her handlers than a manufacturer of puppies. A money-making machine. A mother dog who never knew true happiness.

Just as the rescuer stepped out of the door, the Chihuahua from Cage 49 yelped at the plastic garbage can. He was leaving now and going into a whole new world he knew nothing of. Two quick yelps. They were yelps of gratitude. Yelps of love. That he would make the best of things. He would live life fully. It was the Chihuahua's way of saying goodbye.

Chapter 5

A key twisted in the ignition switch. Roger pulled the car from the curb, moving slowly up the street. Crumbling homes. Broken down vehicles. Little money to make repairs. People barely getting by. Limited resources made for desperation. Crime was too often a way to make ends meet. Poverty caused wrongdoing. Earners caught and sent to jail. More poverty, more crime. A cycle holding the slum dwellers with a cruel force.

The late morning sidewalks were mostly empty. A man donning a black parka coat shoulder carried a bulging duffle bag toward a dirty-windowed laundromat. Roger surveyed the area. A FedEx truck came and went. A mail carrier worked her route a block away. Ideas tumbled in Roger's head. Ideas that were more like vague notions. He contemplated a return to the area. To go back that evening to get the Pit Bull, save the dog from boredom and cold. A pretend idea. A play notion. A fleeting thought that a dreamer dreams in the way a juggler tosses balls. He knew deep down he would never act upon it. Too risky. Too dangerous. If the police caught him, he would be sent back to prison.

If the dog owner caught him the results would be even worse. Like Jamal said, being in that neighborhood after dark was unsafe. No point in taking any chances. The suffering of the animal bothered Roger, but not to the point of risking freedom or even his life.

A Camry, tricked out in neon green flake paint and mag wheels, approached from the opposite direction. Rap music emanated loudly. A driver and three passengers. Teenage boys. Sideways baseball caps. Snarky smirks. Hip-hop types. They stared curiously at Roger. He was out of his element. Eye contact with the kid behind the steering wheel. The driver mouthed a comment. The foursome broke out in an uproarious laugh. Maybe they thought Roger was lost. In a way, he was.

Roger was glad to leave the street and headed toward the routes would take him to I-195. He drove the sixty miles back to the Jersey Shore, all the time thinking about that dog in someone's backyard. The suffering in those animal eyes. A canine held prisoner by a chain and stake driven into frozen ground. The turned-over plastic barrel as the dog's only way out of the elements. He wondered if anyone would bring the dog inside that night.

A turn onto the short dead-end street past the vacant bungalows. Almost all would stay dark until warm weather filled them with summer residents. He pulled the Subaru into the driveway before glancing up at the single-story, white-shingled bungalow home. In the couple of months since he moved into the house, progress was made. New siding, added to exterior walls before the snow came, brightened the home. Shutters book-ending windows added charm. Rotting porch planks were replaced and painted. It all came about with the deal his landlord uncle made with him. Fix up the rundown bungalow and Roger could stay there rent free. Uncle Ray would pay for all materials and when work was completed, the two would negotiate a lease. Roger jumped at the opportunity. After getting out of prison, living at home was terrible. A father's silent treatment. Mother's meddling. Fights ensued. Roger was miserable. Limited resources kept him from leaving. The Uncle Ray offer was a ticket out.

Roger climbed from the ten-year-old Subaru Outback that he bought from a used-car lot of vertical flags and colorful streamers. What attracted Roger to the dealer was not glittery decorative signs or silly inflated air dancers but the promise of easy credit. For five hundred dollars and a promissory note signature, Roger drove away with his own vehicle.

A car door slam. Roger grabbed letters from out of the mailbox. Eyes drawn to the home across the street. It was the only other house on the entire block of ten bungalow homes with winter occupants. A rusty Kia filled half the driveway. A baby carriage on the porch. Snow-filled plastic riding toys sided the garage less property. Roger turned. An absent walk while flipping through the mail. Frigid air. Weather reports stated that the Canadian cold front would drop nighttime temperatures to the low twenties. Roger's mind was on the Pit Bull. He thought of the dog, picturing what he saw that day. Thin coat of gray. Front paws lifted in turns off frozen ground. *How could anyone leave a pet out like that?*

Quick steps up the porch. Roger opened the front door and walked into the dusty, construction area of a living room. Decades of old plaster torn down. Sheetrock ready for hanging, leaning on bare studs. A six-foot table held tools, bags of nails and supplies. A shop vacuum in a corner. Stacked buckets of spackling compound. The house was a lonesome place. He was lonely. A high school sweetheart moved on years earlier. Many friends abandoned him after the arrest. None visited while he was incarcerated. They gave excuses. The five-hour drive to upstate New York was too far. When he got out, they were doing their own things. Little interest in reestablishing old friendships.

Roger strolled into the kitchenette and dropped the mail onto a faded Formica counter. Eyes surveyed an antique sink and dated cupboards. Remodeling the area was next after completing the living room. New fixtures to be added. Cabinet doors repainted. Walls papered. Wooden floors varnished. It was exciting to have the projects and see the progress. He hoped the headway made his Uncle Ray happy. He wanted his mother's younger brother to feel glad about the deal they made.

An obligatory glance into the refrigerator. Roger reached in, grabbing a couple slices of deli cheese from waxed paper before stuffing the yellow food into an open mouth. A couple of steps into the home's only bedroom. It was a sanctuary from the work dust and in-progress alterations. Roger leaned back onto the mattress. Pushed-off work boots clunked to the floor. He unzipped the hooded sweatshirt and removed it before collapsing onto the bed.

With closed eyes, he thought about the dog again. *Poor dog.* That look the Pit Bull gave him earlier haunted him. Pit Bull woofs that spoke to Roger. He had to save the dog. Help him out of the cold. Take him from a miserable situation. Ideas converted into reality. No longer fuzzy impulses. Roger wanted to do something.

A blind hand felt around for the hooded sweatshirt. The cell phone was pulled from the pocket. Roger tapped the screen before scrolling through the contacts. Stephen was an old high school classmate who joined the army right after graduation. Since his discharge, Stephen worked on the party boats that took anglers for day and evening fishing trips. It was a seasonal lifestyle, working one and two trips a day in warmer months. In the winter, Stephen picked up occasional work going out on cod-fishing excursions when the weather allowed. Roger knew Stephen would likely answer. Cod-fishing trips were spotty. Bad weather or not enough sport fisherman willing to tolerate the cold often kept the boats dockside. Roger held a grudge against several old friends for never making a prison visit. Stephen would not likely have made the trip either, but overseas military service gave him an excuse. Roger hit the green phone icon. Stephen's number was dialed. Phone rings. Then an answer.

"Hey, man," came an excited voice.

"Hello," said Roger through a smile. "How are things?"

"Great, man. I'm on unemployment and doing a little handy work on the side. All under-the- table type stuff."

"No party boat trips?"

"The Queen Anne is going out but not many passengers. Captain Herb is going out with a two-son crew, keeping it in the family. That's it. If things pick up, they said they'd give me a call."

"Well, I need a favor."

"What's that, Roger? You need some help working on that house? I saw your uncle at the docks. He told me what you're doing."

"I don't need any help, not with the house that is." Roger never wanted help working on the house. He only trusted the remodeling to himself. "Well, actually I do need some help," said Roger as he stared up at the ceiling. "I need help getting a dog."

"Getting a dog? You're getting a dog? That's great. What kind?"

"I think it's a Pit Bull."

"You think it's a Pit Bull?"

"Yeah, it's complicated. This dog, you see. He's kept outside in the cold, so I am going to get him and bring him home."

"Get him?"

"Yeah, get him. From someone's backyard."

"Wait a second. You're going to steal this dog?"

"Not exactly steal the dog." Roger knew it was stealing. "I am going to save the dog from someone who leaves the dog out in the cold."

"Like a Humane Society type thing?"

"Yeah." Roger liked answering the question.

"Why don't you just call the Humane Society?"

Roger rolled eyes. He hated defending what he was doing. If only he could get some easy help. "It's complicated."

"Where is the dog?"

"Trenton."

"Trenton? All the way out there?" asked Stephen in a raised voice.

"Yeah, Trenton."

"You want me to go out there with you today? It sounds a bit risky."

"Tonight."

"Tonight? That sounds even riskier. Do you really think you need a dog that bad?" said Stephen who followed with a laugh.

"It is dangerous. I just need a getaway driver. That's all. I will do the rest. Basically, you'll be out of it. It's all on me. I take all the risk. You will be behind the wheel while I go get the dog. Once the dog is in the car we take off. That's it."

"Man, that sounds a little wild. I mean the dog obviously belongs to someone and to just take the dog …"

"Listen, I need your help. Remember when you were buying your car a few years ago and I loaned you that twelve hundred dollars."

"Oh, man, stop trying to put the guilt thing on me."

"You still owe me seven hundred and it has been five years, actually six years."

"I told you man, I am working on it."

"Well, I need your help tonight. Can you be ready at midnight? I'll get you then."

"Midnight? My old lady is not going to like this," said Stephen, referring a live-in girlfriend.

"Can I count on you?"

"Yeah, man. The living room light will be on. I will be lying on the couch. Just come get me. You know where I am, right? Bradley Trailer Park. Green single-wide, all the way in the back. Number 38. You will see my car. Still got that old Impala."

"All right, I will call you when I am in front of your house. Be ready."

"Okay, I will."

The phone went dead. Roger then called another friend. Colin was a surfer buddy. A guy that looked up to Roger for his surfing prowess. A younger kid. Someone that Roger taught surfing moves to. Not a real close friend, but someone Roger thought he could recruit.

"Hey, Colin. Its Roger."

"Man, I know who it is." Colin was a stoner and sounded high.

"Colin, Stephen and I are going up to Trenton to get a dog. Can you come with us? Help us out?"

"Oh, man. I just smoked half a joint. When do you want to go?"

"Not now. I can get you just after midnight. Right after I get Stephen." Roger wanted to ask a second friend in the event Stephen bailed out on him. He was not totally confident that he could rely on Stephen, especially with his girlfriend's control over him. Colin was mostly useless, but he was better than nothing.

"Yeah, man, I can be ready. I will come down from this incredible high by then. I will be ready. But what is this about a dog? Are you getting a dog? That is kinda cool."

"Yeah, I am saving a dog from the cold. The owner does not take care of him, so I am going to get it."

"He's letting you have it?"

"Listen, I will fill you in on the details when I get you. Just be ready. I will call you when I am outside."

"See you after midnight, bro."

Chapter 6

THE blanket-draped Chihuahua got the first looks of life existing past the doors of the puppy mill. Outside was a foreign land. Crisp air tickled the dog's nose. Silvery sun beams reflected off ice glazed snow. The Chihuahua blinked away the stinging discomfort. Squinted eyes surveyed the area. Beef cattle stood nearly motionless in an open field, exhaling cloudy breaths and chewing hay. Barns and farm tractors. Faraway trees. Birds darting between rooftops and wires. The Chihuahua was like a hatchling seeing the world for the first time.

A lift into an empty travelling crate of the idling van. Other dogs hardly barked. The calmness felt when the rescuers arrived stayed with the puppies. There was hope. Fear was lifted. An odd sense of relaxation. A certain assurance that a corner was turned. They each survived the horrors of the puppy mill. Life was about to get better.

Two more dogs were brought in. Two long-haired Chihuahuas whose sad eyes and matted fur was evidence of what they suffered. The Chihuahua from Cage 49 yelped at the two dogs placed in their crates. They were yelps of confidence. Dog talk. A signal that they needed to hang in there. Their situation was improving. The actions of the rescue workers assured as much. He heard it in the way they spoke their words. All the dogs were going someplace so much better. He knew it.

The van door was slid shut. One of the rescuers climbed into the driver's seat. The transmission placed into forward. The movement caused a nervousness among the four-legged passengers. A rocking motion, then a bump. Each dog settled in for the ride. Silence fell inside the cabin. No more yelps. Only trust.

The vehicle pulled up to a garage building with a sign saying *County Animal Rescue Building*. The door rolled up. The van entered a bright room. More rescue people in their green uniforms. The Chihuahua recognized one from the puppy mill. He peered out while a rescuer began the task of removing the dogs. Rescuers spoke among themselves.

"Some of these poor pups are in bad shape. Underfed. Matted fur. Eye infections. Lots of the typical stuff."

"Let's get them out and start fixing them up."

"The mothers and their babies will be on the next van. Some of those poor moms are in awfully bad shape."

The other rescuer looked down. A shake of the head. "They usually are. They take the brunt of these situations. Puppy mills are the worst."

The Chihuahua watched as the other puppies were taken out of the crates and handed to a waiting worker. Each was brought to one of a few tables where they were examined by a veterinarian. Most of the long-haired Chihuahuas were shaved of their filthy matted hair and given their first real bath. Not like at the puppy mill where the fat man would simply hose down the dog-filled cages. It was his insensitively lazy way to clean the little prisons. The poor dogs were left in soaking fur to suffer the chills of a drafty building.

Rescuers and volunteers provided warm shampoo baths. Relief from dirty fur. Clean warm water. People doing. Others assisting. Care everywhere. The Chihuahua did not yelp. He did not bark. He simply watched and waited his turn. A building full of kindness and help.

"Come on, baby." Soothing first words of the rescuer who opened his crate and lifted him out. "Ahh, you poor thing. You need to be fed. You are a little bag of bones." She stared at him directly. "No eye infections. You are a little better than some of your brothers and sisters."

April wore a T-shirt saying *Happy Yappers Animal Shelter*. A head of blue hair. She was a volunteer helping with what was known in rescue parlance as *after-raid*. She walked the Chihuahua into the bright surroundings as rescuers, other volunteers, and veterinarian staff

worked to check the stages of illnesses, insect infesta-
tion and malnutrition. The Chihuahua shook for no
apparent reason. He was not scared. An air of confidence. He watched other dogs. They were enjoying the
care they were receiving.

The Chihuahua was laid down on a paper covered
table. A veterinarian in a white medical jacket turned
toward April before looking down at the Chihuahua.
"Male or female?"

"Male."

"How is he?"

"Better than some of the others. He is malnourished, as you can tell," said April. "They were all
underfed."

The handsome, dark-skinned veterinarian shook
his head. "What is it to feed these dogs properly?
They're all Chihuahuas. They don't eat much. But they
still starve them." He made a face of disgust.

A county rescuer who was at the mill earlier recognized him. "He was in a top cage, so he did not have
pee and poop raining down on him. The cages were
really small, but he was the only one in it."

The Chihuahua's body rattled. The rescuer stroked
his head.

"I wonder why he is shaking? Is he scared?" asked
April.

"He could be a little nervous being around such

strange surroundings. But Chihuahuas often shake. Especially if they have been traumatized. This little guy has been through a rough time. They take the puppies away from their mother too early and lock them up in a cage twenty-four seven."

"Ahh, poor Chihuahua," said April as she took a turn petting his head.

"Let me take a look," said the veterinarian.

The Chihuahua felt the cold instrument probing each ear. The veterinarian used gloved hands to pull jaws open. A human face that got close. The Chihuahua pulled back. The veterinarian laughed. Strong hands.

April stroked his back. "It's okay, Buddy. The doctor only wants to see if you have any bad teeth."

"Is Buddy his name?"

"No, he doesn't have a name yet. I just call him Buddy because he looks like a Buddy," said April.

"Well, his mouth looks good. Let me look at his eyes."

The veterinarian held an instrument close to the Chihuahua's face. The Chihuahua tried to control the shakes. He sensed the people were trying to help him. A veterinarian thumb on each side of the little dog's forehead wrinkled back the skin. The white light from an ophthalmoscope blinded him. The little dog shook uncontrollably. A yellow screen of blindness. Lines swam in the Chihuahua's eyes. "The eyes look good. No infections. One of the lucky ones."

April picked up the Chihuahua. He liked being held. The woman's body warmth. Loving energy reminded the Chihuahua of his own mother. He cried a little.

"Is everything okay, Buddy?

The Chihuahua smiled up at April. He felt better. She reminded him of his mother. The same warmth and caring.

"Bath time," said the veterinarian.

The Chihuahua saw others getting baths and they were calm and collected. Even with that, he was frightened of water. Memories of the cruel, fat man hosing the cages only made the Chihuahua cold and wet. He wanted nothing to do with what that man used to do to the puppies. To the Chihuahua, water meant misery.

He was laid in the tub and began weeping puppy cries. The Chihuahua anticipated the cold water running thorough his coat of short hair fur. He stood trying to be brave. April's soothing voice helped.

"Don't worry, Buddy. It's just water."

The voice was not enough. The Chihuahua still shook. The puppy tried not to shake but could not help it. Then a feeling of ecstasy. Warm water caressed his entire body. A feeling even better than a warm blanket. Warm like a mother's stomach. Massaging fingers lathered him. Heated water rinses. Grime washed away. A drape of a dry towel. A lift into April's arms.

"How was your first bath, Buddy?"

He felt the love, a woman's touch. There was love throughout the room. Each person doing their part to care for every canine. Tender holding reduced the shaking. The Chihuahua fared the puppy mill experience better than some of the others who were being treated for eye infections, stomach ailments and other issues. Several puppies showed symptoms of red mange, likely contracted from their mothers. Some dogs may have been suffering from heart disease, kidney disease or other illnesses that take longer to diagnose. The breeder dogs certainly endured lives of multiple sicknesses.

The Chihuahua was traumatized by having been separated from a mother so early. The worst was the ghastly sight of his poor mother being killed. Physically, he was better than most of the other dogs. Although malnourished, he had experienced his captivity without infections. The veterinarian treated the puppy with a de-worming medication as a precaution.

The veterinarian turned back to April. "He seems pretty good. He washed up well," he said with an amused smile. He placed a pen on the clipboard. The Chihuahua felt the soothing head caresses of the veterinarian hand. "I think you could send him over to Happy Yappers. You people are good at finding homes for these guys. The director said they could take three healthy Chihuahuas. Send him there."

April looked down at the Chihuahua. He looked up at her caring eyes. "Did you hear that, Buddy? You are going where I volunteer. You are going to like it there. We are going to find you a home."

"You keep calling him Buddy. Do you want to give him that name?" asked the veterinarian.

"Buddy? No. I just call him Buddy because I don't know his name. He probably doesn't have a name."

"The health sheet just says 'short hair Chihuahua, Cage 49. Tan and white colored.' That's the only identity."

"Ahh," said April in a motherly voice. "Poor puppy. He does not have a name. None of these dogs have names. They won't get names until they're adopted."

"Well, let's make an exception. I'm going to write on the health sheet that his name is Buddy. How's that?" said the veterinarian.

"Did you hear that?" The Chihuahua looked up again to April as she spoke to him. "You are Buddy. Do you like it?"

Buddy moved his head toward the veterinarian who wore a generous smile. He then looked at all the dogs who were being helped. So much happened since the morning. From the unbearable cold experienced in the earliest hours to the routine hunger and a mother's violent end. Now there was care and warmth. Love and nurturing. The Chihuahua had a future. And into the unknown he would take with him a name.

He was Buddy.

Chapter 7

ROGER pulled the pasty compound over the drywall seams with a silvery putty knife. An evening project. Spackle a wall and let it dry. The next day he would go to work sanding down imperfections to the point of smoothness. A glance to the cell phone. It was close to midnight. Roger turned off the shade less lamps used to illuminate the room. He washed up before donning a ski jacket. Gloves were grabbed. A knit cap pulled from a drawer. Earlier he made a home-made leash with yellow rope found in the basement and metal clasp stored in a toolbox. A thought stopped him. Roger considered wearing a hoodie to blend in the neighborhood more easily.

He caught himself. Roger was overthinking things. The walk to the backyard and getting the dog would take no more than two or three minutes. To be successful he would have to operate quickly. The thing was to not be seen at all. Timing was everything. The dog could not get upset or draw attention. A couple of short barks may not disrupt the neighborhood. Or someone may look out a window. Even worse, it could startle the dog owner. Roger's presence could scare the dog enough to attack him. The operation would not work without the Pit Bull's cooperation.

There was so much on the line. He was doing something wrong. Trespassing on someone's property. Stealing a dog. He could get caught, be arrested. A clear parole violation. No judge would see Roger's altruism in securing the welfare of animal. They would say that he could have called the Humane Society or like organization and let them handle the matter. That is what they do. He would be sent back to prison. The notion caused hesitation. Thoughts of being seen by someone living in the home and calling the police. Or those living in the home taking matters into their own hands. Would someone mistake him for a rival drug dealer or gang member? Roger could be physically attacked or even shot. The whole idea was crazy. Both mother and father could never forgive him for getting into trouble over a dog. His father never forgave him for the arrest and the shame it brought. In the eyes of his father, Roger was a family embarrassment. Then he thought of the Pit Bull. The animal needed help. Roger swallowed the apprehensions, pressed down on the fear. He opened the door walking out into the dark cold, leash in hand.

Roger got in the car and steered the vehicle toward the Bradley Trailer Park where Stephen lived. The plan was set in Roger's mind. The trio would make the midnight trek to Trenton. They would get to the neighborhood. He would not drive by, looking to see the dog. Going back and forth could draw suspicion. It may make them look like someone's rival looking for trouble. Darkness made it unlikely to get a clear view of the backyard from a moving car anyway. It was better to park quickly and go to work. A stealth operation. Stephen behind the steering wheel. Colin as a lookout. Roger walking up the sidewalk. When he got to the front of the home, eyes adjusted to the darkness would search the backyard. Maybe the dog was brought in at night. In that case, the mission would be aborted. Not a complete waste of time. There would be some peace of mind that the dog was not always stuck out in the cold. If the dog were there, he would give Colin the high sign, letting him know that the plan was a go. He would duck behind the broken-down Mercury Marquis. From there, he would try to gain the canine's trust.

Unpaved trailer park roads made for a slow rocky ride like a vessel plowing through rolling seas. The park was situated a block past the pier. Trailer homes were aged, rundown facilities. Fishermen, clammers and others tolerated the conditions to take advantage of the lower cost housing. Dirty pickup trucks with lobster pots and nets lined the sides. Roger followed the directions Stephen gave. He did not bother looking for a trailer number. Roger only looked for Stephen's car. The old Impala that Roger loaned Stephen money to buy. A loan with an open balance. Roger saw the banged-up vehicle ahead. He stopped and peered at the darkened windows. Eyes bounced to each blackened pane in the hope of noticing a reflective trace of a glowing television set. There was nothing. No movement. Only stillness. No occupants were awake. The same with the surrounding trailer homes. The whole park was sound asleep.

Roger dialed Stephen's number. It went to voice mail. "I am outside waiting for you."

Colored lights twisting the unpainted rails of a front stoop blinked on and off. In nearly three weeks it would be Christmas. Roger expected Stephen to hear the cell phone ring. Then an interior light would signal Stephan's emergence from bed. Nothing. He tried again. Again nothing. Roger left the warm car. A cold slap of night air. Eyes rose to the sky. Twinkling shards of light surrounded by endless blackness. Hands fumbled for deeply pocketed gloves and slipped them on while exhaling plumes of smokey breath. He shivered. *How could a dog survive in such weather?*

Four steps up the rickety stairs to the front door. He peeled a glove off and gave the flimsy aluminum storm door a bare-knuckle knock, rattling the trailer park silence. A little tap dance to circulate warm blood. Nothing. Another knock. He was not going to let

Stephen off that easily. Help was needed. Maybe he fell asleep on the couch. Determined knuckles rapped the door harder. Louder knocks. A light went on in a trailer across the path. Roger woke up someone else.

The sound of a door being unlocked. Stephen? A pull open. Standing there was Jade. Bleach-blonde bed hair. Pajama pants. Bare feet. Nose ring. Roger forced eyes above braless breasts pointing a white undershirt. An annoyed expression lay on her face. She unlocked the storm door and pushed it open so they could talk.

"Stephen's asleep."

"He said he was going to help me tonight."

"I said he is asleep, Roger," she said evenly.

Roger never cared for Jade. Self-centered and never friendly.

"I know he's asleep. You just said that. Wake him up. Stephen said he was going to help me tonight and I need him out here."

"C'mon, Roger. He is asleep. Besides, what are you up to, getting a dog in the middle of the night? Is this a drug deal you are doing? Stephen is not getting involved in your drug nonsense. Forget it."

"Wait a second … " He said it loud enough hoping Stephen would be nudged out of bed. Jade slammed the door. Roger stood there watching his breath in the nighttime cold.

It sunk in. Shoulders slumped. Head dropped. No

Stephen. Roger walked off the steps and took the icy path back to the car. He waited in the idling vehicle staring dejectedly at the trailer. He really wanted Stephen with him. Stephen was smarter than Colin. Roger only asked Colin to come along to be a lookout. Now he had to rely on Colin all the way. Roger backed out of the spot onto the dirt path road.   Rear tires crackled ice-topped mud puddles. He looked back for the one last chance hoping a sense of duty caused Stephen to step from the trailer. Instead, the windows remained dark. The only action was the blinking of colored lights.

Chapter 8

DOWNCAST, Roger drove to the edge of town where Colin lived with his brother. A turn onto a narrow street. Cars and SUVs crowded the narrow lane. He slowed his vehicle, allowing it to crawl to the front of the American Foursquare-style home with its boxy structure and dormer windows. He glanced at the dashboard clock. The time was 12:35 a.m. Roger leaned over the passenger seat and looked up at the third floor where the two brothers lived. No light. A bad sign. Roger grabbed the cell phone and called Colin. Like the call to Stephen, it went to voicemail. Feelings of disgust. People were unreliable. Friends were unreliable. *Were they even friends? How could friends do this?* Roger got out of the car and walked up the icy driveway. Steep stairs sided the three-story house, added when each of the three floors of the single-family home were converted into separate living quarters. Like a cat burglar, Roger ascended the steps sneakily to avoid awakening the residents of the other apartments. The consideration did little; dogs from the first floor sensed a presence. Barking. If anything, the sound may awaken Colin. Roger rang a doorbell.

No answer. He tried again. Then door knocks. Still no answer. Discouragement. Both friends were letting him down. He went downstairs and around to the rear of the home. A circle of lawn furniture left out in winter. Empty beer bottles and snow-filled ash trays.

A second-floor light was on, something not noticed before. Roger knew where Colin's bedroom was. He tossed pebbles at Colin's third-floor window. Tap. Tap. Nothing. Then a silhouette. A curious house cat jumped up on the sill of Colin's window, searching the outside. Roger was certain Colin knew he was outside. How could both brothers sleep through the doorbell ringing, knocks and pebble taps? They were not close friends. More like acquaintances. Just surfer friends. Roger still believed he could count on Colin.

A second-floor curtain was pulled back. A middle-aged woman with a bed mop of red hair. She pushed a window open before leaning out. Sleepy eyes searched the outside. Freezing air caused steamy breath. She found Roger. He gave her an embarrassed wave.

"Excuse me. Are you lost, honey?" she called down, attempting to hush her voice. She gave Roger a sarcastic look.

"I'm looking for Colin. Do you know where he is?" asked Roger, trying to add levity to the odd situation.

"Nooo," said the woman. "How would I know where he is? Maybe he is asleep in his room?"

"I thought the same thing. He's suppose to go somewhere with me and I got a feeling he's asleep."

The woman leaned out farther. Then a turn up to the unlit windows above before looking back to Roger. "It's almost one in the morning and the apartment is dark. What would give you the idea that he'd be asleep?"

Roger felt the sarcasm. He woke her up and likely the people on the first floor whose dogs barked.

"I know, I know. I am sorry. Colin was suppose to be ready. Looks like he is sleeping in."

"Did you call him?"

"Yeah, did that when I got here. He did not pick up."

"I think you need to realize he's not going to meet with you," said the woman with a voice hinting of anger. "You need to run along, okay? You woke me up and I have to work in the morning."

The woman pushed the window down before slapping the curtain closed. Roger understood that the woman would be mad. He could not blame her. Roger stood in the cold darkness of the backyard. Like Stephen, there would be no Colin. Neither was going to help him. The winter chill made him think of the Pit Bull. Roger's footsteps crunched across the frozen grass. A retreat to the car. Thoughts of what to do. *Maybe the dog was brought inside*. Roger contemplated going home. Then he thought of the turned-over barrel. A dirty straw bed. The frigidity of the nighttime air. Roger put the transmission into forward. He was heading to Trenton.

Chapter 9

THE empty highway of late hours. Three more Tuesdays until winter solstice. People were not out. Like Colin and Stephen, most of the local world was in a warm bed. Thoughts of anger mixed with craziness. The mission was absurd; Roger knew it. He was heading to a city he hardly knew to save a Pit Bull owned by someone else. A dog he had no right to. A dog not his. The thoughts repeated themselves. He could end up in a lot of trouble. That was the way it was. That was the law. Whatever the ethical or legal consequences, he convinced himself that saving a dog from suffering trumped everything else. It was that thought that fueled the engine of perseverance. It was what kept him from turning around.

Back to the grimy fringes of the state capital. Trenton darkness. Driving alone. Thoughts of what law enforcement may think. Could he get pulled over just for driving? Would a cop think he was there to make a drug deal? What would any logical person think? Roger's eyes darted around looking for a patrol car that he did not want to see.

Deep breaths, an attempt to calm down. Roger

tried to convince himself that being alone was better. He could control the whole situation. Maybe too many people could mess things up. A group of guys in a car might draw more attention. It was better this way.

The late-night streets of winter Trenton were lonely. No one out. Even the homeless were hidden away in the dark corners of the city. A couple of blocks up, he saw the white and red lights of a vehicle cross through an intersection. One-handing the cell phone, he turned it off. Roger buried it deep into center console. He hid it beneath a phone charger, pens, miscellaneous receipts, and a bottle of water. If he got pulled over, he would tell the cop that earlier that day he lost his phone. That he thought it may have fallen out of a pocket when he went to the car, so he was returning to where he parked that morning. The story was crazy but there was a needed narrative. Something to say in the event he was questioned.

A turn onto a dark Liberty Street. A dry mouth. Rhythmic chest poundings felt like an overworked bilge pump. Gentle brake taps slowed the Subaru to a sneaking speed. Roger's mind a blender of thoughts. A new strategy. No look out. No one to drive the vehicle away. He was on his own. He would leave the vehicle unlocked. Just get the dog into the back and drive away. He could do it.

Few cars lined the street. Roger easily maneuvered

the Subaru to the curbside, several car spaces behind the black Escalade shining beneath a streetlamp. It stood out among the broken-down older vehicles hugging the street sides. It was clear to Roger that whoever owned that late-model Cadillac was someone important. He recalled what Jamal said in the meeting the morning before about gang bangers and drug dealers living in the area. Roger's eyes fell to the dashboard. The time was two fifteen. Breathing accelerated. Blood pulsed in Roger's ears. He was getting himself into something hot. Time to stop overthinking. A need for action.

Roger pulled the gloves over each hand. He grabbed the homemade leash off the passenger seat. An exit from the vehicle. The door was closed quietly. He opened the back door and dropped the back seats down so the Pit Bull would have plenty of room in the rear compartment. Quick steps around the vehicle. Roger hid on the sidewalk between the car and an empty lot that was a dumping ground for household appliances, mattresses, and garbage. A narrow walking trail of exposed cement was carved into the snow by pedestrian traffic. Getting ready to make the move, Roger noticed a pair of headlights turn onto the street. Roger ducked behind the Subaru before lifting eyes above the edge of the door. A peek through the car side windows. The silhouette of an approaching patrol car. He watched as it neared. Paranoia set in. Did someone call about him? Two

police officers in a car. Slow but steady, like a passing
ship. Swivel heads turned robotically investigating the
area. The vehicle continued up to the next corner until
it disappeared.

Slow breathing. A way to calm himself down.
Roger straightened cramped legs while remaining bent
down by the car side. The street was middle of the night
quiet. Eyes studied the surroundings. No one around.
Roger thought about what would happen. First, he
needed to know if the dog was even in the backyard. It
could be sleeping in the barrel. Dogs are wary animals.
No matter how quiet Roger was it is almost certain
that the Pit Bull would sense Roger's presence. He was
concerned with how the Pit Bull would react. Would
the dog recognize him through the darkness? The Pit
Bull could start barking, even attempt to bite him. The
dog needed to cooperate or the whole operation would
fail.

Roger stood up and looked over the roof of his car.
He knew some gang members in prison, guys moved
from the overflowing maximum-security facility to
the medium-security prison where he was held. Tough
guys. Muscled, tattooed. They looked violent. They
were violent. Men who thrived on the danger of living
the gang lifestyle. They would not think twice about
killing you if caught stealing from them. No questions asked. Roger glanced over at the black Escalade.

Whoever owned it was someone special. Maybe a gang leader. Possibly a successful drug dealer. More thoughts of what he was doing. It was a crazy idea. He no longer feared the police he saw just before. Roger convinced himself that they were only on routine patrol, not looking for him.

He studied the surrounding homes. Unlit windows. The neighborhood slept. A trio maneuvered the sidewalk more than a block away. Big parka coats. Wool hats. Teenagers on the move. They were far away. Roger stayed cloaked in the darkness. Roger looked up, staring at the streetlamp. Light blocked the path. He would have to walk through it. No other way. He walked toward the house. A sidestep behind the rusted Mercury Marquis. Roger hopscotched iceless spots. He got to the front of the old worn-out vehicle. Ears pulsed with every heartbeat. This was it. Roger was committed. He looked in the backyard. Darkness. Roger did not see the Pit Bull, only the black silhouette of the barrel.

Eyes were drawn to an upstairs open curtain window. The green glow of a computer lit up the room. In front of the monitor a man sat studying the luminescent rectangle. Broad powerful arms decorated in tattoos sided the man's torso. A comely woman with long wavy hair mingled in the background. Yoga pants and a T-shirt clung to curves like paint. Roger focused on the man's arm. He recognized the Roman numeral XI. Roger knew what that meant. He was locked up in prison with some of the Romans. It was the nickname used for soldiers in the Eleventh-Hour Gang. Roger learned that they were a relatively small gang that chose members very carefully. Business minded, they protected territories ruthlessly. The criminal organization started in Newark and spread its tentacles to other cities at the behest of the Mexican cartel with which they partnered.

Four stars were tattooed over the Roman numeral XI. Roger also knew what that signified. The second highest position in the gang, just below the drug lord himself. This guy was the territory head. He was the Eleventh-Hour Gang leader for Trenton and the surrounding area. Shocking waves of fear drifted through Roger's body. No longer did he notice the frigid temperatures. Dread easily overtook any sense of discomfort resulting from the cold night air. He thought it better to leave. The situation was getting way more dangerous than he originally thought. It was real. It was treacherous. It was reckless.

Resting on a knee, Roger lifted from a crouching position. Just before moving to return to the car there was a motion in the backyard. A head toss toward the barrel. Through the middle-of-the-night blackness Roger saw something stirring. It was the Pit Bull exiting the barrel. The sharp, hard, clanking of the chain. Roger's eyes adjusted to the sight. The dog stood still. No sound other than panting dog breath. Frosty clouds of exhale. Then a low throaty woof, as if the canine spoke to Roger. A signal that he remembered him. He knew who he was. That the Pit Bull was ready to go with him. Not a warning, but an acknowledgement.

Roger stayed motionless, only raising eyes to the bedroom window. The couple was still distracted by their little bedroom activities. The woman pulled a brush through long lengths of hair. The man kept eyes affixed to the computer monitor. A right hand jiggling the mouse. No indication that they thought anything was amiss. Roger's gloved hand tightened to the leash. A hard swallow. Then another louder woof.

"Shhhhh!" Roger reacted. The dog was anxious. The longer he hesitated, the greater the chance the clandestine mission would be uncovered. The Pit Bull waited. The dog took little steps back and forth, as if to move paws from frozen ground. Forward pulls unslaked the chain. A couple of more woofs. The Pit Bull was suddenly getting impatient. Roger froze. He looked up to the window. The woman was out of view. The man remained studying the screen.

"Shhhh! Stop it," said Roger in a forced but hushed voice.

Roger stopped before proceeding. A sneak walk. Footsteps sounded the crispy snow. More woofs.

"Stop!" whispered Roger. The dog then growled.

"It's me," pleaded Roger in a low voice, as if the dog would fully understand human language.

Roger reached out a gloved hand. Would the dog bite him? Roger got closer. A lowered arm. The hand placed on the dog's crown. A welcoming. The glove crossed the Pit Bull's head. Roger believed he was gaining the dog's trust. A slow step closer. He petted the dog's abdomen. Skin rippled the ribcage of the underfed animal. More hand strokes to calm the dog. Another woof. The other gloved hand lifted the dog's chin. A pulled back head. Roger looked down into the Pit Bull's eyes.

"Please stop" said Roger in a hushed but forceful voice.

A look toward the lit room. The window facing the backyard was empty except for the woman's shadow projected on the back wall. Roger bit a glove tip before pulling his hand out. Nimble fingers clicked the metal clasp onto the collar loop. Roger unhooked the chain, freeing the Pit Bull from the tethered prison. A gentle tug of the leash.

"Quiet," whispered Roger in an unsteady voice.

Quick steps across the yard. The Pit Bull cooper-ated. No woofs. He stayed silent. It was as if the dog sensed something. A connection. That he knew Roger was only there to help him. A slip behind the Mercury

Marquis. Another look to the side window. The man busied himself with the computer. The woman worked fingers over the man's upper back. Her tight body stripped of clothing.

The Pit Bull broke the silence. A low growl. Something alarmed the canine. The teenager trio seen earlier mingled at the driveway's end. They stared over. Confused looks. Far enough back that they could not see the couple in the window. Eyes peered at Roger and the dog. The teenagers waited for him. A quick glance to the window. No change. The Eleventh-Hour Gang leader and woman still did not detect Roger's presence. He needed to get off the property. The kids were in the way. Panic set in. Steps forward.

"Yo, man. What are you doing with Spider's dog?" yelled one of the teenagers.

"He's got Spider's dog," said another.

Roger walked toward the teenagers.

"Spider?" said Roger nervously. Then wished he could eat the words. "Yeah, Spider. I am the dog walker. Got to go."

"Hey, motherfucker. You got Spider's dog. Spider ain't gonna like that."

Roger took quick steps toward the car, leaving the teenagers behind. The dog was quickly coaxed into the back of the car while Roger heard a commotion by the home. One of the boys yelled something about the Pit Bull and some bearded guy. He was found out. Roger jumped in behind the wheel and brought the car forward into the street to make a quick U-turn. No point in going back. With the car turned around he floored the accelerator. Spinning wheels screeched the silence. A look into the rearview mirror. In the shine of the streetlamp stood Spider. Shirtless. Flip-flops. Shorts. A sinewy outstretched arm. A strong grip on a handgun.

A crack of gun blast. The rear window shattered. The terrified Pit Bull howled. Another blast. The metal pinging of ricochet. Then another shot. A metal cling sound. Roger kept the gas pedal down. The car barreled down to the end of the street. A twist of the steering wheel sent the vehicle into a violent turn. Momentum flipped the Pit Bull off four legs. Roger pinned to the door. The rear of the vehicle spun wide. Brakes slammed. The car stopped. Roger straightened the steering wheel and hit the gas. The Subaru raced toward the highway and out of Trenton.

Chapter 10

THE poor Pit Bull woofed. Roger thought he knew why. The dog was forced to step onto the crystal shards sprinkled by the explosion of glass. Heat cranked high provided some warmth, even if cold air freely leaked though the broken rear window. Eyes darted to the side mirrors. Fear that Spider would jump in the black Escalade to go after him. So far, no headlights. No sirens or flashing of blue and red. Nothing but a long, dark, empty stretch behind him.

Roger welcomed the entrance to NJ-29S, the highway that would take him out of the city. Three miles before the New Jersey Turnpike took them toward Route 195. Then across the state to the Jersey Shore. There was an urgency to pull over. Roger could not let the poor dog step around sharp pieces of glass. The canine cried with pain. Roger had another thought. A bullet may have hit the dog. Not just that, the spider-webbed rear window with a fist-sized hole could easily draw the attention of a highway patrolman.

An orange and brown sign said Wawa. Roger drove the car to the rear of the 24-hour convenience store, far away from customers who dropped in during the late evening hours. The Pit Bull was whimpering. Roger hid the Subaru behind the building and got out to open the rear hatch. An interior light shone onto a blanket of crystallized shards. The Pit Bull hobbled to Roger with a lifted paw and dropped a bulky head into the crick of Roger's neck. A pet of the dog's cheek. The dog was in pain, but still wanted to show Roger affection. He gripped the paw and lifted it to his face. A sliver of glass stabbed into the dog's foot pad. Blood trickled from the injury. Biting the glove tip and pulling it off, Roger used freed fingertips to pull the glass out. A quick tug to minimize the pain. The sting from the improvised surgery. Dog cries. Roger pulled a tissue from a coat pocket and dabbed the paw.

"Hang in there, my friend," said Roger in a calming voice.

Cradling arms lifted the fifty-five-pound Pit Bull from the rear compartment of the Subaru, placing him gently onto the ground. Roger inspected the dog all over and found no evidence of additional injuries. Roger searched a dumpster. He tore some cardboard off a discarded box to use as a makeshift shovel. A sweeping coated arm pushed the granular pieces into a corner. Glass was scooped and disposed of in the steel trash bin. He went to work on what was left of the rear window. A peel away of the shattered tempered safety glass. Some broke off in chunks. Other glass cubes rained to the ground. The Pit Bull watched calmly with a lifted paw.

Something in the passenger headrest drew his attention. A hole in the vinyl. He leaned on a stiff arm. A reach with the other. Fingertips poked the opening. Pinched fingers worked onto the spongy hole. The slug was removed. Roger stared at the projectile, a tiny lead sculpture of compressed metal. He thought about it. The bullet easily could have hit him or the dog. As bad as the night went, Roger realized how fortunate they both were. He dropped the spent bullet into a pants pocket to be kept as an odd souvenir.

"We got lucky, my friend. We got lucky."

From the corner of Roger's view, he saw a state trooper vehicle come slowly into the parking lot. Suddenly, a racing heart. Was he looking for him? Roger leaned into the shadows. A held breath. Careful eyes watched the cruiser disappear in front of the building. Roger took long quiet strides to the other side. A woof-woof.

"Shhhhh! I am not going anywhere," said Roger to the dog.

A peek around the corner. The trooper vehicle exited the parking lot. The cruiser sped off. Roger exhaled a sigh of relief.

Roger turned. The dog was right at his legs. He had followed him.

"I'm not going anywhere, my friend," said Roger in an assuring voice.

He walked the dog over to a spotlight illuminating the rear area. A look at the dog's paw. The bleeding stopped. The hobbling told Roger that the dog was still in pain. He lifted the injured dog into the back compartment. The dog looked at him. In those eyes Roger saw a reconnection. The same sort of contact that occurred earlier that day. Those dog eyes spoke to him. The look said that he would be forever loyal to Roger. That Roger was now his caretaker. The Pit Bull was ready to be Roger's best friend. A hobbled step forward. A bulky head rested on Roger's shoulder.

"Ahhh! Everything is going to be okay." Roger ran a petting hand over the dog's back. Rhyming bumps of a ribcage. "You were not fed well. We'll fix that. You will never go hungry with me."

Roger closed the back hatch. The window was missing now. It looked much better than cobwebbing glass and a fist-sized bullet hole. The idling vehicle pumped heated air throughout the Subaru's cabin. He knew the dog was likely hungry and thirsty but, rather than go into the Wawa convenience store, Roger returned to the highway. In his mind it was better to get as far out of the area as he could, as fast as he could. Roger drove a couple of more miles down I-29 to the Turnpike. Curious eyes lifted to the rearview mirror. The Pit Bull was curled up in the back and sound asleep.

Once back on the Jersey Shore area, he stopped at a convenience store to purchase dog biscuits and a couple of cans of Alpo. Roger made it back to Bayshore town where streets were rolled up for the evening. The Pit Bull continued slumbering. Roger wondered when the last time was that the poor dog had a decent sleep. He backed the car into the driveway and walked the groggy, still confused dog into the home. The dog climbed the stairs awkwardly, still favoring the cut paw. Once he got the dog into the home, he cut a plastic square from a drop cloth and retrieved a roll of duct tape from the living room's makeshift work area. Roger turned to go back outside. The dog followed him.

"Just a minute. I have to cover the back window," he said to the anxious dog.

Roger turned the doorknob and squeezed through the door so the dog could not get out with him. The dog started to cry.

Roger dropped his head to the dog. "I will be back in a moment. I am not leaving."

Roger hated to have to go outside again. The frosty air was still. Only a couple of more hours and the sun would rise from the ocean's edge. *What a night.* He laughed to himself as he sealed up the window. He would not tell anyone what occurred, what he went through to save the Pit Bull. No point in alarming anyone into believing he was in the drug business. That is what people would think. Roger knew that would be the conclusion. Instead, he would keep the events to himself. The truth was too unbelievable, anyway.

Chapter 11

THE next morning, Roger woke up to the Pit Bull sniffing an extended hand. It was early and the dog had to go out. A new experience. He was coming to realize the morning responsibility of a dog owner. A few pats to the dog's head before swinging legs over the bedside. Roger donned rumpled clothes worn the night before grabbing the homemade leash.

Roger took the dog out the front door. His attention was pulled to the bungalow home across the street and one house over. The home where the young woman with two kids was residing. He often saw her wheeling the stroller up and down the dead-end street. There was something about her. A curiousness that rumbled inside. What it was he could not be sure.

The injury inhibited the dog's ability to stroll far. Roger took another look at the injured dog's foot pad. It was getting worse. The foot swelled overnight. The cuts caused the Pit Bull to whimper in pain. He decided to take the dog to PetSmart to see if he could purchase lotion that could clear up what might be an infection. In the meantime, Roger took a first aid kit and wrapped the foot with gauze and white medical tape.

A look at the car and the missing rear window. With the benefit of sunlight, he inspected the back of the car. He poked his finger into the bullet hole that was just above the rear light. Roger remembered three shots. One went through the glass, the other was the hole in the back. He searched the back part of the car. He looked and looked. Maybe the one shot missed all together. Nothing there. He thought he'd heard a ricochet. Or did he? He looked at the roof. There was a chip in the paint. A slight indentation.

He got the Pit Bull into the front passenger seat and headed over to PetSmart. When they got to the parking lot, the still-timid dog was reluctant to leave the car. He stayed close to the front passenger seat. Roger figured the Pit Bull was afraid that he was going to leave him somewhere. He reached in and petted the dog. Roger tugged on its collar. Roger held his head against the dog's. He spoke to the Pit Bull in a soothing voice. It was his way of gaining the dog's confidence.

"What's the matter, there? We're just going into the pet store to get you some things."

Roger picked the dog up and placed him on the ground. Then he slow-walked the Pit Bull into the store. The dog still hobbled around with its injured foot. Roger maneuvered the aisles in a scattered-like search, unsure what to get first. He needed a bed for the dog, and a good leash. Dog shampoo was thrown in the cart. Then a dog jacket for the cold days. He even grabbed a dog toy to help keep the Pit Bull occupied and a chewy bone because it looked good. He found dog ointment. Roger read a box promising to clear up cuts and relieve pain.

Then there was the food. Roger lifted a heavy bag of what appeared to be the most premium dog food in the store. If this underweight Pit Bull suffered from a lack of food, he was now going to be well fed.

Roger pushed the cart toward the front of the mostly empty store. Only one checkout lane was open, which was attended by a young woman. A thin frame and narrow face of smooth, milky skin made her look nineteen or twenty. She wore dazzling blue hair and mischievous smile. Roger was suddenly intrigued. Items were placed on the conveyor.

"Are you a Treats member?"

"A what?"

"A Treats member. Are you a Treats member?"

"I don't know what that is."

The cashier gave half a laugh. "It's our awards program. I guess you are not, if you don't know what it is."

"I will sign up for it the next time I'm here."

"You need to feed your dog more. He is way too skinny. And why does he have a problem walking?" The cashier took another harder look. A grimace crossed her face. "That dog is emaciated."

Roger was embarrassed by the comment. He realized then that people may see him as a neglectful dog owner. "Oh, well, I just got the dog. Just last night. I never had a dog before. And the Pit Bull stepped on broken glass and cut up a foot."

"You just got him? Just last night? Where? Was he a rescue? I am surprised they would give him away looking so underfed and injured the way he is."

"A what?"

"What do you mean 'a what?'" said the cashier with a confident smirk.

"You called the dog something."

The cashier gave a breathy laugh. "A rescue. Is your dog a rescue? It must have been. They don't sell mature dogs like that in pet stores. Did you get him in a dog shelter?"

Suddenly, Roger realized he would have to explain the dog's origin. He never thought about it. It would not be good to tell the truth. That he stole the dog and was nearly killed in the process. He continued placing items on the conveyor belt. "It's complicated."

The cashier gave Roger a curious smirk. "Well, looks to me like you need to get that dog to a vet. I can recommend someone. She's great. She does a lot of work at the dog shelter where I work. As skinny as he is, he is a big Pit Bull. Bigger than usual."

"I didn't get him at a dog shelter. Although, he

should have been there. He was outside, and it was cold. Real cold. Too cold for a dog or a person or anything else unless it only lived outside."

The cashier held up a compromising hand. "Okay-Okay, I will stop asking questions. I suspect the dog is much better with you then with someone who wasn't caring for it. I do not need to know all the details."

Roger was relieved by the retort. He did not want to explain any more. "Thanks. Maybe one day I could give you the details, just not now."

"Call Dr. Crowe. Alice Crowe. Tell her April sent you. You need to get that poor animal there. That dog has been neglected and who knows what is wrong with him. That paw might be bad. He also may have worms or something. Could need antibiotics. Who knows? In fact, you may want go there right now. With that foot, you probably do not want to wait."

"You work two jobs?" Roger's mind was jumping around. "I am sorry I don't know much about dogs. I guess I have a lot to learn."

"That's fine. I work at the Happy Yappers Rescue Shelter. I work there and sometimes they team me up with the County Rescue when a place gets raided. I work for pay sometimes and sometimes I'm a volunteer. They're a non-profit so it depends on how the donations are coming in, whether I can get paid or not. That's why I do this gig as well. "

"Oh, yeah. I'll have to check that place out. Not that I need a dog. I have one. But maybe I can stop by one day."

"I'd like that," said April with a wry smirk.

Roger enjoyed the flirting. It had been such a long time that a woman took an interest in him. During junior year of high school, he sat next to a raven-haired beauty with a smile that could light up the room. She was smart and giggled at the jokes he told. Roger became instantly smitten by the coquette. Alyssa was a cheerleader and guys were gaga for her. Roger was well aware of the competition. Efforts to excel on the grid-iron were not so much for the fans, coach, or father, but instead a way to garner her attention. It worked. She attended the junior prom with him and joined Roger to spend the latest parts of the evening down hidden away at the beach. That summer and senior year, the two were as inseparable as two kids on the edge of adult-hood could be. Alyssa helped Roger with the fledging T-shirt business. Roger joined Alyssa and her parents on college visits. She helped him study. He taught her how to surf.

When Alyssa went away to college, Roger saw the change. She met new friends. As good a student as she was in high school, Alyssa became more studious in college. She often talked about her future. She wanted law school. A personality change. She belittled him for not going to college. She said that a T-shirt business was not a career. That it was not even a real business. That her friends were going to be bankers and executives. On weekend visits to the college, Roger often felt like a fifth wheel. Alyssa had more in common with classmates than with him. Phone calls became shorter and more infrequent. Roger suspected that Alyssa was seeing other guys. When Roger was arrested, Alyssa's father called to say that his daughter no longer wanted to be contacted by him. Now the blue-haired sex kitten named April was expressing her interest.

"Well, I will stop by; I promise. By the way, you have a cool name, April."

"Thank you. I have had it my whole life."

"And you?" asked April with a questioning look.

"Roger."

"Oh, Roger the Dodger," joked April. "How perfect. I ask you about the dog and you dodge my questions." She ended with a laugh.

"I will tell you everything once I know you better. I promise."

"You make a lot of promises," said April dryly.

"I guess I do," said Roger nervously.

"You have a nice beard. Beards are popular now."

"I started growing it after I got out of … " Roger stopped himself.

"Out of what?"

"Out of … " Roger could not think of what to say.

"Yeah? The military?"

"No, not that. I started growing it six months ago. On a lark. Just started growing it for fun."

April looked at Roger suspiciously. "What's your dog's name?"

"Name?"

April burst into a laugh. "Yes, name. He has a name, doesn't he?"

"Oh yeah. I guess he does. I just don't know it." Roger stumbled on his words. An entertained grin crossed April's mouth. The beep-beep sound of scanned items as April finished the order.

"Well, when I was just a youngster, I always wanted to have a dog and name it Cyrus. We didn't have a dog because my mother was allergic. I still live with my mother and still never had a dog."

The name tumbled in Roger's head. It sounded like a good name. He even thought that the Pit Bull looked like a Cyrus. There was a tough quality to its sound.

"Well, if you don't mind, Cyrus will be his name. His new name. I like it."

"That sounds good." April circled around the conveyor belt. With two hands she palmed Cyrus's head and spoke to the dog's face. "You are Cyrus. And you have quite an owner. I know he will take good care of you."

"Thank you for saying that. And I will. I will take good care of Cyrus."

"Cyrus means 'one who bestows care'. Don't be surprised if he takes as much care of you as you do of him."

"Dogs have a way of taking care of people, that's for sure."

"He's a Blue Nose. Did you know that?"

"No, I didn't. What's that?"

"It's Cyrus's coloring. The blackish-gray nose. The bluish-gray coat. They are uncommon. Someone paid a lot for him."

The comment stung Roger. It made him feel like a thief.

"Now all you have to do is pay us," said April, "and get him to the vet."

"Oh, yeah." Roger reached for his wallet and transacted the sale.

"I'd like to see you at that dog shelter," reminded April.

Roger studied the cashier. Her pixie mouth. The outlines of her curves. The softness in her face.

"The dog shelter? Oh yeah, I will come by one day."

Chapter 12

THE sign on the building said *Rex Collision – Rex Fixes All Wrecks*. The name and slogan were ubiquitous to the area. Billboards and television commercials advertising the establishment helped the company be the area's most successful vehicle bodywork facility. Rex Colleti was the owner and familiar to many for acting in the company's silly television commercials. Roger knew his son from high school. He was an unusually smallish kid who was often the target of cruel taunts. Bullies often called him "Little Glen." One day after classes Roger drove past the lake adjacent to their high school. Several teenagers surrounded Glen in an act of intimidation. It appeared that they were attempting to toss him into the water. They could easily overpower the diminutive sophomore. Several girls implored the ruffians to stop, to no avail.

That day, Roger slammed on the car brakes and sprang into action. The screeching wheels got the bullies' attention. Roger yelled out. He charged the group, pushing his way in until facing off with the biggest of the group. Roger slammed hands into a guy's chest, then raised a clenched fist. He figured that if he showed a willingness to tussle with the toughest then the others might back off. It worked. A few words were exchanged but the ruffians gave up, quickly withdrawing. Glen was shaken up. Roger gave him and the girls a ride home. For the rest of his senior year, Roger became a bit of a protector of Glen. The very fact that students knew that Glen was a friend of Roger, the star football player, was enough to temper bullying activities. The small sophomore always acted grateful. Now Roger was driving around in a shot-up car and decided to call in a favor.

Cyrus was in the front passenger seat, breathing happy pants. Dr. Alice Crowe examined the paw earlier, which led the veterinarian to find what caused the pain. She discovered a small sliver of glass remaining in the front foot pad. The doctor cleaned out the cut, added some antibiotic ointment and wrapped the paw. The veterinarian was confident that in a few days the foot pad would heal completely. She gave the Pit Bull a full examination. Shots given would fight any infection and parasites homed up in the dog's system. Dr. Crowe noted Cyrus was underweight, but with a few weeks of being fed a high protein diet the dog would gain back those needed pounds.

Roger and Cyrus entered the Rex Collision office. The room reception area was painted in a tangerine and baby blue motif, marking the company colors. A long-haired, heavyset guy with tattooed arms stared into a computer screen sitting on the counter. Walls displayed thank-you plaques and sport sponsorship recognitions. At the side, massive windows allowed customers a fishbowl view of the repair activities inside the facility.

The counter guy lifted working eyes to peer at Roger. "Can I help you?

"I need to speak with Glen Colleti."

"In reference to what?"

"In reference to I am a friend of his and need to speak with him."

"Is there anything I can help you with?"

"Yes, you can ask Glen to come see me."

"He's busy."

"I'll wait."

"You're going to wait? Does this have to do with fixing your car?"

Frustrated, Roger turned toward the glass windows. Anxious eyes searched the garage where busy technicians operated on several cars in different workstations. Glen happened past the windows, wiping hands into a rag. Roger took a couple of quick steps toward the former high school friend. A tap on the glass. Glen stopped. Twisting his abdomen toward the window. A confused look crossed the technician's face. Roger held up an open hand in a wave. Glen waved back still looking bewildered. Roger suspected that he did not recognize him. A cupped hand waved Glen in.

"He's busy, dude."

Roger turned back to the counter to give the guy an exasperated look. Glen entered the waiting area.

"Glen, its Roger. Roger Wilson from high school."

"Roger!" sang Glen. "I only realized who it was when I came through the door. The beard threw me off. How are you? Last I heard you were … " Glen stopped himself. A blush of embarrassment filled his face.

Roger looked down at the ground gripping Cyrus's leash with both hands. There was an awkward silence.

"Yeah, I got myself in some trouble. I've been out for six months. But I need some help today. Can I show you something?"

"Show me something? Yeah, Roger. Your car?"

"Yeah, my car," said Roger with an amused grin.

"Okay, let me get my coat." Glen grabbed a jacket off a coat hook and followed Roger to the parking lot. "What's wrong with your dog?"

Cyrus was still hobbling on a bandaged foot. Roger had put the Pit Bull in a dog coat to keep the dog warm, but also so that people would not see how skinny he was.

"He stepped onto some cut glass and cut up his paw. I took him to the vet and he will be okay."

"Looks like he needed a vet. A doctor to wrap that paw. He looks like he is hurting."

"He'll be okay. Really. The vet pulled out some glass and added some ointment. I take good care of my pooch."

Roger did not like having to explain about Cyrus, much less making what might sound like an apology. They got to the car. He wanted to refocus on the damage.

He pointed to where a lead slug punctured the vehicle's metal body. "Look at this."

Roger stepped up on the bumper and pointed at the ricochet dent in the roof. Glen joined him.

"I think you can see the window was shot out."

Glen looked astonished. "Shot out?"

They both stepped to the ground.

"Yeah, shot out. But its not what you think. I'm not in trouble. I happened to be in a gang area when some shots hit my car. It had nothing to do with me. I just do not want to have to expound on it too much. Especially, since I'm still out on parole. I need you to fix this for me without anyone knowing. Not even your father."

Glen stood frozen. Then a hesitant nod. A faraway stare.

"Listen," added Roger, "I know what you are thinking. I'm not in trouble. I promise. I stepped into something bad but need your help. Can you help me?"

"Yeah, Roger, no problem. I can fix the holes and replace the window. I'll call around to a couple of salvage yards and see who has the back glass. Everything will be done on the q.t."

Glen peered into the inside of the automobile. He spoke while looking in. "Is that a bullet hole in the passenger seat headrest?"

"Yeah. That's the bullet that blew out the window. A miracle that neither me nor Cyrus got hit."

"Were you in a war zone?" said Glen with a wry smile.

"I guess you can say that."

Glen looked inside the car then turned to Roger. "I'll patch that."

"Thanks, man. I'll pay you whatever you need. Just get this fixed for me. I don't need anyone asking questions. And can I get a loaner car? I need transportation."

"Yeah, we have a loaner car that you can use. And don't worry about the money, Roger. The glass won't be much and I will do all the work myself. It won't cost you anything, This one's on me." Glen held up a balled fist as an invitation for a knuckle bump.

"Really, free?" said Roger through a screwed face. He bumped knuckles.

"Yeah, man, free. Free for my friend."

Chapter 13

MUTED, wintry sunlight shone down on Roger and Cyrus as the two went out for their morning walk. The pair came across many well-meaning pedestrians who could not help asking about Cyrus and the injured paw. Roger looked forward to the next couple of days ahead when the foot would be healed, and the bandage removed. No longer would he have to repeat the lacking-in-detail explanation of a dog who stepped on glass. Some along the way commented on Cyrus's unusual large size for a Pit Bull. Others could see past the dog coat and remarked how skinny he was.

"Don't you feed him?" one woman asked.

"Of course, I feed him. But he's a very active dog and burns off lots of calories," responded Roger defensively.

Cyrus ate meals ravenously. Soon the dog would put on the needed weight and Roger would no longer need to explain the slim canine physique. It was apparent that he could not leave Cyrus alone in the house all day. With Roger away for at least ten hours doing shift work at the Amazon warehouse, Cyrus was left outdoors. The conditions were better than in Trenton. The dog was not tethered to a chain but could roam the yard freely. Roger left plenty of food and water for Cyrus and made a cloth bed on the covered porch for the dog to rest on. He clearly saw the irony in having the dog outside in the cold all day or even worse, all night. That is when he came up with the idea of a hinged doggy door. Roger removed the backdoor and cut in a hole and added a flap. No longer would poor Cyrus be stuck outside waiting for Roger to return to let him in. Cyrus was given the freedom to access both the indoors and outdoors whenever he liked.

Christmas was Roger's favorite holiday. He loved the decorations and the excitement that the coming day brought. Roger missed three Christmas home celebrations while in prison. He still dreaded the Christmas Day that would arrive in less than three weeks. Roger's mother called several times to remind him when he was to arrive at the home. She would try to treat him normally, but his father was another story. Roger anticipated the glances of disdain from the father seldom shy about reminding Roger of the shame he brought the family.

April found her way into Roger's mind. The thin-waist sexiness. A certain arrogant self-confidence. The hippie, free-spirit type. She could just come and go. A liberated woman. It was who April was. Roger wanted to know more about her. He allowed Cyrus to climb into the back of the Subaru. Rear seats were always left down to give the dog more room. No more bandage. A healed foot. The dog paced excitedly in the back compartment. Cyrus loved driving in the car. An open rear passenger window allowed the dog to feel the rush of oncoming wind in its face.

He went to PetSmart to buy Cyrus more food only to learn from the manager that it was April's day off. It was the second time he returned, and she was not working. The news was disappointing. He was anxious to see her again. He recalled what she said about the rescue shelter. She could be working there that day. A switch in plans. The shelter was a few miles west in a more rural part people called horse country. It was dubbed that for its many thoroughbred farms supporting the horse racing industry. Roger lifted the heavy bags of dog food onto the conveyor belt.

"Are you a Treats member?" asked the associate.

"Yes, I am."

Roger and Cyrus returned to the car where the Happy Yappers Rescue Shelter was inputted to the GPS. The lady voice directed Roger during the fifty-minute drive to the converted feed storage building with a full parking lot. More cars edged the country road. Roger drove past the rescue facility to leave the car at an abandoned gas station of peeling paint and broken windows. He opened the back of the car and, after leashing Cyrus, allowed him to climb down. Open skies. Sunbeams heated the earth. Rooftop snow converted to melt water that cascaded into gutters. Potholes filled with dirty slush. The warmer weather break was welcome.

Roger and Cyrus were greeted by a chorus of dog barks. So many humans enlivened the canine residents who yearned to be noticed. A couple of dozen dogs pranced excitedly around a common area. The canines were drawn to the waist-high plexiglass barrier each time someone approached. A beauty pageant of canines vied for notice. Barks, struts, jumps. Pants and tail waggles. Every dog doing its best to be taken to its forever home.

Roger and Cyrus walked down a hall where there were more dogs displayed in roomy cages. Some had their own special swagger. They, too, barked or pranced where they could. Cyrus rubbed noses through the cage openings with some of the dogs who footed *take-me-home* dances. People pointed and discussed the canines they might adopt. Little children there were just as excited as the dogs. The few puppies got the most attention. Volunteers and workers at the rescue shelter busied themselves speaking to the many people expressing an interest in a particular dog. Roger pretended to show interest in the dogs without any direct contact with the rescue workers. Eyes darted around for April. Nothing.

Just a sign pointing in the direction of the cat area. He moved around some more people before seeing the easy sight of blue hair. April was busy caring for some of the dogs in the background. Roger moved in closer, an attempt to be seen.

"Hey there!"

April was passing through an inside gate and into the common area. Many dogs surrounded her yelping and barking. She laughed at the attention she received. Then a welcoming smile.

"They think I have a treat for them."

"Do you?"

"Not at the moment. They were all fed earlier. I will give them dog biscuits in about an hour."

April shifted feet to maneuver through the mix of dogs, a shuffle that kept her from tripping over any canine in her path. She went to Roger with arms spread before leaning over the barrier to give him a hug.

"Oh Roger, it is so good to see you again. Thanks for stopping by." April leaned over to Cyrus. A head tilt. Then a voice used like she was talking to a small child. "And who do we have here? Is this Cyrus? Do you remember me from PetSmart?"

Cyrus used front legs to push his upper body off the floor and lay paws into April's open hands. She continued with the childish pet talk.

"Awww. I see the vet helped you, Cyrus. You really needed it. Yeah, you remember me, don't you? Don't you?"

Cyrus licked April's face. She giggled to the dog's affection.

"He remembers you, all right." Said Roger.

April then dropped the paws before leaning over farther grabbing the sides of Cyrus's face. "You are such a good dog. You've gained a little weight. You look so much better than when I saw you a week ago."

April held her hands there to a grateful Cyrus for a few moments before looking up. When she raised eyes, Roger was reminded of how beautiful she was. That smile was a heart tug. The features of nature's grandeur. A comment fell from his lips. "I bet guys hit on you all the time."

She sang her response. "All the time."

Roger smiled. The collective sound of barking got his attention. "Will you find homes for all these dogs?"

"That's the objective. We are not a kill facility. If a dog is not adopted, they just stay with us. The older ones are harder to find homes for. It can be heart-breaking. We do our best to love them all."

"I know you do. I can feel the love here. Everyone appears so dedicated."

"We are. We're all dog people. That goes without saying. And cat people too. We even have some rabbits. Everyone does their best. If the money was here, I'd work here full time. There are more dogs and cats than there is money. But like you said, there's lots of love. Boat loads of it."

Roger noticed a dog from the corner of his eye. It was patched in black, brown and white longish hair. Short legs kept its body close to the ground. The dog came close to Roger. She did not bark, but instead brought her nose close to the glass and touched the clear barrier near his legs. A tan and white Chihuahua was at her side. The little dog yelped. Roger reached down and pet the bigger dog and ignored the Chihuahua.

"She is a Pembroke Welsh Corgi. She's a full breed. But she's old."

"How old?"

"She's ten. That is old for her breed. We've had her for two years. I think she will be with us forever. Her owner died at home. Neighbors called police when they did not see the old man for a couple of days. Cops found the owner on a couch dead of a heart attack. The Corgi was by the man for three days. No food or water. She was guarding the man. Would not move. She growled at the first responders. She is loyal. She was true-blue to that old man. Lady, that's her name."

"Lady sounds like a good dog."

"She is. But she is up there in years."

Roger looked curiously at the Chihuahua. "What's the deal with the little guy?"

"He was born in a puppy mill out in Warrenburg. The place was terrible. Poor dogs. The police and county rescuers raided it a couple of weeks back. The authorities spread the dogs around to a lot of shelters. We got three and were able to find homes for two. This one latched on to Lady. He does not move from her. He even sleeps with her."

Roger laughed. Cyrus bounced his nose on the Plexiglass as if to reach Lady and the Chihuahua. "I guess he likes older women."

"I suppose," said April with a seriousness. "The poor dog never had anyone to love him except his own mother. They take the puppies away from the mothers too soon. The mothers' bodies are nothing more than puppy factories."

There was a pause.

"I am sure that poor Chihuahua went through a lot."

"I'm sure he did. We worry about him. He really is attached to Lady. No one will likely adopt that old girl. She really likes him. You can see she likes taking care of him."

"What's going to happen if someone wants to take that little guy?"

"Buddy? It's what we worry about. It's going to be bad when we have to break them up. It will be hurtful to Lady to not have him around. Buddy won't want to leave Lady. She has become a surrogate mother to him. We do not want to traumatize the little guy anymore than he has been."

Roger tried to think of something to say. "If I didn't just get Cyrus maybe I would adopt them. But I can't, not with him now."

April's eyes opened wide with the suggestion. "Why not? You're a good dog owner. You have a good heart. You would be great with three dogs."

The idea did not seem feasible. The interior of the house was under construction and the idea of having three animals seemed unrealistic. Roger looked at the eyes of Lady. She exuded goodness. The story of her standing sentry to her deceased owner for days impressed Roger. It even made him feel a little sentimental. And now she provided protection to the young and traumatized Chihuahua puppy.

Roger looked back to April. She crossed arms beneath a calm, hypnotic stare. A hip bend and wanting facial expression. He knew exactly what the sexy sorceress was up to. She was attempting to cast a spell.

And it was working.

Chapter 14

BUDDY was confused. The man with the beard laid him onto the front passenger seat of the vehicle and walked away with Lady and the other dog. April was outside as well, helping the man. He yelped. He yelped for Lady. He yelped for the mother he still remembered. A yelp for April who took good care of him. He yelped again and again. Sudden panic. Circle turns. Body shakes. A commotion toward the back of the vehicle. Then a door slam. He saw the other dog. He saw Lady. She pushed her upper body onto the center console. She panted happy pants. Buddy touched noses and licked her face. He could tell she was happy. Happier than he ever saw her. This made him feel less nervous. He relaxed a little. If Lady was happy then he thought, he should be happy.

The man with the beard entered the car. He reached over and pet him. He brushed the side of his thumb over his forehead like he had done an hour earlier. April gave the bearded man a couple of leashes, some dog food and paperwork. The man made him feel comfortable. Lady made him feel comfortable. *Were they going to a better place?*

April was at the driver's side window. "Thank you, thank you, Roger. You are my hero. Take good care of the fur babies. I know you will."

"You have nothing to worry about, April. They are in good hands. I'm excited to have them. Now you'll have to come over and see them."

"You know I will. Of course, I will." April lowered her head and gave Roger a surprise kiss on the lips. "You deserve that. You are such a good guy." She then spoke to the dogs playfully. "Lady, Buddy, this is Roger and Cyrus. You're going to be very excited with your new home."

"You owe me a date you know," said Roger through a smile.

"I haven't forgotten. You have my cell phone number now. It's in with the paperwork I gave you. Give me a call."

"I will."

Buddy was happy with the ride to Roger's house. He never felt so free. No cage. No restrictions. He stood on hind legs with paws on the dashboard seeing the world through the windshield. Trees, buildings, cars. So much to see. The stimuli caused the Chihuahua to shake. They were good shakes. Happy shakes. All Buddy wanted to do was to look out and take it all in. An hour drive before turning onto the dead-end street. They got to the bungalow house.

Roger let Lady and Cyrus out of the back of the vehicle. Then he came over and opened the passenger side of the car. He reached in and picked up Buddy and held him inside the crook of his arm. Buddy got scared. He was not even sure why he was scared. Maybe the newness of it all. So much happened in such a short period of time. The puppy mill. Then the rescue shelter. Then a car ride. Now a new place. The newness of everything was frightening. Not scared like when he was at the puppy mill. Even less scared when first getting to the animal shelter and seeing all the barking dogs. But scared, nonetheless.

He was relieved that Lady was there. But he still shook. Shaking is what he did. He did it when he was cold. He did it when he was scared. Sometimes he shook for no reason at all. If he was separated from Lady, the shaking spells were more frequent. Lady was unleashed as was the other dog. They were in the small front yard. Cyrus sniffed around. Lady did the same, as if to discover some new surroundings. Roger petted Buddy's head which had a calming effect on the timid puppy. Then Roger climbed a few steps and went to the front door. He turned back and called the other dogs.

"Cyrus, Lady, come on up."

Cyrus ascended the stairs with ease. The Pit Bull was young and muscular. Long legs and built like an athlete. Cyrus mingled on the porch. Roger laid Buddy onto the decking floor. He under-armed the mail to use a free hand for the keys. Buddy went to the edge of the porch and looked down. Lady was still on the sidewalk.

"You're having a little bit of trouble with those stairs, eh?" said Roger to Lady.

Lady looked up at Buddy. Eyes connected. Lady seemed unsure of the stairs. She was not used to them or had not climbed steps in a long while. Buddy knew Lady had a problem. She was not moving. Only staring. Buddy yelped. Quick little barks of encouragement. Buddy's way of helping Lady. Lady stayed fixated on Buddy. She moved back and forth a little, then a leap to the first step. Then another, then another until she reached the porch. Lady was there. Her eyes reassuring. They signaled to Buddy that everything would be okay. That they both had a real home now. Lady paced quickly around. She returned eyes to Buddy. The sound of jiggled keys. A doorknob turned. An open door.

"C'mon, Cyrus. We're going in. You need to show your friends around."

Buddy investigated the surroundings while Cyrus checked them out as if getting used to the new two. Roger took the back door off its hinges. Cold air came into the home and the Chihuahua followed Lady and Cyrus out the back opening into the yard. There were dog toys out there just like the rescue shelter had. Lady picked up a red plastic toy. She paced around the perimeter of the yard that was closed in with a chain-linked fence. Cyrus pulled the toy from Lady's mouth.

"Hey, Cyrus, let her have it!" yelled Roger.

Cyrus dropped the toy on the ground, but Lady did not take it.

Buddy looked up on the porch and watched Roger use a circular saw to cut an additional square opening. It was smaller than the existing hole and lower toward the bottom. Roger attached a door to the smaller opening in the same fashion as the larger opening. Roger rehung the door.

"Okay, I am not going to be here all of the time. So, you three will have to go in and out. This will allow you to go and come back."

Roger trained Buddy in using the flap door. He held up a recognizable box of dog biscuits. He shook the box. Buddy yelped for the biscuits. So did Cyrus. Lady paced back and forth panting with a smile on her face. Roger walked to the door. He pushed the pet flap and it rocked back and forth. He then put his hand on the knob and walked outside. Roger disappeared behind the door. Cyrus, already experienced, ran right through the passageway. Buddy was excited with the challenge of learning something new. A hand pushed the box of biscuits. The carton danced on the floor. Buddy and Lady looked at the curiosity. Buddy barked at the dancing box. Lady panted and looked on. More barking. More faux attacks at the box. Then the box disappeared behind the flap. Cyrus rushed back though the door, as if helping train him and Lady. Cyrus then disappeared though the larger door. Lady took a careful slow walk through the opening.

Buddy was unsure of the small door. Small doors were all over the puppy mill. Those small doors kept dogs trapped. The little canine paced back and forth. He did not want to be alone in the house. Fear. Loneliness. He paced some more. He barked. Loneliness overcame the fear. He went to the flap door with head down and pushed through.

"How's that, Buddy?"

Roger awarded Buddy a treat. Canine jaws crunched the delicious biscuit. A smile between Roger's whiskers. Broken biscuit pieces fell to the porch floor. Paws used to push the bigger parts. Buddy's tongue scraped up the crumbs. He felt the bearded man's hand against his back. A lift into his arm. Buddy was petted affection-ately. He responded to the attention with quick pants.

"How did you like your dog biscuit?" asked Roger.

Buddy yelped.

A laugh. "Yeah, Buddy? You liked it?" Roger held him closer. "You know something? You are going to like it here. All day long you can come and go from the house to the back yard. Much better than the puppy mill you came from. Here you have your freedom."

Buddy's glassy eyes looked up at Roger. The bright smile shining through his beard was reassuring. Buddy felt the love through a caretaker's grasp. There was a happiness within the house. Buddy was not shaking like before. There was a feeling of security. A loving owner. A warm home. Two dog friends.

Chapter 15

THE Subaru slipped into the driveway. Roger's schedule was not constant, some day shifts, more night shifts. It was exhausting. Sleeping at different times. Extended work shifts to keep up with the Christmas rush. Lots of overtime. The money was good. Roger was young and in shape. He would do what he had to keep up. Make the cash while he could. That was the thinking. Things would normalize after the new year.

Roger wanted to go into the house and collapse on the bed, but knew the anxious dogs would not allow it. They would want to go for a walk, so any needed sleep would have to wait until the three canines got their fill of strolling through the neighborhood and beyond. Roger entered the home to the daily canine welcoming committee. Cyrus, by far the biggest of the trio, threw two front paws on Roger's chest. Buddy yelped in place. Lady paced back and forth with a happy tongue hanging out the side of her mouth. All were hungry for attention. All were hungry for food. Roger overflowed the dog food bowls to buy a few moments of time. Roger went to the bedroom. He laid back on the mattress without ever taking off the ski jacket. Legs dangled off the edge. Eyes mercifully closed.

A quick drift into sleep. Only a few minutes before the dogs entered the room demanding to be walked. Cyrus learned how to grab the leashes by standing on hind legs and taking them from the wall hanger. All three got into the habit of dragging their leashes around when they wanted Roger to take them out. A couple of barks. Roger's tired body stayed pinned to the bed.

A head lift to see the trio. "I know, I know. You guys want to go walking. One minute."

Roger dropped his heavy head back. A long walk and the dogs would be satisfied. Roger knew it. Cyrus, Lady and Buddy would let him sleep when he got back. They were okay with a closed bedroom door and a lazy afternoon in the back yard. Roger scooped up the leashes that the dogs dropped on the ground. A hook to the collars before herding the excited dogs out the front door. He took them up the dead-end street to the main road. Roger walked them a few blocks down to the piers to be around some people activity. It was there that party boats with sterns backed in were ready to take on day anglers. Gray waves splashed through sturdy pilings. Captains hawked their boats' different offerings. Half-day trip. Three-quarter day trip. Whiting. Ling. Cod. Heated rails. Warm cabin. Fast boat. Fishermen carried fishing rods and coolers down the docks. Money exchanges. People welcomed aboard.

Roger easily recognized a face of one of the deck-hands on a boat called the *Miss Took II*. There was Stephen in waterproof bib overalls, hooded sweatshirt and stocking cap. He busied himself with a filet knife, cutting squid into bait-sized pieces. He enjoyed some playful conversing with customers who passed behind him lugging fishing gear. Roger stood and watched the unsuspecting crewman as he worked. Thoughts of being stood up by a friend boiled inside him. The more he watched, the angrier he got. Not a friend at all. Just another guy who pretended to be a friend.

From the bulkhead Roger yelled over, "Hey, Stephen, I missed you the other night."

Stephen looked up. Eyes widened. A hint of embarrassment crossed his face. Stephen just shook the knife in the air in place of waving a hand. The gesture said he was too busy to talk. That he was too occupied by the task at hand.

"Don't forget my seven hundred dollars, Stephen. I do expect to be paid back," said Roger in a louder voice. The point was to shame Stephen. He also was not going to let him skate on the money that was owed. Some of the customers looked over. So did the captain who turned back and looked at Stephen curiously while his deckhand remained looking down. Stephen just kept slicing the sea life of elongated tubular bodies and tentacles into pieces small enough for a fishhook.

Roger was done. He let himself be known. Who knew if he would ever get the seven hundred dollars owed him? That was not the point. Roger was there in Stephen's time of need. He learned that guys like Stephen and Colin were unreliable. Roger knew most of the guys he grew up with could not be counted on. Time to shed friends like that. Roger took the dogs farther down the pier where the commercial fishing boats tied up. Some boats netted fish. Others dragged the ocean floor for scallops, clams and flat fish. Lobstermen piloted sloops spotting the water surfaces with buoys tied to baited lobster traps. He looked for the ninety-five-foot *Lady Mora*, the commercial fishing vessel that Uncle Ray owned. It was a boat that went out on ten-day scallop trips to the Georges Canyon. Scallop fishing was a profitable enterprise and *Lady Mora* was phenomenally successful. The vessel known for its lucrative catches earned the moniker "Lady Moolah." It was tough work with little sleep. No one denied that the money was good. There was a waiting list for those who wanted to crew on Uncle Ray's boat.

Roger even got a taste of it one high school summer when he crewed on the *Lady Mora*. He saw how many of the commercial deck hands lived. To Roger, those who worked the fishing boats were their own community. Misfits and others on the edges of regular society. Ocean cowboys. Renegades. They were almost a different breed. Adventurers who thrived on that sense of disconnection. Some had suspicious histories. Many with past run-ins with the law. When they were on the boat, they were away from everything. It was their world out there, not someone else's. The work was very tough. Some said it required a back of steel with a hinge in the middle. Other times it was exhilarating. The crew shared in the bounty. The more scallops harvested, the more money everyone made. When crews got back, they left the docks with pockets full of cash. Outstanding bills were paid. Refrigerators got filled. Drug dealers contacted. Bar crawls. Partying ensued. Morning breakfast with the children. Dealings with wives or girlfriends. Sometimes both. Trouble never far away. More partying, more bills. When money got low, the captain got calls. *When are we going out to sea again?*

Fun walks. Tangled leashes of excitement. The dogs loved going out. People coming and going, boat activity, seagulls lifts and landings were all enough stimuli to keep the canines energized. Cyrus pulled hard. Lady took her time, focusing longer on local action. Buddy was a bundle of energy, zigging and zagging, yipping and yapping.

Three-strand nylon ropes held metal-hulled *Lady Mora* tight to the bulkhead. Roger brought the dogs closer. Steel dredges stained the trawler sides rusty red. Iron pipe masts supported a winch and drum system ready to haul catches harvested from forty fathoms of depth.

A station wagon sporting years' worth of scratches and dents was backed up to the vessel. Deck hands unloaded grocery bags to pass to an onboard crewman. Forty-five-year-old Uncle Ray issued captain orders while busy hands tested the hydraulics. He was fit like an athlete. Narrow waist, strong arms. Not an ounce of fat. A brownish face weathered by years of sun, wind and cold. Crisscross complexion lines showed the toll the sea can take on a man. From the neck down, Uncle Ray looked thirty. From the neck up he could pass for sixty.

A cigarette cornered the captain's mouth. Feet filled white rubber boots darkened by use. A sheathed knife strapped belt side. Blue jeans and flannel shirt. The cool-blooded eyes of a man in charge.

"Hey, Ray. You should wear a jacket, its cold out today."

Uncle Ray leered over. He was busy and looked hurried. "What you got there?"

"Me? Just some dogs." Suddenly a realization that maybe bringing the dogs by was not a good idea. There was never any discussion about pets. He did not have dogs when he moved in his uncle's bungalow.

Uncle Ray looked annoyed. That was not unusual. He could be especially tense when ready for a trip. "Dogs? You have dogs living in my house?"

Roger's heart sank. He quickly worried that having animals at the house could be a problem. He tried to think of something to say.

"They are clean dogs. And they keep my house protected. I mean your house protected. You should see what I am doing there. I have taken down the old plaster. No more water stains. I am replacing the old walls with new Sheetrock."

"We never talked about pets. Who said you could have dogs in the house? I don't want pets messing up my house."

Roger recognized some of the six-man crew. None greeted him. That was the way guys like that were. They were cliquey. Either you were a crewman, or you were not. Some exchanged amused glances as if tickled by the troubling exchange.

"These dogs are good. I put dog flaps in the back door so that they can come and go when I am gone. Real good dogs. They don't t make a mess."

"You're cutting holes in my door?" said Ray without looking up.

"I can always replace the door."

"I'm not charging you rent. The least you could do is ask me before you bring animals into my house," Uncle Ray shouted from the boat. Again, the deck-hands traded smirks. One laughed silently.

"I'm sorry. I should have thought of that. I promise

to keep things real clean. You'll see. The house is coming along real good. The walls are nearly done. And you saw the siding I put up. And the shutters. The shutters sure makes the place look better. Everyone says it. Just some more Sheetrocking, then I can hit the floors. I pulled up that old carpet and the hardwood floors underneath are beautiful."

"I know the floors are good in that house. That house was built right after World War II. That's the way they did things back then. Not like today," said Uncle Ray dismissively.

Roger stood nodding in agreement. He decided it was best to end the conversation. Roger waited a few moments as Uncle Ray went back to issuing commands to the crew who remained busy. Then he spoke.

"Have a safe trip, Ray. I hope you catch lots of scallops."

Uncle Ray was distracted with a mechanical issue. He did not answer but instead disappeared into a side door of the cabin. Roger walked away dejectedly.

The dogs twisted around Roger's stationary pose. He switched leash handles between hands to allow some slack. He looked down at the dogs and spoke.

"You guys want to keep our walk going? I think we should."

Roger began to walk back toward the end of the pier. He saw a woman pushing a stroller. He knew who she was. Roger recognized her as the only other winter resident on their short, dead-end street. She and her two kids lived catty-cornered from where he lived. As he neared the woman, he realized who she was. She was the younger sister of a high school acquaintance. A skateboarder that Roger used to know named Devon. It was his sister. Roger knew a little bit about her. Like April, she was three or four years younger than he. Roger vaguely remembered her as pudgy and socially awkward. She used to wait tables at a hot spot restaurant where the then teenager met a much older waiter who got her pregnant. The last thing he heard was they were married. Roger quickly recalled never seeing a man come or go from the house across the street. He remembered Devon's sister as Melissa.

He walked toward her. She stood looking toward him, rocking the carriage back and forth. Both toddlers had winter in their cheeks. One of her children leaned forward, pointing to a seagull pecking the insides of a broken clam shell. More of the ocean birds rode overhead winds. She spoke first.

"Howdy, neighbor!" said Melissa kiddingly.

Roger smiled and waved.

"Are you dog-sitting?" she asked.

"No, these are my dogs. You are out early."

"Yeah, I have four online classes today. Thursday is my busiest day so I have to get the girls out now because we will be stuck in the house the rest of the day."

"I see."

Melissa brought the conversation back to the dogs. "All three dogs are yours? Really? Did you get them recently? You must have. I've seen you with the bigger one but not the other two."

Roger walked up to her and stopped. Cyrus sniffed at the three-year-old Sophie, while the two-year-old Emma looked on. Emma appeared a little apprehensive.

"You can pet him if you want. He won't hurt you."

The three-year-old put out a spread hand and petted Cyrus on the head. A gesture that he welcomed.

"Ah, Sophie. You found a friend," said Melissa with her eyes bouncing between her daughter and Roger.

The attention Cyrus gave Sophie caused Emma to begin crying jealous sobs. Roger lifted Buddy to the younger girl so she could pet him and when she did, the crying ceased. The little girl petted Buddy's head and giggled. Lady paced back and forth in front of the stroller.

"My two girls like your dogs."

"I can tell."

Roger looked straight at Melissa in a more serious way. She was attractive with short dark hair, bright brown eyes and a pixie smile. Roger knew her brother and calculated Melissa's age as twenty or twenty-one. There was a sexy rasp to her voice. The old weight was gone. She was now fit. It was why he never recognized her from a distance. "My name is Roger. I know your brother, Devon."

"Yeah, Devon mentioned you."

Roger hesitated; unsure what Devon may have said.

"All good things, by the way." Her facial expression changed to a more serious one. Her face dropped. "Although he mentioned you had some troubles. But that's okay. I know what that's like. "

"How is Devon doing?"

"Devon went to Seton Hall for a year and was kicked out for bad grades. He's talked about joining the army until he got a drunken driving arrest."

"I heard about that. No doubt you heard about me."

"Everyone heard about you, Roger. It was so unlike you. But heck, we all make mistakes. They say it's best to make the mistakes while we are young. We have our whole lives ahead of us."

"Oh. And what did you mean when you said you know what troubles are like?"

"Me?" Melissa lowered her voice as if she wanted to tell the story but not have the girls hear. "I made a lot of my own mistakes. I met a guy four summers ago when I waited tables at Captain Henry's. He was an Albanian guy in his late twenties."

Roger, already knowing some of the details, pretended to be hearing it for the first time. "Oh yeah, Captain Henry's Seafood. It's a good place."

"Yeah, I was making a ton of money there. But meeting Prek was the worst thing."

"Prek?"

"Yeah, Prek. That is an Albanian name. Some people at the restaurant called him Peter. But if his mother named him Prick it would have been better."

Roger politely smiled and let her continue.

"He was a real asshole. But I was young and thought he was great. He was much older than me, twenty-eight when I met him. I just turned sixteen."

"A real cradle robber."

"Tell me about it. My parents hated him. He got me pregnant when I was just seventeen. Right away he wanted to get married. Not to do the right thing, but so that he could get a green card."

"Then what happened?"

"We got married and moved into Strayer Apartments up in Atlantic Cliffs. You know where I am talking about, right?"

The three dogs liked the attention they were getting from the two girls in the stroller.

"Strayer Apartments? Oh, sure. People sometimes call them Starter Apartments. A friend of mine lives there."

"Yeah, I know. It seems like everyone starts out there. Rents are reasonable and they only ask for one month's security."

"So, what happened to that Prick guy?"

"Prek was his name," said Melissa with an embarrassed smile. "Anyway, he was my husband. But he and his two brothers were into stealing cars and shipping them to Eastern Europe. I did not know anything about it. Although, Prek always had a nice car and treated himself to fine wine. He went out a lot. I was stuck home with the babies. But he always had money. Even though he was a waiter."

"So, what happened to him?"

"One night they tried to steal the wrong guy's car. The guy caught them in the act and beat the shit out of the two brothers. Prek was the lookout. Not such a good lookout, I guess. He managed to escape without a scratch. The cops think he is hiding out in Canada. They said he won't be back. If he did come back, he would be thrown in jail like his two asshole brothers."

"Wow, I am sorry to hear that."

"I was sooo naïve. Insecure and unsure of myself. I was swept off my feet by a handsome European who always smelled nice and drove a cool car. Now I have two children and am back living with my parents."

"But you are in that bungalow across from me?"

"Yeah, I know. I really live with my parents. That bungalow is an investment property my parents rent out in the summer. They are letting me stay there for the winter. It gives them a break from us and us a break from them."

There was a pause in the conversation. The weight of her circumstances showed in her pressing of a curled lip. Snow flurries began to swirl. Melissa spoke.

"It has been a cold fall. I can't believe we had two snowfalls already." She leaned forward toward the front of the stroller. "Sophie, Emma, you found some friends." Melissa turned back to Roger and smiled. "I am liking my time in the bungalow. I see you are doing some work to yours."

"It really is not mine. It is my Uncle Ray's. He's a fisherman. He owns the *Lady Mora* up the pier." Roger tilted his head in the direction of the trawler. "They are going out on a trip today. They dredge for scallops."

"Wow, kind of cold to be out in the ocean." Melissa hugged herself in a mock expression. "And so close to Christmas."

"They are making a lot of money harvesting scallops. That's why they are squeezing in a trip before the holiday."

Melissa bounced her head up and down in a nod of understanding. She then spoke again.

"I was upset that your business closed. I even have a couple of your shirts. I got them as gifts. People told me your business was doing really well but then … "

Melissa's candidness jarred him.

"My T-shirt business did great. I was making a lot of money. The business was growing faster than I could keep up. In the slow season, money was going out faster than it was coming in. Then I did something really stupid and basically ruined my life."

Melissa's eyes dropped to the ground. Her mouth became more serious. "I see."

"Money can make us panic ... or a lack of, is what I mean. It can make us do stupid things."

"How long were you in jail?"

Roger was taken aback by the question. "Well, I got ... I got ..." he stammered, "I got sentenced to six years in state prison but was released after two and a half years for good behavior."

"How was it in there?"

"Tough. Very tough," said Roger, who also searched the ground.

"You didn't ruin your life. You can always bounce back."

"It's not easy."

"How long have you been out?'

"About six months."

Melissa turned her attention to the bay as if searching for something to say.

"Who said its going to be easy? Life isn't easy unless you are born rich or win the lottery. Look at me. Pregnant at seventeen. Teenage mom. A husband on the lam. No job prospects. Not even a high school diploma. I used to feel sorry for myself. That I had no future. That welfare momhood was my destiny. Then one day I said to myself I can either wallow in pity or do something. That's when I worked on getting my G.E.D. Now I am taking nursing courses at the community college. A lot of the work I do is online."

"Wow, that's cool."

"I made a decision that I wanted my two girls to be proud of me. That they saw me as a worker. Someone who did something. Its not easy, but what is?"

"You make a lot of sense."

"I am almost twenty-one. In the spring I will have my associate's. Straight As. In the fall I start going to Kean College to get my four-year degree. My goal is to be a nurse practitioner."

"You are a real go-getter."

"I can sit around and feel sorry for myself or I can do something about it. There is an excitement in working toward a goal. I do it for them." Melissa tilted her head toward the front of the stroller where the girls played with the dogs. "And I do it for myself."

Roger was ready to end the conversation and move on. "I give you a lot of credit. You are doing a lot. It was good meeting you."

Roger tugged on the leashes to pull the three dogs from the stroller. "C'mon guys. We need to keep going."

Melissa was not finished. "Don't believe you have ruined your life, Roger. You can fix it. You do have a choice."

"I hope you are right."

"I am right. It is a thinking thing. A reset thing. Don't let your arrest define your life. You made a mistake. Learn from it and move on."

"You are a wise girl – I mean woman."

Melissa let out an amused laugh. "I've had to do a lot of growing up in the past three to four years."

"Well, I will remember what you said. Its cold out here. Coldest fall I ever remember. We're going to keep going. I'll see you around. Bye, girls!"

Roger started to walk away. Melissa called to him.

"Roger, if you ever want to do anything, I'm around."

Roger stood there and pursed his lips. He did not say anything. A tricky silence.

Melissa spoke again. "I know guys are hesitant when they see a girl, or a woman with two kids. But I would not be a burden. We could just go out. My mom can watch the girls."

Roger stayed quiet without adding a facial expression. He nodded. "Thanks, Melissa, Thanks for letting me know."

Roger gave a perfunctory nod, then turned walking the dogs away. He heard Melissa speak to his back.

"Make sure you take care of your babies."

"I will, Melissa. And you do the same with yours."

Chapter 16

WHITE-COLORED lights spiraled the Christmas tree. Roger added the plastic ornaments and silvery tinsel to the evergreen branches. Roger was glad to have the tree, feeling it added warmth and holiday spirit to the home. The dogs seemed curious about having a tree in the house and kept up a routine of sniffing the needles and poking at it. They found the evergreen a real attraction. Roger made a point of driving a nail in the wall and tying string to use as an anchor. It was a matter of preventing his coming home to a knock-over accident.

The inside of the house was coming along nicely, and he worked on it more diligently than ever. Completion would mean a true common area instead of walking into a construction zone. Most of the rest of the walls were all freshly Sheetrocked, waiting to be spackled. Some other walls were smoothed with compound and sanded, ready for paint. He also hurried, as he wanted to impress Uncle Ray, to try and get back on his good side. There was a good side to Uncle Ray. Roger had seen it when working for him on the *Lady Mora* and his giving him a place to live. On the other hand, Roger knew that Uncle Ray's good side could at times be hard to find.

Roger took a quick coatless walk out the front door to see how the tree looked from the street. He knew few passersby would ever see the decorated evergreen through the window, but Roger still wanted that feeling that the place had Christmas décor people could enjoy, it even if it may only be a mail carrier, or parcel-post personnel. As he stood on the street admiring the decorating work, there came a raised voice over his shoulder. Melissa was on her porch. She was coatless as well, standing with crossed arms in her own defense against the winter chill.

"Your tree looks good, Roger. I am glad you put it in the window so people can see it. We need some decorations on this street. It is so dead on this dead end."

"I had to get a tree," said Roger in a voice raised enough that she could hear him. "The inside of my house is a construction site. A Christmas tree makes the place feel more like a home."

"Where did you get it?"

"I found it in the woods behind the house and cut it down."

"You are kidding me," said Melissa, finishing with a laugh.

"I kid you not. I was walking around there recently with the dogs and happened upon the perfect tree. A few days later I went back there with a saw and cut it down. It was meant to be."

"Could you go into the cellar and get my tree?"

Roger was not expecting an extra chore. Melissa did not wait for a response. She just went to the door and opened it up as if she were too cold to stay outside any longer. She turned to him just before disappearing inside.

"C'mon Roger. It will only take a moment. I need your help."

Roger smiled at the assertiveness. He walked over and ascended the steps before letting himself in. The first thing he noticed was how tidy the home was. Walls looked freshly painted. Varnished floors so clear they looked like they could be skated on. A computer screen resting on a corner desk glowed. A pulled back desk chair and open book indicated Melissa was working moments before. Above the desk hung a framed poster that said: *One step beyond fear is excitement!* The girls were on a couch in their pajamas watching cartoons.

Melissa stood there with a smile on her face. An open cellar door was an invitation. "Can you go downstairs and bring up my tree? It's assembled with a sheet over it. Your help is appreciated."

A walk downstairs to the musty brick basement. The space was identical to the one beneath Uncle Ray's bungalow. It was not surprising. All the homes were identical. All built by the same developer in the late forties. All with the same layout: five bungalows on one side of the street and five on the other side. The unevenly settled brick floor was familiar. A washer and dryer in the same spot he had his. In the corner was the artificial tree kept upright by its stand, covered in the white bed sheet like a Halloween ghost.

Roger held the tree in front of him, blindly walking it up the steps. He gently struggled with its bulkiness but managed to get it through the basement door. The girls took their eyes off the television set to watch the activity. Melissa helped get the tree upright before removing the sheet. There, for all to see, was a holiday decoration of green PVC plastic held by twisted wire connected to a wooden pole.

"Can you set it up in the corner?"

"Sure." Roger walked the base of the artificial tree to the other side of the room. "How's that, girls? Your mother will decorate this, and now Santa will have a place to leave your presents."

"We don't have a chimney, so Santa is going to come through the front door," said Sophie.

Roger smiled at Melissa. "Don't worry, Santa always finds a way in. That's his job," he said.

"My grandmother passed away last summer, and this was something I got from her house. My parents got most of the inheritance, but my brothers and I were allowed to take things before the garage sale. I took a radio and the tree. Some decorations. That was it."

Roger was momentarily at a loss for words. "Well, at least you did not have to buy a real tree."

"Neither did you," said Melissa through a laugh.

"Well, I was glad to help." Roger pointed a thumb in the direction of his home. "I am going to get back to my bungalow."

Melissa responded as if to extend the conversation. "This bungalow used to be my grandparents.' My father and his brothers and grandparents summered here in the sixties and seventies. My grandfather worked for GM in Livingston and would commute to the plant in the summer while the rest of the family stayed here and vacationed."

Roger politely looked around the bungalow. It showed Roger the possibilities there were in fresh paint and new varnish.

"It's a nice place."

"We keep it neat but don't put a lot in here, as we don't want the renters breaking a lot of stuff. My parents put in here what they need. That's it. At the end of every season my dad paints all the walls and shellacs the floor. I like it here. I wish I had it year-round."

"Like I said, I am going to go back. I have more work to do on the walls. I have to finish. The old carpeting was recently pulled up and thrown away. Next week the floor sanders come. Good-bye, girls."

The two girls suspended their attention to the television to say good-byes to Roger.

"Thanks for your help. I was going to make you some fajitas. Couldn't you stay?"

Roger took a step toward the door, before looking back at Melissa. A dimple smile brightened the neighbor's face. Twenty years old. She was wise beyond her two decades. More grown up. More focused than most people the same age. Someone with a life plan. More together than Roger knew he was.

Melissa's structured life was spawned from a rough beginning. Roger recalled the chubby high school girl who did not fit in with the other teens. Someone who ranked low in a teenage caste system. Such rejections fostered vulnerabilities. A girl who was too easily taken in by an older man's attention. Wanting to believe things that would never be true. Wedding bliss was ephemeral. A farcical union that was nothing more than a way to obtain permanent resident status. A future togetherness never really existed. A marriage license with an expiration date. For her beliefs in true love, she was given two toddlers and no means of supporting them. She outgrew her chubbiness and naivete. She kept herself in shape. There were goals and a path of achievement. A devoted mother. Roger found her resiliency attractive. He felt heartstrings gently pulled. A part of him wanted to stay, to learn more about her.

Then there was April. Roger had only begun dating the PetSmart cashier. Head and heart debated. He did not want to be unfair to April. "No, really, I need to get back."

"Is it the kids? It usually is. Guys don't want someone with kids."

Roger detected a voice crack.

"Its not that. I am just a bit mixed up. I am just trying to get my act together. You know, between the fixing up of the bungalow and adopting the dogs and I work a lot at Amazon, not to mention my monthly meetings with my parole officer."

"Those aren't reasons; they're just excuses."

Roger smiled. He felt the warmth of a face blush. Something inside kept him from mentioning April. "Maybe you are right. I will think about it. Not tonight, but maybe some other time. Maybe."

Roger felt regret in his throat as he said the words. It was not good to lead Melissa on. Not good to give her hope when she would inevitably see April come and go on the short dead-end street of ten homes. It was a bad habit of his. An appeasing of people just to manage the moment. To please someone without regard to future consequences. What was said was said. One day Melissa would see April and then she would know.

Melissa's face registered disappointment. "All right, I'll look forward to some other time. Goodnight, Roger."

Roger went to the doorknob. He left the home, walking in the catty-corner direction toward the bungalow house where he lived.

Chapter 17

THE next day, Buddy looked out a front window with two forward paws laying on a couch arm. The piece of recently delivered furniture was draped in plastic to keep it from dust and paint drops. All three dogs welcomed the couch. There they sometimes took afternoon naps in lieu of using the on-the-floor dog beds or sunny parts of the afternoon porch. It also gave Buddy a perch from which he could view the outside. He saw Roger loading bags of gifts into the front passenger floor of the car. Roger slammed the door as a car passed the house, turned around and stopped at the curb.

The driver was a woman Buddy recognized. He yelped to her. No indication that she heard him. More quick yelps. The Buddy barks drew the attention of the other dogs. Cyrus and Lady walked and mingled at the front door. Her attention was on Roger. She wore a pink, puffy, winter coat and a wool cap. Her smile was broad. She embraced Roger. They then stepped back just far enough to talk face to face. They spoke through smiles. Excited conversing.

Buddy liked April. She had provided much human

affection when he and Lady were at the Happy Yappers
Rescue Shelter. It was her lap that he sat in when he first
got there, shaking uncontrollably. He wanted to stop
the shaking but couldn't. He shook and shook. April
held him. She petted and spoke to him. She comforted
the shakes out of him. He was scared then. Very scared.
The rescue shelter looked like another puppy mill but
with dogs of all sizes and breeds. The people were all
gentle. Not all the dogs were. Some dogs were bullies.

The common area had a garage door. Opened, it
led to a back yard. Buddy and the other dogs would go
out there for the day. The world was so new to Buddy.
He never knew any life outside the confinement of the
breeder stall or metal-meshed cage. He did not know
what grass was and initially was unsure of the spiky
vegetation. Other dogs raced around on it. A trepid paw
tested the greenery. It was soft. A second paw moved on
the cushioning blades of plant growth. He dropped a
curious nose to fill his nostrils with the sweet scent. The
smell was reassuring, comforting. He entered the green
carpet of real grass. Its fragility. Its coolness. Its warmth.
He trotted around the yard.

Everything was so different. In the puppy mill
he had been confined but surrounded by dogs that
looked like him. In the rescue shelter he was free
around dogs of all different temperaments and sizes.
The canines were curious of the tiny Chihuahua dog.

Dogs approached him. Menacing stares. Wet noses and barks. Rambunctiousness. It all frightened him. There was one dog that did not scare him. It was a Pembrooke Welsh Corgi the rescue help called Lady.

Other dogs often frightened Buddy. That is when he got near Lady. She shielded Buddy from the rougher dogs. The loud barkers. The toy thieves. When Lady befriended him, things got better. He felt safer. Lady barked and growled at dogs that neared Buddy. Some were macho dogs; they could easily show off a toughness to a pint-sized pooch. Others were simply curious, wanting to investigate the smallest breed in the domesticated dog kingdom. They wanted to follow him, smell him. Some meant no harm, but still frightened Buddy. Their presence made him shake. He would hide behind Lady. Her body was a buffer, a wall of protection. Lady could stand up to all the dogs. Normally, she appeared a bit passive, maybe a little meek. But if she sensed Buddy's fear, she would show a protective side of her that lay within that docile exterior. When dogs got too aggressive or began poking around the tiny Chihuahua, Lady sprung in action. She showed off canine teeth, gnashing them at the interlopers. Growls and more growls until the dogs learned it was not worth mixing it up with the Pembrooke Welsh Corgi. That they could find something else in the yard to interest them.

There were so many dogs with different levels of

playfulness and assertiveness. But the people there were gentle. They cared for Buddy. The building was consistently heated. There was food. Good food. Better food than what he was fed at the puppy mill. There was light. Not like the puppy mill that was usually left in near darkness. The rescue facility had light, consistent heat, food, and most of all love.

Buddy watched out the window. He saw April and Roger step along the sidewalk gently bumping shoulders along the way and laughing. Buddy yelped happy yelps. He was excited to see the caretaker from the recue facility. Tail wags and happy smile. The couple climbed the steps and neared the door. Lady and Cyrus, sensing the couple's approach, neared the front of the home and waited. Roger opened the door from behind April, allowing her to enter first. Buddy paced back and forth along the sofa. More joyous tail wags. The woman's face lit up. Roger held an entertained smile. April spoke with hands spread. "How are my furry friends?"

Chapter 18

ROGER drove the car to his parents' house with a mix of cheeriness and dread. Christmas was his favorite holiday. The colored lights, passing decorations and caroling music flowing from the car radio all brought the holiday spirit. The evergreen scent of the Christmas tree reminded him of happier times when he and his sister opened gifts in their pajamas. The crackling warmth coming from the fireplace would bring back memories of a home that brought holiday happiness. He knew what to expect. Savory smells of roasted pork and sweet scents of apple pie floating on the air. Most of all, it was the togetherness. The enjoying one another's company. There was the dread, though. He missed three home Christmases due to the incarceration.

Prison Christmases were a little better than a usual day. Work, classes and appointments were all suspended. The warden allowed an extension of leisure times. More card playing and ping pong games. The weight-lifting area was occupied all day. It was tradition that the guards each chipped in money towards bags of fruit, candy, magazines and playing cards. Each prisoner got a sack of Reese's Cups, Hershey bars, candy canes, Three Musketeers bars, raisin boxes, periodicals and more. The cafeteria deviated from the usual bland fare of spaghetti with red sauce or dried-out ham and peas. Christmas lunch included tasty turkey with all the trimmings. Many families entered the "dance floor," which was the large visiting room where loved ones joined inmates. Roger's parents declined to visit him inside the barbed wire fences on Christmas Day. The father explained that they were not going to disrupt their holiday for Roger's arrest. Instead, Roger's mother and father drove up the weekend before Christmas. Mr. Wilson would sit in the car and read the newspaper, while Mrs. Wilson went in and visited her son. The couple would then go out to lunch before heading back to the Jersey Shore.

Roger drove the Subaru up to the house where a blow-up Frosty the Snowman and Santa Claus wobbled on the lawn. White lights twisted around the bare branches of front yard fruit trees. Exterior speakers filled the yard with holiday music.

He got out and went to the rear of the vehicle before opening the back hatch, allowing Cyrus to leap to the ground. Wrapped arms lowered Lady to the icy street, while Buddy spied the activity from between the front seats. Roger grabbed the handled bags of gifts from the floor and took Buddy under an arm. Roger felt the hesitation in each step. He wondered how his father would react to his arriving. Roger pondered how the day would go. The arrest was a festering wound that was not healing. The incarceration brought shame to the family. The incident made all the local papers. Articles made it sound as if Roger was part of a drug ring, when the truth was that he was recruited for a one-time drive. The whole bust, trial and imprisonment was too fresh. The loss of the T-shirt business. The parents' mortgaging of the home to pay Roger's legal bills. Roger's disqualification from ever becoming a professional firefighter. Roger knew too well the disappointment felt by his father. The relationship was rocky before the arrest. No football scholarship. No visits to a Marines recruiter. Things Roger's father wanted for him.

Roger knew who was in the house. Younger sister Christine, a senior in high school, was there. Snowbird grandparents on his mother's side, who drove to Florida every January 2 since retirement, would be couchbound. Neighbor Gerry never missed a holiday celebration at the Wilson home. The childless widower and Vietnam vet had no other place to go.

Roger walked up the uneven sidewalk; the two older dogs followed. He opened the door and let the dogs in. Roger's mom agreed to let him bring the dogs rather than have them stay alone in the bungalow all day. The dogs were home alone enough as it was when Roger worked was the pitch given in a phone call days earlier. He entered the split-level home from the downstairs side door. The kitchen, master bedroom, living room and dining room were all upstairs. Christine moved into Roger's old room downstairs which included a den and bathroom. Roger liked that room when he had it as it provided a private living area.

A faux question was yelled by Roger's mother from the kitchen. "Who do we have here?"

"Hi, Mom," shouted Roger from downstairs.

Roger heard talk coming from the living room. They would be sitting around on the sofas, enjoying cocktails.

"Come on up, Roger. I just put out some cold shrimp. Tell your sister to come up."

Roger's sister Christine walked out of his old bedroom. An open door revealed soccer posters of female athletes scoring goals and chasing soccer balls. Christine was a star athlete and was the apple of their father's eye after receiving an athletic scholarship to Duke University. Her blonde hair touched her shoulders. A body tight and athletic. The dogs were quiet and calm.

"Hey, Christine."

"Hi, Roger," said Christine through a pearly smile. "You have your family with you."

"Yeah, got some dogs. They are all good. They keep me busy."

"Dad said Uncle Ray is mad about the dogs. Keeps saying things."

"I saw Ray about the dogs. He is not upset about the dogs. Just upset I didn't tell him. That's all. But I have been really fixing the bungalow up. The place needed a ton of work, but it's getting there. The dogs are good. They spend most of the days outside."

Roger hated having to explain everything to people. He wished actions spoke for themselves. But the arrest put him in a guarded position. Too often, normal things had to be explained. People thought the worse.

"I am sure they are good," said Christine, looking down at the dogs. She stepped forward and the dogs naturally positioned themselves to get some attention. Christine ignored the dogs and went over and wrapped arms around Roger, a welcome he deeply needed. A gesture of true affection before the mixture of perfunctory greetings and slanted looks waiting for him upstairs. Christine showed the compassion that was nonexistent in his father and lacking in his mother.

She squeezed Roger tightly. "Dad is tough on you, I know. I am almost surprised you are here."

"He always was tough on me."

"It's the Marine in him."

"Marine? He was a Marine for four years. It like defined his whole life. He still wears a crew cut. Let it go."

"He is what he is, Roger." Christine let go of the embrace. "Just warning you. The dogs are still an issue with Dad. He thinks you should never have gotten them."

"Dad is against everything I do. What else is new?"

"Just hang in there, Roger. Things can get better. Maybe you can open another store. Maybe start your business again. One day you can do it."

"I've thought about it. I don't have any money right now. But who knows?"

"Dream big, Roger. That's what Dad taught me. I was going to go to a small college, but Dad told me to always dream of the big school and the things that were there. I put it in my head that was where I was going. And things fell into place. I am not saying it is easy, but what is? You can bounce back. You are not a warehouse guy. You are an entrepreneur. A businessman."

"A convict, a felon."

"Oh c'mon. There are many famous people who committed crimes and made it to the top. Hell, Bill Gates was arrested when he was a teenager. Martha Stewart went to jail."

Christine went to taking turns petting the dogs while looking up at Roger. Roger welcomed what she said.

"Where are you guys? We're waiting." Their mother's voice came from upstairs.

Roger lifted his head back and yelled, "We'll be right up, Mom."

"Maybe put the dogs outside," was his mother's retort.

Christine smiled at Roger. "The dogs are an issue."

"I know, I know. I can put them outside for a little while, but they will want to come in."

Roger looked down at the dogs. He was relieved that they were so well-behaved. "I better do this," said Roger, lifting his head toward the upstairs in a gesture. "But I am bringing the dogs upstairs."

The dogs led the way up the steps of bulky carpet.

Roger's father was in the kitchen pouring a bourbon on the rocks. He leered at Roger without saying anything.

` "Hi, Dad."

"What are you doing with so many dogs?" said Roger's father evenly.

"Taking care of them; that's what I am doing," said Roger defensively.

"Just taking care of them? You mean temporarily?"

"No, not temporarily. They are my family. I will take care of them forever." Roger did not like arguing but he did get some strength from defending his canines.

Gerry was in the living room with the grandparents. "Merry Christmas, Roger," said Gerry, raising a can of beer as a gesture.

The grandparents sitting on a couch twisted shoulders in unison to see Roger. The dogs entered the living room. Roger walked in and gave hugs to the older couple.

"Merry Christmas, Gerry." Roger was glad for the momentary distraction. His mother patted down her apron while walking forward. His father sipped the brown liquor without responding.

Roger's mother spread arms before wrapping them into a big hug.

"Take your coat off, Roger," said his mother with a Christmas cheeriness. "Did you hear about Christine? Your sister got her SAT scores back. She scored very high. She got 1440. You know she applied to Brown and Dartmouth. The University of Virginia and Boston College too. She's been offered sports scholarships and the whole shebang. But I think she likes Duke. They really recruited her the hardest."

"You already told me all that. I know all the details." His mother had told him all about the scholarships a few weeks earlier. Hearing it again was painful rather than informative.

"All the colleges are recruiting her," said his father. "That's what you should've done. College football. That's a dream come true. Not like selling T-shirts or working for Amazon," said his father dismissively.

"I don't want to go over this again, Dad," said

Roger with anger tingeing his voice. "I would never have gotten onto a Division I team. I was too small and too slow. I would have been on a Division III team, and I do not like playing football enough to do that, anyway."

"If you think like that, you will never have or be anything. You should think like your sister."

"Why do you always have to start like this? Its Christmas."

The dogs took turns getting familiar with Gerry and the grandparents.

Roger's mother spoke up as Christine entered the room. "Roger's right. Let's just try to get along today. Let's not focus on the negative. Talk about the positive. Here's Christine." There was a chorus of welcomes. The mother stepped back into the kitchen area.

Roger pulled off the ski jacket and hung it up while the dogs huddled around his legs.

"Your uncle is upset about those dogs," said his father with even annoyance in his voice.

Roger's mother leaned her body out of the kitchen while wiping down a plate. She spoke before Roger could.

"My brother felt a bit blind-sided, Roger. He's doing you a favor by letting you stay at that house. You should have told him about the dogs. Actually, you should have asked him."

"Mom, Mom. I am fixing that dump up. You should see what I'm doing."

"My brother isn't charging you rent. He told me that."

Roger was getting annoyed and heard his voice rise. "Mom, the place was uninhabitable. The place could never get a CO. A city inspector would never give it. I shouldn't even be there but at least it's getting better."

"Its still his place," interjected his father. "He could have gotten a certificate of occupancy. One call to the city is all it would take. Old Ken Crowley, the building inspector, would have signed off on a CO. I've known him thirty years. He would do me the favor. Don't act like you know so much when you don't. You should have made arrangements before bringing in three dogs."

Roger regretted going to the house. The arguing confused the dogs and Buddy and Cyrus yelped and barked.

Christine joined the dogs to give support to Roger. A way to cause a distraction. "I love Roger's puppies." She fussed over the canines.

"They aren't puppies. Well, Buddy sort of is. But the other two are much older, especially Lady. She's the Corgi."

"Oh, I know. I am just playing," said Christine.

Roger nodded.

There was an awkward silence. Then Christine broke it.

"Mom, Dad stop being so hard on Roger, its Christmas."

"Let me take the dogs outside," said Roger, needing an escape. He grabbed the ski jacket and put it back on. He followed the dogs down the stairs. Christine went along, as well. He went through the den to open a sliding glass door leading to a patio. The edges of an overhead deck dripped snowmelt as temperatures rose above freezing.

Roger turned to Christine who had not put on a jacket and stood in the open doorway. "Do you see now what I am talking about. This is what I put up with. It is the same old thing over and over. And Mom says to focus on the positive, then a moment later she gives me a hard time. Oh, brother."

"I know, Roger. I know and its Christmas. And I have not forgotten how Dad treated you after the arrest."

"How about before the arrest? How he pushed me into sports and was always yelling on the sidelines and making a fool of me and our family."

"Dad is a passionate man."

"Passionate? He always had the coaches and umpires mad at us."

"But you were great, Roger."

"I wasn't great. I was good. Maybe a little better than good."

"Roger, your senior year you were All-County in both baseball and football. I was only All-Shore in soccer."

"Dad always took the joy out of everything. I could hit three for four in a baseball game and on the ride home all Dad would talk about is the one time I grounded out. In football he was the same way. He would talk incessantly about the game and analyze every play in excruciating detail. That is what I was up against. That's why I started to hate sports."

"You were great at sports."

"That's why I didn't go to college. I couldn't go through what I went through in my younger years. That's why I love surfing. It's not competitive. At least not in an organized way. You just go out there. You and the waves. You compete against yourself, not even against the wave. I always thought of the wave as my partner. This momentary partner, we are either going to have a good ride or we aren't. It's mostly up to me. The wave provides the opportunity. If I am fast enough, skillful enough, agile enough, then who knows?"

Roger flailed hands for emphasis. "I may get a good ride on the back of a wave. In a few fleeting moments that partner, that wave is gone, dead. Not forever, though. It comes back a little different but with much the same personality. Like an incarnation, but seawater instead of a person."

"Wow, that's philosophical."

"I suppose when I am out in the ocean waiting for a wave, I connect with things. These thoughts pop up in my head. I am relaxed. Open to my God or Source or whatever. Not like organized sports where I was always stressed out by Dad."

"I know, Roger. Dad resented the fact that you didn't pursue a college scholarship. I was surprised when you said no Division I schools wanted you. I would have thought they would have given you a look."

"They did give me looks. I lied. Recruiters from Temple and Rutgers both spoke to me, but I told them I wasn't interested. I told the football coach to keep recruiters away. That I wasn't going to college. I was not going to be miserable in college. I wouldn't allow it."

Cyrus, Lady and Buddy searched the yard, sniffing around the way dogs do.

Christine walked out onto the patio crossing arms against the chill. "Oh, Roger." She put her arm on his shoulder and squeezed half a hug.

"I sort of did like sports, especially football. I mean, you know. Everything we did, Dad could take the joy right out of it. He wasn't so bad with you, but with me it was torture. I loved to play, but he was so serious about that it. I mean does he ever smile?"

They both laughed at the comment.

"I mean, how does Mom stand it? He is so serious

about everything. Its like he can't enjoy life. Everything is competitive. Everything has to be better. Should have been better. He even analyzes the dinners that Mom and he have out. It's exhausting."

"Mom is a saint, let's face it. But she adores him. You see she goes along with what he says. They are soul-mates. I can't wait to go away to school. Just to be away from the madness. I'm going to Duke. That is where I want to go. They are giving me a full scholarship. I don't even have to wait to hear from some of the other schools."

"I don't blame you," said Roger through a smile.

"You know Dad was always jealous of you. The way you were natural at sports, and even your creative side. Do you remember Dad made those tacky-looking plaques with pictures on them and tried to sell them out at the flea market? He sold like two. They were horrible. He spent all that money and the idea turned into a bomb. Then you started your T-shirt company, and it was successful from day one."

"I think that's why he never mentioned my company. He never complimented me on it ever. I know you are right; he resented it."

"He did, Roger. He did."

The sliding sound of a window opening. Roger and Christine looked up past the deck. Their mother poked her head out.

"Roger. Christine. Where are you guys? Your dad is lighting up the fireplace."

Christine tilted her head back and yelled, "We'll be right up."

Their mother ducked back into the house and slid the window closed.

"Don't let Dad bug you too much. He is who he is. The ex-Marine. The fireman. Now he drives Mom crazy with his retirement."

"Mom said he might go fishing with Uncle Ray."

Christine rolled her eyes. "She told me. Poor Ray. Poor crew. I don't think Uncle Ray wants him. It was Dad's idea. Probably Mom's idea too. Get him out of the house for a few days. But it wouldn't work. Dad is wound too tight for those guys. He would be admonishing them for cigarette smoking, for the way they work. There would be a mutiny. The crew would throw him overboard."

Roger laughed. Cyrus lifted his head to Roger's hand. Roger rolled his open palm around the dog's face.

"We better get upstairs, Roger. You know Mom is going to call us again in a moment."

Roger shook his head in dismay. "Why don't you go upstairs. I can't handle too much Dad. I might hang out here for a little while."

"Sure. I can run interference while you get the will to come up and deal with Dad and Mom. Just don't wait out here too long."

Christine skipped through the sliding glass door and pushed it closed. Roger laid back into one of two pieces of chalky wrought-iron furniture that were heavy enough to withstand winter winds. He looked absently into the back yard surrounded by a bare board fence he helped his father erect. The same back yard where he created a pitcher's mound and tossed balls against the side of the shed to hone the pitching skills used in high school.

The fireplace scented the air with the smell of chimney smoke. Soon the dogs became bored with a blind yard and no toys to play with. The three canines huddled around his legs seeking a petting hand. He picked up Buddy who rested affectionately in his lap. Then the too familiar sound of a window opening. He did not bother to look up but kept focused on the dogs. He knew what was next.

"Roger, why don't you come up and join us? Your father just built a fire."

Chapter 19

BUDDY easily settled into the daily routine. There were always morning walks with Roger. Sometimes Roger leashed him, Lady, and Cyrus when he returned home from the occasional night shift. Usually, he took the three of them out in the dark hours before the sun came up. That morning, Roger got out of bed and took the dogs on the daily sojourn. When they returned, Roger fed Buddy and the other two dogs before refilling clean bowls with enough food and water to hold their hunger at bay until returning from work. Roger said good-byes, leaving the home wearing the yellow safety vest required of all Amazon warehouse employees. The hours ahead would be like most mornings and afternoons when Roger was gone to work. Just a lazy day of wanderings in the backyard. Indecisive forays through the flap doors. Buddy would go out for a while until the cold urged him back inside. There he would sit on the couch until that bored him, then he would return to the porch and down the steps. Cyrus stayed out longer, spending more time outside satisfying an interest for moving things. The Pit Bull patrolled yard boundaries searching the woods for creatures going about their business. Maybe a butterfly or errant plastic bag would float by with Cyrus responding with barks and jumps. Nearby squirrels and rabbits had long ago learned that the chain-linked fence kept them safely from any Pit Bull danger. Lady often stayed on the porch corner where warming sun rays angled onto floor planks.

It was early afternoon and Roger was long gone. After a short nap, Buddy went to the kitchenette for a few dog-food bites and sips of water. He passed through the flap door to see what the other two dogs were up to. Lady was curled near the steps. A slow lift of the head. Drowsy eyes. The sound of a swinging door was enough to awaken Lady from a fragile nap. The old girl yawned before returning her head back down in an act of no concern. Buddy watched Cyrus police the sides of the yard. The Pit Bull peered at a muskrat making its furry way across the backwoods floor before hurrying into a tree trunk. A dark cloud of starlings descended on the bare limbs of a sycamore, doing nothing to arouse Cyrus's attention. A lowered snout. The Pit Bull went back to poking and strolling the fenced-in lawn.

Something suddenly alerted Cyrus. The Pit Bull moved along the fence before stopping. A piqued interest. Unknown. Unidentified. A stirring hidden inside the trees and brush. Cyrus kept focused. Eyes peeled. Statue stillness. A countenance of concentration. Something beyond the curtain pines and hardwoods.

Buddy took full body leaps down each step and trotted across the grass to be near Cyrus. He shared the sense of possible threat. A scent of human odor traveled a gentle breeze. A rustle of dry leaves. Whispers. People approaching.

Eyes studied the trees. Ears followed the sounds. Olfactory glands sniffed the smells. Lady joined Buddy and Cyrus. The trio waited, anticipating the approaching humans. Then two men revealed themselves. Each carrying an end of a homemade ladder. The duo appeared to be the same age as Roger. Slow steps. Deliberate crouching the way a feral cat stalked its prey.

Cyrus let out a woof. It was a warning bark. The same woof Cyrus used when he would see a red-tailed hawk circling the yard, a species known for attacking small dogs. At those times, a warning woof could send a panicked Buddy scrambling to the safety of the back covered porch. This was not a hawk. The trespassers approached their home. They headed in the direction of the narrow easement between the houses, a skinny lane of beige cement sided by identical chain-linked fences. Cyrus gave a double woof. Buddy joined in with his own rat-tat-tat of yelps. The barks did nothing to deter the intruders. They continued their advancement.

Buddy saw how Cyrus was uneasy with the prospect of people coming through the woods. The dogs were used to the activities of letter carriers and UPS delivery personnel in the front of the home. The UPS driver leaving a package on the front porch might get a friendly bark. The letter carrier seen so regularly no longer triggered dog reactions. This was nothing familiar. Maybe nothing friendly.

Cyrus transitioned the barking into a low, throaty growl. Buddy paced back and forth. He then stopped. The young Chihuahua mimicked Cyrus by giving his own warning barks. He wanted to be tough like the bigger, older Cyrus. Lady stayed close to Cyrus, watching the event calmly like a wise elder. She stayed quiet. Lady was not one to waste barks.

With the instinctive inclination to protect the property, Cyrus increased the menacing growls. The pair continued their sneaking progress toward the narrow easement. The two men entered the alley way of neighboring chain-liked fences and cement path. Buddy ran toward the porch and ascended the steps to be at a higher position. He yelped at the two men. Cyrus showed clenched teeth. He snarled. Buddy never saw Cyrus so mad. The young Chihuahua went to the side of the porch to be nearer to the men. He stuck his miniature head through the bars of the porch railing; he barked and barked.

The men chuckled. "Look at that little one there. Is that a dog or a barking cat?" The other man laughed covering his mouth.

Slamming the weighty full force of chest and paws Cyrus rattled the chain links.

The second man carrying the ladder looked directly at Cyrus, whose head peered just over the top of the yard enclosure. "Wow, getting a little hostile, aren't you, mister?"

Cyrus responded with loud, wet barking. Pasty white saliva cornered the dog's mouth. Menacing snarls. Buddy continued yelping. Both dogs intensified the barking. Buddy's body shook with the sounds he made. Neighborhood silence was gone. The air filled with the warning calls of two canines.

"I wish they'd shut up," said one of the men.

"Why don't you shut up so we can make this quick?"

Buddy descended the steps to join Cyrus and Lady. The two men passed between the houses. Cyrus growled some more. Buddy did the same. Lady stood between the two animated canines and watched the two trespassers go about their suspicious business. The cold no longer bothered Buddy. The action warmed him.

"Shut up," said one in a hushed voice." The barking annoyed the intruders. One leaned the ladder against the house. The two men looked around. A deserted neighborhood. A stealth mission. The perfect place to perform a crime. One man walked to the edge of the house, peeking around the corner to survey the street.

He called back, "No one around. Let's make this quick. These stupid dogs are too noisy."

The other man climbed the ladder. Using a screwdriver, he inched up the window enough to get fingers underneath. The window was pushed open.

Cyrus growled as he watched. Buddy yelped.

"Hurry up!" said the man on the ground. "I don't want these dogs drawing any attention. Just get in and pass me the power tools. Electric hand tools only. Make sure to put the tools in the cases before handing them out."

"I know, man, I know. Its not my first break-in."

The man on the ladder pulled his body through the window. Two spread legs hung out like a pair of open scissors. Then a slither. The man was in the house.

Cyrus turned. A dash to the porch. Buddy went in hot pursuit with the older Lady bringing up the rear.

Cyrus rushed through the dog flap. Then Buddy, then Lady.

A scream.

"What the fuck!"

"What?" came the voice of the man outside.

"The dogs are in the house."

"In the house? How'd they get in?"

"How do I know?"

Cyrus went for the burglar. The ambushed intruder was pushed back. Shoulder blades driven into the corner. Fear lit the man's face. Curled arms and a pulled leg. The terrified man pressed into the joining walls in a protective stance. "Get in here!"

A quick pass through the window and over the sink. The second intruder reached for the broom leaning on a wall. He lifted it in the air. A hammering down. The weaponized broom handle slammed against the sturdy back of the Pit Bull. A dog cry of pain. A turn. Cyrus had fire in his eyes. Confusion. Injury.

Anger coursed through Buddy. A flash of puppy mill memories. Confinement. Abuse. The fat man. The attack on his mother.

Cyrus used menacing growls to push back the broom-wielding man. A bump into the Christmas tree shed glass ornaments that shatter-popped on the hard floor. Seeing Cyrus distracted, the cornered man attempted to inch away. Buddy stiffened into an attack stance. He was enraged. Mad at the men for invading their home. Furious for the strike on Cyrus. Buddy was more than a toy dog. He came from a long line of hunters. A descendant of proud Mexican canines. There was more inside of him. There was more to the Chihuahua than twenty thousand years of domestication. Deep inside the dog DNA was a wolf.

Sensing a movement, Cyrus reacted to the burglar stepping from the corner. The Pit Bull growled him back.

Hair on Buddy's neck bristled. A rhythmic growl. A charging stance. He went full force toward the man swinging the broom. The handle came down. The sound of cracking wood. Wood splintering. A Cyrus cry of pain. Buddy's jaws clamped down on the man's ankle. Teeth penetrated the skin. A taste of human blood. A man scream.

"Awww!"

A hobble. Two limping steps. The man's face went red with rage. A foot cocked. Buddy was kicked clear across the room. He hit the wall. Stunned by the concussion, Buddy struggled back to four feet. Pain. Dizziness. Quick pants an attempt to revive. He looked over. Cyrus made quick, tail-chasing turns, eyeing up both men. Lady watched the action. She barked rare barks, doing what little she could do to help Cyrus. The Pit Bull went back to cornering the man. Growls. Snarls. The terrified man pushed harder into the walls. Loud woofs. The metallic cracking sound of teeth-on-teeth snaps. The other man lifted the broken handle in another act of aggression. Buddy charged again, nipping the man's ankle. He yelled, "Damn it!"

A stumble forward. Lady moved strategically and calculated. She put her body in the man's path. A long abdomen. Short legs. A canine tripwire. The man fell over the Pembrooke Welsh Corgi only to crash into the six-foot table holding power tools and supplies. The table flipped to its side. Electric handsaw, power drill, cordless sander fell to the ground. A can of nails twisted and turned in midair. Hundreds of pieces of sharpened hardware scattered across a varnished floor like escaping insects. The broken broom handle loosened from the man's grip, rolled toward the wall.

Chaotic sounds distracted Cyrus, and in that moment the cornered man made a break for the door. He ran out, with the second man in quick pursuit. Cyrus and Lady both followed the duo outside. Buddy joined the two on the front porch watching the burglars dash through the front gate and into the street. One sprinted toward the main avenue before turning into the yard of a vacant bungalow, then disappearing. The other hobbled along favoring the injured leg. "Wait up, wait up."

The three dogs continued barking until the second man vanished between two houses. When both burglars could no longer be seen, the barking died down. Then Buddy and the two other dogs went silent. The three canines waited while looking up the street, just to assure there would be no return of the two.

Buddy stood proudly as part of a team. What the trio did that day was noble. It was brave. A battle won. Most of all it was dutiful. It was done together. Part of their canine heritage. An instinctive thing that dogs do.

They protected their home.

Chapter 20

ROGER walked the parking lot toward the Subaru. The massive Amazon building was white and utilitarian, two football fields' worth of size and blandness. He was tired of the job. Actually, he had been tired of it almost from the beginning. The work was robotic and predictable. For many employed there, that was a good thing. The security of knowing what was ahead when reporting to work. Conditions were mostly good for the workers. Clean, climate-controlled warehouses of hard, smooth floors and miles of back-and-forth conveyor belts. People working alongside robots. Yellow carts filled with product. Organization and efficiency was the culture of the workplace. Military-like obedience to the tasks at hand. Full-on working between start and quit buzzers. Cameras and supervisors watched every move. Many people thrived on it. Get the job done and there would always be benefits and a check at week's end. The money was good. Still, Roger felt out of place. Christine was right. He was an entrepreneur. A businessman. Working for himself was who he was. Creating things that people would pay money for was what he thrived on. The marketplace had its trade-offs, but for him uncertainty was better than monotony.

When Roger was in prison, he took a job painting the walls and cell rooms for near-nothing wages. It helped pass the time. It took his mind off the incarceration. He spent the earnings in the commissary buying canned tuna, crackers, and apples. Roger was afraid of the cafeteria selection of strange-looking food and ate little of it. Prison coffee and toast in the morning. A banana if there was one or a bowl of cereal was safe. All other meals were consumed in his cell. The limited diet caused a loss of weight. There was thirty pounds less of him when he was released. Roger did not care. There was no appetite for mystery stew or strangely colored scrambled eggs.

In a short time, Roger earned a reputation as an excellent painter. Working hard ingratiated him with the guards. They knew he was a good worker and left him alone. He labored efficiently, covering walls like a skilled artisan. Bored guards allowed him to work alone, knowing the painting was getting done. Those responsible for watching the inmates were just counting minutes, adding them into hours and bunching the time into a shift. Guards and prisoners were all part of the same mind-numbing experience, a system where killing time was everything.

The Amazon job came along shortly after a successful parole hearing granted him early freedom. The world's largest online retailer was hiring and

needed people. Roger became accustomed to the
work. His athleticism helped handle the squatting and
lifting and seemingly endless walking. He was good at
what he did. But the job actions were too mechanical.
Too programmed. The managers controlled his every
actions. Time was meticulously measured. Scanners
traced people as much as they tracked boxes. Cameras
watched every movement. For Roger, it was dehuman-
izing and hard to accept. He knew that the supervisors
liked him, but he never got used to the never-ending
surveillance. It was a job. It was money. Maybe employ-
ment there never made Roger happy, but it did make
him grateful.

The shopping mall-sized parking lot was filled
with hundreds of cars. He found the Subaru and began
the trip home after the ten-hour shift. Roger looked
forward to being back with the dogs that always greeted
his return. It was so much better than the days when he
went to an empty house. The hour long drive back to
the bungalow home allowed Roger's mind to float to
the plans for New Year's Eve. April was invited to the
big event held at an eight-bedroom mansion up on the
hill. Every year the massive old home was the stage for
a party attracting more than a three hundred revelers.
The guy who threw the bash was a fellow that people in
the hamlet all knew as Barefoot Harry.

Harry Merten inherited the stately home from

well-to-do parents, Victor and Elena Merten. Unable
to have children of their own and very devoted to
the world of art, the couple adopted Harry as a baby
when both husband and wife were in their early fifties.
The two kept busy running their famous Leo Belgicus
Auction House in midtown Manhattan, which was
known worldwide as Belgian Lion. Roger remembered
the couple as sophisticated and upper crust. Elena was
a former French model of blazing red hair who never
lost her svelte shape or accent. Victor carried himself
with the stately demeanor of a European diplomat.
Outwardly charming, the Belgian dressed nattily in the
very image of class and dignity. The couple celebrated
artists at their castle-like home of stone and imported
timbers with lavish parties that were chronicled by
the *New York Times,* as well as local newspapers. The
likes of Jack Nicholson, Diana Ross, Henry Kissinger,
Chris Plummer, Nancy Sinatra, Sidney Poitier, and Joe
Namath had all attended events at the home.

Although together they associated with many
wealthy and famous people, they were salt-of-the-
earth approachable. It was nothing for them to chat up
a letter carrier or a dog walker. The couple earned a
well-deserved reputation for generosity, having donated
to many charities. Their travelling to New York City
each day in a chauffeur-driven Rolls Royce made them
celebrities with the locals. Even Harry enjoyed some

"Richie Rich" type fame for his being left in the care of a cook, nanny and housekeeper.

When Roger had been a Cub Scout, the den had gone to the home to view some of the famous art lining its walls. This arrangement was likely made by mothers more interested in touring the museum-like home than providing any art education to a bunch of eight-year-olds who could not appreciate the works. The home was like nothing Roger had ever seen. The commercial kitchen containing all stainless-steel appliances outsized the entire downstairs of the home where he lived. Furniture was large and gaudy, appearing to be more for show than to be used. Elena certainly enjoyed discussing the works of art even to a group of youngsters and mothers whose main concern was what each was serving for dinner that evening. At the end of the tour, the Cub Scouts went outside to play on Harry's playground (by then he was in college) with jungle gyms and swing sets that outrivaled what was at the local school. The housekeeper brought out freshly made apple juice and a plate of baked goods shipped in from a Manhattan bakery.

Victor and Elena Merten sent Harry to some of the best boarding schools in the hopes of one day getting him into an Ivy League university. A consequence of his away-school experience was that it kept Harry from forging strong local friendships. Many local kids only knew Harry as Victor and Elena's son.

As it turned out, Harry was not so up for the rigors of elite boarding schools and struggled at a mix of them. Regardless of Harry's less-than-stellar academic achievements, the couple adored their adopted son. Harry eventually went to the University of Miami, where he traded blazers and preppy ties for tie-dyed shirts and well-worn jeans. Curly, dark hair was grown long and wild. A penchant for travelling the campus without footwear earned him the moniker Barefoot Harry. He held on to the shoeless habit and brought the nickname home with him. Instead of being referred to as Victor and Elena's son, everyone eventually knew the long-haired guy living on the hill by the sobriquet *Barefoot Harry*.

A few years back, Elena died in the New York show-room of a stroke. Victor was so overcome with grief that, three months later, the broken-hearted husband followed Elena to the grave after firing a pistol into the roof of his mouth. Harry inherited the mansion home, auction house and much accumulated wealth. He sold the auction house and became flush with cash. Nearly friendless most of his life, Harry wanted to be wanted. He was exceedingly generous and there was no shortage of those wanting to take advantage of Harry's good nature. The home became a sometime flop house as Harry allowed people down on their luck to live in one of the many bedrooms. Neighbors complained about transients and loud parties. Roger only knew Barefoot

Harry as someone he said hello to, a well-known and friendly local character. He thought of Barefoot Harry as a good guy. A man with a big heart. Someone who would not hurt a flea. For a span of ten years, the long-haired guy with an aversion to shoes threw a big New Year's Eve party. It was an invitation-only event that brought many friends and acquaintances and more than a fair share of party crashers. Roger did not know Barefoot Harry well enough to ever get an invitation and was not one to just show up. But April showed the folded card requesting her and a guest to attend the annual get-together. Harry was a big donor to the Happy Yappers Animal Shelter, and April knew him well enough to be invited. "See, we are invited to Barefoot Harry's party." The invite featured a pencil drawing of the bottom of two bare feet. A caption exclaimed *Barefoot Harry Invites You to Welcome in the New Year*.

Roger glanced over to Melissa's home as he drove down the street. The rusty Kia was in the driveway and the stroller out on the covered porch. As much as he liked April, he found himself often thinking of the single mom. Roger found something mysterious and intriguing about her. He had the desire to know more about her. He shook off the thoughts. He had a girlfriend. Time to get the mail and greet the dogs. He flipped through the letters walking distractedly along the cement path to the porch steps. In front of the door, he pulled the keys from a coat pocket. The metal chamber twisted without resistance as if the lock were not engaged. Roger wondered if he forgot to secure the home before leaving that morning.

He turned the knob and pushed the door open. The dogs were there but did not greet him in their usual way. Instead, they shifted back and forth curiously. The living room was in disarray. Not the organized remodeling worksite he left. The worktable was knocked over. Power tools and countless of nails covered the floor. A dent in the wall. A disheveled Christmas tree. At first Roger thought the dogs got a bit rambunctious causing the mess. It happened before that Cyrus and the sometimes over-confident Buddy fussed over a toy. Growling and anger would ensue. On such occasions, Roger needed to intervene. *Could the two dogs have gotten that out of control in his absence?*

Roger felt cold air pushing in from the kitchenette area. He walked over. The window was open allowing outside air to cool the house. He got closer and noticed a pair of two-by-four wooden beams leaning on the ledge. He lifted himself over the sink to take a closer look.

"Holy crap!" yelled Roger.

He fell back to the floor bouncing like a gymnast. He closed the window and walked toward the dogs. It was then that he noticed two large swellings and a small reddish gash on Cyrus's back. Eyes darted around the room. The broom was broken, and the larger part of the handle lay along the base molding. Roger examined Lady and Buddy. Both were less jovial than usual. Buddy was even shaking a little bit. Roger figured that all three were traumatized by what occurred earlier. Lady and Buddy did not appear to have sustained any injuries the way Cyrus did. Roger's mind fit the pieces of the puzzle together. Whoever entered the home was surprised by the dogs. They did not realize that the house was fitted with flap doors allowing the canines free access to the inside. It was the nature of dogs to defend their territory. The broom handle was used against the most threatening of the trio.

"Who was it, Cyrus? What did he look like?" asked Roger, as if Cyrus could provide an answer. Roger paced around. Eyes continued to survey the chaos. Coat pockets were searched for a cell phone. Police needed to be alerted.

"Hello!" sang a female voice.

Roger turned around. Melissa stood in the front door holding three-year-old Sophie by the hand and clutching two-year old Emma in an arm. Her face was made up with cosmetics and lipstick as if she did it for someone. All three dogs went right over to greet the neighbors.

"Hello, Melissa. Did you see this? We were broken into."

"I know."

"You know? What do you mean, you know?" asked Roger urgently.

"Yeah, I know," said Melissa as she guided the three-year-old in and shut the door behind her. "You had burglars."

"How did you know? Did you see them? Did you call the police? I need to get the police here if they haven't been here already," said Roger hurriedly.

"I did see them. The burglars, that is. No police have been here. They don't know what happened. The dogs chased the two guys out of the house. I don't think the two guys realized the dogs could get in. I think they broke in because they thought the dogs were stuck in the backyard."

Roger was stunned and confused. A tight circle walk. Head down, Roger rubbed a temple corner as if in deep thought. A sudden jerk of the head. Roger stared at Melissa.

"You saw them? Did you call the police?"

"No, I didn't. I heard the commotion of the dogs getting excited. I saw the two guys running out of the house. One was limping pretty badly like he got bitten or injured himself. He may have twisted an ankle. The dogs continued to bark at the two guys until they were gone. I don't think anything was stolen. They ran out empty handed. Like they were running for their lives."

"Then what happened?" asked Roger.

"They kept running. They went up the street. I lost sight of them but guess they ran between the houses and into some woods."

"I don't get it. If you saw them," Roger's voice was raised with agitation, "why didn't you call the police, Melissa? Why not call them and give a description?"

Melissa was calm. She put Emma on the ground so she could pet the dogs. "I saw them. I got a good look at them. Like I said, they ran up the street. When they were gone, I ran over without the girls, who were napping. Not even a coat. The dogs were coming and going from the open door. I guess they were checking to see if the burglars were returning. Of course, they wouldn't after what the dogs put those two frightened guys through. I herded them back inside and shut the door. That's all I did."

"Wait, wait. Back up," said Roger, sounding even more upset. The phone was in a hand ready to call law enforcement. "You saw the two men who broke into my house run up the street and you did not call the police?"

"Roger, I quickly came across and got the dogs back into the house and shut the door. That's all I did. I guess I was more concerned with the dogs being unattended on the front porch. And all your heat being let out."

"The heat? The window was wide open. How about

the two guys? Do you see what they did? My house is turned upside down and I have to see what they stole."

"They ran out of your house empty-handed. And I had my reason for not calling the police."

"Oh, yeah, Melissa? And what is that?" said Roger in a voice full of frustration.

Melissa looked blankly like she was being spoken to in a way that she did not deserve. Shoulders slumped. She waited a moment before answering. Her response was careful. Her voice shook. "I did not call the police because I knew who the two guys are. One was my brother Devon. The other was Chris Harmon."

"Devon and Chris? Why? Why would they burglarize my house?"

"I didn't tell you before, but Devon is a drug addict. OxyContin, Percocet, those sorts of drugs. Maybe even heroin, who knows? They probably wanted to steal the power tools so they could sell them for drug money."

"So, he has to steal my power tools? I know Devon. We had classes together."

"Roger, drug addicts steal from everyone. Devon has stolen from my parents, my parents' neighbors. Everyone. They don't care. They need a fix, and they will do what they can. I don't think he knew you lived here. But I am not sure that would have stopped him."

Roger stared at the ground. Thoughts spun around his head.

Melissa spoke. "I couldn't call the cops on my brother. I'm sorry."

Roger felt himself calming down. He looked around. There was the damaged wall, but that could be fixed. A quick visual inventory assured him that nothing was missing.

"All right," exclaimed Roger with hands on hips and walking in a wider circle. A hand dropped to pet Cyrus's head. "I won't call the cops either. I'll let this go. From now on, the windows will be locked," said Roger, turning a slightly tilted head toward the kitchenette. A sheepish smile crossed his face. He liked Melissa. She had her vulnerabilities and yet she had street smarts. It was appealing, the way Melissa wanted to protect her brother under the circumstances.

"Thanks, Roger. I came over after my brother and Chris ran away. The dogs were barking. Really mostly Buddy and Cyrus. Lady was mostly quiet."

"She never has much to say."

"I saw what happened and ran across and let the dogs back in the house and shut the door. I didn't lock it. Maybe I should have. But the girls were in the house taking a nap and I wasn't really thinking."

Roger held up an open hand to stop her. "Don't worry about it. Nothing was stolen and you helped me out and I appreciate it."

"Mommy, I am hungry," said Sophie.

Melissa looked down at Sophie. "Okay, honey, we're going to go." Melissa looked up at Roger. "The kids are hungry. They eat around now."

"Go, go," said Roger. "Thanks for all you did, Melissa."

"And thank you, Roger."

"Thanks for what?"

"Thanks for not getting the police involved. You are not going to get the police involved, right?"

Roger figured there was no point in making such a big deal of the break in. He looked at the dogs that really proved themselves. An involuntary smile crossed his face. "No, no. No cops will be called. Although you know those two will break into another house."

Melissa looked at Roger blankly, as if getting the message but still wanting to keep things as they were.

He was sure she made up her face for him. Roger found her attractive, with and without the make-up. He spoke again. "But yeah ... I mean, no. Of course, I won't call the cops."

Roger walked to the door and opened it for them. "Good-bye, girls."

The two little girls responded with good-byes and childish waves. Roger stood in the doorway and allowed his eyes to follow them home as the three dogs huddled at his feet.

Chapter 21

MUFFLED sounds of rock music filled the winter air as Roger led April by the hand. The already narrow street was reduced to an alley as it was lined with parked cars on both sides, forcing the couple to leave the Subaru three blocks away. Roger convinced himself that he was looking forward to the party. Not so much for the revelry but to experience the event. To know what it was like. He was curious if the gathering would meet expectations. To know, once and for all, if all the hoopla about the party was true. For him it was a one-off event. He would do this one time, tolerate so many people and never come back. At least he was with April. He had someone for New Year's Eve. A year earlier, he welcomed the New Year from a jail cell.

"I hope no one lights off any fireworks around my house, I mean, Uncle Ray's house."

"Stop qualifying your statements about the house you live in. It is your house; you live there."

"I know, April; I just don't own it."

"That does not matter. Besides, Uncle Ray is lucky to have you. You said that old bungalow was a real mess before you got in there. Now you are making it so nice.

And the dogs will be okay. No one shoots off fireworks where you live. Hardly anyone lives in that area in the winter."

"I know, I just worry about the dogs."

"Stop worrying. They will be okay."

Roger thought about the home and the improvements made. He contemplated next year, when the living room and kitchenette were finished rooms instead of construction sites. Next year would be different. He imagined serving brie and chardonnay. The two would dine on prime rib, green beans and roasted potatoes cooked in a real oven, not the two-burner, camper-style stove there now. The romantic dinner would end with brandy-soaked cherries with vanilla ice cream in a delicious Cherries Jubilee. He and April would snuggle on the couch watching TV, seeing the Times Square ball drop. It was not April's typical idea of New Year's Eve. She liked crowds and activity. He even told April of the home celebration idea. She said it sounded boring. That she would never go along with that. A big party was her idea of ushering in the New Year. She was excited about getting an invitation to the party held by an eccentric guy who inherited his parent's mansion. The party was a big deal. At least, to April it was. Roger was not discouraged. There was a whole year ahead to sell her on the idea of a quiet New Year's Eve. This year he was happy enough to let April have her way.

A pass through the wrought iron gates. Roger looked at the mysterious home of stony exterior and towers pointing into night darkness. Rocking sounds of a four-piece band spread out to the front lawn. They helped themselves through the over-sized oak door hung on ancient metalwork hinges. Two dozen people huddled in the entrance way, escaping the crowds and noise coming from the great room. Many were older and dressed more formally, as if they were going to a nice restaurant. Roger suspected some may have been friends of the Mertens. Other cavernous rooms were stuffed with revelers holding cups of alcohol while making conversations over the elevated sounds of music and voices. The crowding and beer cups reminded Roger of college parties he attended with his former girlfriend, Alyssa. Roger and April continued to the great room. The arched ceiling and high stained-glass windows gave the space a feeling of being in a cathedral. The band played to a shoulder-to-shoulder audience pushing to the front. Those closest to the quartet bounced up and down in mosh-pit fashion. Roger smiled, shaking his head. He knew Victor and Elena Merten would be horrified that their beloved living space was transformed into a concert venue. It was the same room where former Beatle Paul McCartney gave an impromptu solo performance to a reception for Mikhail and Raisa Gorbachev.

A petite female partier with an unlit cigarette dangling from a mouth corner pushed through the bodies with a plate of wiggling Jell-O filled custard cups. She approached Roger and April, holding the multi-colored tray of gelatin under their chins. She raised her voice above the noise.

"You want one? They're spiked with Finlandia vodka."

Roger waved off the offer while April grabbed the jiggling shot of gelatinized alcohol and slurped it down with enthusiasm. She then turned to Roger. "You're not going to try one?"

"I'm driving."

April turned to the woman. "My boyfriend is a nerd."

"That's okay," said the woman. "There's beer kegs out on the patio." She then went to other attendees who cleared the plate.

"You want to get a beer?" yelled April.

"We better see your friend first."

"That's a good idea."

The couple squeezed their way through a sea of people to the swinging doors that led into the kitchen. It was the way he remembered it. Metal pots hanging from a ceiling rack. Restaurant-sized appliances lining the walls. That night, white clad caterers scrambled to get hors d'oeuvres onto the trays of waiting servers.

Barefoot Harry leaned against a stainless-steel table holding court with several attendees.

April interrupted the conversation by entering the circle. She threw arms around the neck of a Hawaiian shirt-clad Barefoot Harry. The people surrounding the homeowner sidestepped to allow Roger in.

"Harry! Thank you again for inviting us." She released the hug and stood back.

"April. I am so glad you made it."

"Harry, this is my boyfriend, Roger."

"Whoa! I thought I was your boyfriend," said Harry in an entertaining way.

"You are. I have a lot of boyfriends; you know that," said April through a laugh.

Harry reached out and put his hand to Roger. Right then another couple came, vying for Harry's attention. That gave April and Roger the opportunity to head outside. "We'll be back," said April.

The change in temperatures was dramatic. The house overly warm with so many bodies, and the outside freezing with shivering people sipping drinks and smoking cigarettes. There was also a relief from the noise. Roger grabbed a red cup and began pouring a beer while April lit a cigarette. He saw some faces he recognized. People from around town or high school that he only knew in a distant sort of way. He felt the stares. Roger was compelled to say something to break the little standoff.

"Nice to get out of there for a moment. Its loud in there."

"Loud and warm in there. Cold and quiet out here," said someone to Roger's back.

"I don't know where to go. Here or there," responded Roger to no one as he handed a cup to April. More noise spilled out when someone opened the door.

"Lots of people showed up," said someone trying to make conversation.

"Yeah," nodded Roger while getting a beer for himself. "Quite a crowd."

"Barefoot Harry always invites a lot of people. But my guess is that half of the people are crashers."

Roger nodded before responding. "That's what I always heard."

"You were invited. Right?" asked the guy.

Roger laughed. "Oh yeah, I am invited. Well come to think of it, I really wasn't. I am here with April, who was invited. She knows Barefoot Harry from Happy Yappers."

"Rescue?"

"Yeah, the rescue center."

"Oh, yeah, I know that place."

April was in a separate conversation and did not hear Roger or the other talking.

"Oh, then you're invited. I mean, there a lot of people who just show up to Harry's New Year's Year bash."

"I think the ones April is talking to are crashers." Roger leaned his head in April's direction.

"Well, I guess it's going to happen. At midnight, some people set off fireworks."

"Does Harry allow that?"

"Not really. People just do it."

"Poor neighborhood dogs; dogs don't like fireworks. It scares them."

Marijuana smoke scented the air. The smell alarmed Roger, who was under strict orders from his parole officer to stay away from any drug use. Inhaling second-hand smoke was enough to trigger a positive drug test result.

He turned to the group that April was in conversation with. A joint was being passed around. "April?"

She knew the situation. April promised to never light up in his presence.

"What's the matter?" responded April with a wry smile on her lips.

"What's the matter?" said Roger, hearing a little panic in his voice. "Don't you remember what I told you?"

April pushed the joint to pierced lips and inhaled. "Oh, yeah, you can't smoke pot. Or you don't smoke pot. One of those," said April in short sputters, attempting to hold the smoke in her lungs. A childish laugh squeezed from a tightened mouth. Then a full laugh. A grayish cloud. Roger dodged the illegal smog like avoiding a swarm of stinging insects. He ducked the cloud with a protecting shoulder.

Out of the way, Roger turned to the people he was just speaking to. "I'm on parole. The last thing I need is a positive test. Jamal would freak out. I'd find myself back in a jail cell."

"Jamal?"

"Yeah, Jamal!" said Roger forcefully while moving to the deck railing. "My parole officer."

One of the people in the group spoke up. "You're Roger Wilson. I heard about that."

"Oh, I know," said Roger, who took backward steps toward the railing. A crowd huddled in front of the steps, blocking an escape. He grabbed the railing and swung legs over the bar like a gymnast crossing a pommel horse. He landed two yards below on two even feet. Startled revelers leaned over the railing.

"What's up?" said one of the guests.

"I need to get away from that smoke."

"Where did he go?" Roger could hear April asking through a cough. Then a plethora of answers. Roger circled around the deck looking up at the people above him. April looked down. "You can be weird, Roger Wilson."

"Weird?"

"Yeah, weird."

"I'm not going back to prison. If I tested positive …"

"Yeah, yeah. We all know. I'll see you inside." April turned toward the gathering of friends and disappeared.

Roger walked along a driveway that hugged the side of the house. He ran into an old acquaintance from high school, Travis. Travis had been a stoner in school. A small following surrounded the guy with bloodshot eyes and long wiry hair held down with a wool cap. He spoke with a stoner drawl.

"Roger, my main man." Travis gave Roger an unsolicited hug. "How the hell are you? I heard you had some trouble. I saw your mom. She told me about it. You're out now; is that right?"

"Well, either they let me out or I escaped," said Roger awkwardly.

"Ha-ha. Oh, man, they made you wear stripes? Ha-ha."

"Hey, man, that ain't funny." The comment annoyed Roger. One of the guys looked at Roger and shook his head as if embarrassed by the slight. "I'm out. Did my time. They made us wear yellow jumpsuits, if you have to know. We called them bananas. But yeah, as you can tell, I'm out."

"That's cool, man. And no hard feelings. I was just messing around. You got mixed up with Quincy. That kid. Man, he spilled his guts, and nothing happened to him. Man, you took all the grief. Man, that sucks."

Roger just gave a stiff shrug allowing his eyes to follow the two guys and a girl standing there. They looked on with serious smiles. "Life happens, I suppose."

"No, man. Its not like that. I mean, Quincy got you involved in his enterprise and then when things got bad and the cops didn't like what you guys were up to, he acted like you were the bad guy. But he was the bad guy. He saved his own ass. Whatever happened to Quincy? "

"Oh, man, I don't want to talk about it. I don't know where Quincy is. Last I heard he moved to Florida. That's all I really know."

"He's bartending in Fort Lauderdale," piped in the girl standing there. "My sister still sees him on Facebook. Good-riddance. I never liked that guy."

"Oh, well," said Roger, zipping up his hoodie before pushing hands deep into the pockets. "It's cold out here."

"You need a coat," said one of the guys bundled up in a snorkel coat and wool hat.

"I didn't think I would be spending so much time outside."

"We're going straight for the beer," said Travis as he lit up a cigarette. "Then we are going inside. The band's really good. See you around. "

The group passed by.

Roger sidestepped patches of snow, preferring the frozen grass. Then back to the front of the house where he re-entered the home. The house was even more congested than it had been just a half hour earlier. He moved into the great room by squeezing through, side shouldered. Roger could not get over how such a large room would be part of someone's home. Eyes traced the walls of fine art and European architecture. He imagined the many dignitaries who were once entertained there, as he moved through the standing-room-only crowd. He reached a side area of oversized sofas sitting on Oriental rugs surrounded by antique floor lamps, a den-like oasis among a sea of people. Partygoers crowded onto the furniture like college kids sharing seating space in a fraternity house.

A cocktail table paralleled two sofas. Two guys stood on it to get a better view of the band; the extra foot and a half allowed them to easily see over people's heads. One of the two men helped a girlfriend onto the table. It bothered Roger to see such disregard for the home. He figured they may be some of the party crashers, although he could not be sure. April said that the invitation list was two hundred people long. Roger estimated that the house and patio contained double that. No respect for the invitations. Little consideration for the interior furnishings. Roger moved in closer. Shoes shuffled on the smooth wooden top. A piece

of elegant furniture constructed by artisans in Italy or
Spain, treated like a soap box. Wherever the table came
from, its purpose was never meant for standing on.
The scene upset Roger more and more. Anger boiled
inside him. It was none of his business. He knew that.
Barefoot Harry hung out in the kitchen as if he did
not have a care in the world. It did not matter. Roger
remembered the Mertens as good people. Hard work
and talent brought the home into existence. It was they
who imported the fine furniture, stained glass, and
decorous drapes. A castle-like home filled with paint-
ings and statues from artists the world over. This was
their making and it needed to be respected. Many lumi-
naries in the fine-art community helped create a history
there. It was all real. Not myth, but truth.

The disrespect was unbearable. People near the
two men and one woman on the cocktail table smiled
approvals at the rude act. Some held cups up in saluta-
tion or simply laughed at the scene. If everyone believed
such thoughtlessness was to be celebrated, Roger was
going to do something. He got close and patted one of
the guy's knees with the back of a hand.

"Hey, man," Roger yelled over the sound of the
music. The guy smiled and nodded before turning back
to the band. "Hey, there." Still nothing. The trio traded
interrupted glances. Their focus was the music. Roger
looked down at the slick tabletop and three pairs of

shoes. More disrespect. More anger. He banged the side of the guy's leg again with increased force. He wanted to get the guy's attention. Roger looked up. Eyes glared down. Glassy eyes. Not just an alcohol shininess. There was something more to the intoxication.

"Yeah?" A response barely audible over the loud music. Irritation on the man's face.

Roger was unsure what to say. Nothing planned. A loss for words. A fumbled mind. He searched for a response. The guy stepped down to the floor. He was taller than Roger expected. Broad shoulders. Made-in-a-gym biceps.

"Do you need to be on there? That's someone's furniture," Roger yelled at the guy.

His buddy stepped down and stood behind him. The guy got closer. A face screwed mockingly. The friend wore a cocky smirk in the background.

"What's your problem, dude?" shouted the guy over the noise of the band. The smell of beer breath.

Roger needed to defend his position. He could not look scared. He learned that in prison. Once they sensed fear, you were done. Half of the battle was psychological. Stand your ground. Hold on. He learned these things. An inmate taught him martial art moves. A Roger favorite was the Bruce Lee straight blast punch. The hardest he could throw. The lessons helped him inside the walls. He learned to hide fear. He knew how to defend himself. There were some scuffles. Inmates mostly left him alone. The guys he faced at the party were high on something. They were drinking. Their actions unpredictable.

"You're on someone's furniture," yelled Roger as the music played on.

"Yeah? So? Is it your furniture?"

The friend laughed.

"No, it's not. How about showing some respect for Harry's house?"

The guy's girlfriend looked down from the coffee table. She waved a hand up wanting the guys back. The rest of the room was preoccupied with watching the band and was oblivious to the confrontation. She yelled down to the two guys, "Forget him. Get back up here."

The guy ignored her. He kept suspicious, glassy eyes on Roger. A menacing, intoxicated curl of a lip. "Why don't you mind your own fucking business since this it ain't your house, dude. It belongs to some guy named Harry. I don't think you're Harry. Are you?" The friend laughed.

The guy turned swiveling his head toward the friend who held the cocky smirk. Both were amused by the going back and forth. The friend in the back emptied a plastic cup to his mouth. With three fingers he removed a wet chunk of ice, throwing it at Roger's face. The guy in front roared with laughter.

Roger wiped the wetness off a cheek with the back of his hand. He turned as if to walk away. In that split second when the front guy's guard was down Roger planted feet and twisted back. A cross body blast punch to the guy's chin. The force threw the man's head back. He fell into his friend's unexpecting arms. The ice-filled cup fell to the floor. A left step and right hook. Roger caught the friend with closed fist to the eye. Then a left jab to the friend's undefended nose. Both collapsed to the ground. The woman on the table screamed. Her voice attracted the attention of those in the vicinity. Roger stood over the two in a victory stance. The woman jumped down to attend to the pair who lay disoriented on the ground.

Roger turned into the crowd. Like a parting of the sea, those who witnessed the fight moved out of the way of the victorious pugilist. A back shove. Roger turned. A partygoer stood with shock on his face. He pointed a hitchhiker thumb toward the two friends on the ground. He yelled, "What the fuck?"

Roger used all his might to push the guy in front of him who fell backwards into other people. Spilled drinks. Screams. Yelling. Then a chain reaction. More pushing and shoving. Suddenly the room turned into a melee. Roger slipped through the crowd on his way out of the great room.

Once in the hall, Roger squirmed back to the kitchen where there were more partygoers. The open door allowed the sounds of cacophony to reach the ears of those there. Conversations ended. Heads lifted. Eyes widened.

"There's a fistfight in the great room!" yelled Roger.

A hulking security guard eating hors d'oeuvres while chatting with a female sever threw a plate on a table and ran past Roger. Another security guard did the same. Some followed while others ran to safety. Roger returned to the back deck.

Sounds of the commotion leaked to the outside area.

"What's going on in there?"

Roger stood safely from any residual marijuana smoke. "Hey, April, let's go. There was a fight."

"A fight?" asked April.

"Yeah, a fight."

Mumbling about a fight among the few dozen people, partygoers exited the home onto the deck. Roger grabbed April by the arm. He pulled her as she puffed a cigarette and held a drink.

"What are you doing?" said April with an agitated face. She pulled her arm back. "Stop!" she said in an amplified whine.

There was continued yelling from inside. There was a disturbance among those who spilled out onto the deck. People were asking what happened. There was talk about a fight and someone or more who got punched.

"April, let's go. This party is over. The cops are being called. I don't want to be here."

"Do you know who started it?"

A preppy guy wearing a corduroy jacket and loosened tie approached Roger. "Hey Bud, why'd you hit those fuckers.? You ruined the party."

"Oh, no!" said April.

"They attacked me. Let's go."

Roger pushed through the sea of people. He overheard people saying that he was the one in the fight. Someone yelled at Roger, "You fucked those guys up, man. They called the police. Thanks for wrecking the party, asshole."

"Someone always does something like that," said someone in the crowd.

Another asked, "Who is that?"

"Roger Something. I can't remember his whole name. He got arrested for drug smuggling."

"I didn't cause the fight, man. It was someone else," yelled Roger. "It was someone else."

Roger and April walked quickly to the front of the house. People were huddled out on the front lawn like school kids practicing a fire drill. Roger and April walked around them. Someone yelled, "Hey, April, where you going?"

"Home," she yelled back. Roger held April's arm and walked hurriedly. Others leaving the area. A police car flashing its lights pulled up and another turned the corner up the road. A cop hurried across their path.

Roger and April got to the car. Cars were speeding away when they could. Two more police cars showed up, with officers directing people away from the house.

April yelled, "What the hell, Roger? What the hell?"

Roger pulled the car out into the street and made a U-turn to avoid the mansion. He accelerated. The Subaru passed a police car from another town, evidently called in as back up. Then an ambulance.

"Did you hear what those people were saying, Roger? They were saying you were in the fight. Were you?"

Roger did not answer but concentrated his eyes on the road.

"Roger, are you listening to me? Did you get in a fight? That was a good party. I hope it wasn't you who caused this."

"I did not get into a fight. I just defended myself. Two guys went after me."

"Oh, Roger. I did not know that about you. Do you get in fights? Do you?"

"No, not at all. Its not my thing. These guys were all over standing on your friend's furniture and I said something, that's all."

"You can't do stuff like this. You could get sent back to jail."

It was what he was thinking, but April's confirmation hit him hard. "I know, I know. But I didn't start it. They started with me."

"You need to learn to walk away, Roger. You need to prevent trouble. You say it all the time. So, what do you do? You get in a fist fight with two guys. Real smart. People know you were in the fight Roger. They know who you are."

"I know, I know."

Roger's mouth dried with worry. "If anyone asks you tell them it wasn't me. That I had nothing to do with it."

April rolled the window down. A rush of cold air entered the cabin. Shaking hands held a cigarette and lighter. The scratch of flint, then the sucking sound of inhaled smoke. Shoulders slumped in indignation. April spoke a whitish gray cloud. "Whatever, Roger. Whatever."

Chapter 22

ROGER lay in bed, clicking through his phone and social media. Facebook users discussed the party. There were comments about the fight. Two mentioned Roger by name but were unsure if he was the one in the altercation. Some posted about a guy in a beard who may have been a part of it. No one seemed to know the other two guys. It was said that they looked beaten up but managed to escape before the cops could question them. Roger took that as good news. There were people at the party who fingered him. No one said he instigated the fight. The rhetoric was not as bad as he expected.

April was still asleep.

The blankets were tossed aside. Roger still worried about the police and what they might ask him. He imagined law enforcement officers knocking on April's apartment door. Police wanting him to go "downtown" to answer questions. They would know his record. Jamal would be contacted. Assault and battery charges. Then the freedom he enjoyed would be gone.

Legs across the mattress. Feet placed on the floor. He got up and walked naked to the bathroom. Roger stared at the mirror. A focus on the beard. *If he shaved it, would it help?* Several people at the party referred to him as the guy with the beard. There were witnesses. They would have spoken to the police. He wondered if shaving the face whiskers would help. Then he thought that it could look suspicious. That he had something to hide.

Roger rummaged through the drawers. The very act made him feel guilty. It was not right to look through the vanity drawers of a woman he only knew for a few weeks. Necessity kept him going. A blow dryer. Scissors. Blue hair dye. Assorted half-used lipsticks. Birth control pills. A razor. Electric hair clippers.

A black cord was untwisted. He still debated the idea whether shaving the beard was a good idea. He wanted to be another person. Not the bearded guy who got in a fight. Not the man who fist-battled two guys. He plugged in the clippers. A glance at his crotch. A big bush of pubic hair. He ran the clippers across the mane allowing the cut curls to drop to the floor. Roger did it again and more hair was clipped away. In a moment all but the shortest hairs were gone. Nothing but bristles.

A lift of the hand. Clippers taken to the beard. Hairs fell into the sink. Roger continued until his beard was short. He then scrounged around for the razor still laying in the drawer. A search of the shower. A rusty can of shaving cream. White foam dispensed into an open hand.

Roger shaved his face clean and massaged the smoothness. He took the razor to his groin area to shave it clean. He stood staring at himself in the mirror. Smooth cheeks. Eyes dropped. It was true about cleaning the pubic hair away; it made his manhood look bigger.

Roger thought of April and the way she acted last night. She was right to get mad. April had looked forward to the party. He second-guessed the behavior. Where did the anger come from? He needed to control it. It was easy to blame other people over what transpired in the last few years, but he made choices and needed to own them. He knew old anger boiled inside. There was Quincy and the arrest. Alyssa who dumped him. A father who resented him and a mother unsure what to do about it. Then there was all that was lost.

Those guys on the cocktail table really were none of his business. If Barefoot Harry let such goings-on to occur, who was he to get involved? The security personnel were hanging out in the kitchen and Barefoot Harry did not seem to care. Who showed up to the party was something that Barefoot Harry could worry about, if he wanted to. It was not up to him. He felt bad for ruining the night for April. It was her night; he should have been more considerate. Roger knew he should have thought of what could happen when confronting the two guys. Instead, he just reacted on his own. It was something he sometimes did. To do things without thinking them out. To not consider the consequences. He convinced himself that is how he found himself in prison.

Roger walked back out into the bedroom. April was awake and pre-occupied with her phone. Speedy thumbs texted messages. The blanket was up to her neck. She realized his presence without taking her focus off the phone.

"You are all over Facebook. A lot of people know it was you who got in the fight. Did you know that?"

Roger did not answer but stood naked in the middle of the floor. He waited for April who remained fixated on her phone.

"Roger, did you hear me?" April asked.

When he did not answer she dropped the phone while letting out an exasperated sigh. She then spoke while turning toward him. "Roger?" She stopped and stared for a moment. Her eyes widened. She broke out into an uproarious laugh while cupping her mouth. The laugh was on him. He did not care. He was happy to hear April's laugh. He wanted her to be glad after the ruined evening.

"Oh, no!" More laughter. Fruitless attempts to hold back the chuckles. "They'll never be able to identify you now!" She laughed some more. "Oh, no. You shaved both beards." More laughter.

"Okay, okay," said Roger with a smile.

April got control of herself. She caught her breath. "Well, Jenny said you really did those two guys. One has a broken jaw and the other a broken nose. What the hell did you do, Roger?"

"They were in my face. One of the guys threw ice at me. I attacked before I was attacked."

"Jenny said they are troublemakers from Syracuse. In fact, both have warrants for drug peddling. They skipped out on court dates. That's why they took off, despite being beat up. They went into New York City and got fixed up in a hospital there. They told the emergency room they were jumped near Times Square. The ER was so busy, it being New Year's Eve, that no cops questioned them. The two then snuck out of the hospital before being released. What a mess. The one guy had his mouth wired shut."

"I guess I don't know my own strength."

April stared at Roger with a smile. She lifted her phone as if to take a photo.

Roger darted back into the bathroom to hide. "That's the last thing I need," he said.

April roared with laughter. "Oh, Roger. I would never do that. I am only kidding. Get out here."

Roger peeked out the bathroom door while gripping the door frame. He stayed there until he was sure there was no threat of an unsolicited picture.

"What? Do you think no one will find you? That

no one can identify you? A lot of people are already saying they thought it was you who got in the fight with those two guys. The people who saw the fight did not know you. Some don't even know you wear a beard. They only know you from high school and then going to jail. But your name is coming up about this. I have been texting people saying that it wasn't you. That a lot of guys have beards."

"When I searched social media, I did not see much about me."

April looked down at his groin. "Wow, you sure are clean-shaven." She laughed again at her own comment. "Happy New Year!"

"I hope those guys don't come back."

"You don't have to worry. Those two are out of commission for a while. There is chatter about you. Jenny is telling people it was not you, that you had already left the party. Besides, those guys need to be worried about the police. They are going back to jail when the law catches up with them."

"You are right, April; I did get lucky."

"The local cops told Harry no more New Year's Eve parties. Things are out of control. I should have left you home," said April sarcastically.

"I'm sorry, April."

April finished a text before tossing the phone to the foot of the bed. She then lifted the covers off exposing the silky white skin that made up her naked body. She swung closed legs across the mattress and sat on the edge of the bed leaning on locked arms. April got up and walked toward him. Roger expected her to fall into his arms but instead passed him on her way to the bathroom. He heard the clink of the toilet seat drop and the whistling sound of urinating. Roger stood still. She spoke from the bathroom. "I don't think you have much to worry about, Roger."

The sound of a toilet flush. The squeaky crank of the shower faucet.

Roger spoke over his shoulder. "Can I get in there with you?"

"I don't know. Can you?" It was the way April often talked. Her way of an invitation.

Roger turned and went to join April for an early morning shower.

Chapter 23

ANOTHER ten-hour night shift at Amazon came to a merciful end. Roger was still grateful for the job. It was the robotic nature of the operation that he detested, the repetitive routines. It was tough work, even for someone who was in as great a shape as he. They liked him there. He did his work well and was a fast worker, although the pressure to produce more was ever present. To Roger, there was little wonder why Jeff Bezos was the richest man in the world. Roger certainly needed the money, but it was not like when he had his own business.

Lately, Roger was thinking more and more about the end. The end of warehouse work and something else. He thought about the T-shirt business and starting it again. He went online in search of T-shirt contractors. All the old business equipment he once had was long gone. Roger had left everything to four employees who agreed to keep the business going until he got out of prison, but that situation never worked out. The business was run into the ground in just a few months. The van, equipment, and all inventories were all sold. Proceeds were split among the former workers. The people whom Roger gave jobs to were never seen again.

Thoughts of restarting Quotable-Ts swirled in Roger's head with increasing intensity. This was even though there was no money to bring back the business. No capital for equipment or payroll or putting a deposit down for rental space. The notion sometimes depressed him. He felt cornered and wondered if showing up to a gargantuan white warehouse was his life. That he would do a job well and find himself drifting along in a career he neither loved nor did not hate enough to leave. Efforts and skill would be rewarded. There would be additional training. He would move up the chain of increasing responsibilities until becoming one of the top supervisors whom he increasingly resented. The company would put him on a trajectory toward becoming one of the people who micromanaged workers' actions by staring into a monitoring screen. It concerned him. He saw friends' fathers and mothers who got jobs in their younger years only to toil for decades in like positions. Careers they simply accepted. Jobs that were rarely inspiring, often tedious. Holidays and vacation time was analyzed with precision. Days between weekends constantly counted. He wondered if he could get caught in a similar career river, only to go with the flow for thirty years. Would he ever be brave enough to swim to the banks and save himself?

There was no money to start a business. He had a car payment and the Amazon job provided health insurance. Housing was free, but when the remodeling was completed Uncle Ray would make him sign a lease and mail rent checks. He needed capital. Some way to get started again. That is what he thought. Or was it? There was no money when he was a junior in high school and launched Quotable-Ts. The first inventory of blank T-shirts was gotten on credit. The initial imprinting was made on a borrowed silk screener. He sold the shirts walking around festivals until vendors complained and management threw him out. It was a gypsy-like existence, but it worked. Soon some stores agreed to carry the shirts on consignment. Roger would go around once a week, collecting money and replacing the sold shirts with new ones. Profits went to the purchase of a used silk screener he set up in his parents' garage. That allowed him to make so many shirts that he rented booths at festivals. There the shirts were a hit. More stores heard about the "Ts" and wanted to stock them. That is when Roger rented a store so he, too, could sell retail in the front and manufacturer in the back. Roger recalled nostalgically the way things were back then. The sales, the growing business, having his own employees. The challenges of constantly having to figure things out, make things happen. It kept him sharp. Challenge is what he thrived on. He never needed drugs or alcohol; success was too intoxicating.

As well as the business did, his father pushed him to

take the firefighter test. It was not something he wanted
to do, but convinced himself to listen. He thought he
could do both firefighting and run a business. Some of
it made sense. Firefighting paid well, had great benefits and a pension. Shifts were twenty-four hours with
three and four days off. It would give him plenty of
time to run his business, and the employees could pick
up the slack when he was at the station. Roger passed
the written exam, physical and was waiting his turn to
be hired. Then the arrest happened. There would never
be a chance to be a firefighter.

He pulled up to the house, knowing the dogs
would be anxious to see them. He knew that the twelve
hours he was gone was a little tough for the dogs even
if they had access to the outside through the dog doors.
Roger would get in and find all the food was eaten
and water mostly drunk and stale. He got in and the
happy dogs were there awaiting him. As down as Roger
could be about his work circumstances, the dogs always
made him happy. Cyrus grabbed the leashes off the
wall hanger and dropped them on the floor. He picked
up his and paraded with it in his mouth as an easy
reminder that it was time for a walk. The other dogs
retrieved their leather tethers, following suit. The sight
made Roger laugh.

Roger freshened the food bowls and provided fresh
water, which all three attacked ravenously. While the

dogs ate, he changed clothes into something warmer in preparation for a walk in the January cold. Roger wrapped the dogs in their dog coats. April was working at PetSmart that day, so Roger considered going over to the big box store. It would be an excuse to see her and there was always dog food to be purchased. He found himself liking her more and more. There was an easy attraction to her sexiness and free-spirited lifestyle.

As Roger got the dogs ready, he saw Melissa walking up the street, pushing the stroller. As cold as it was, Melissa always seemed to get the kids out of the house for a walk. She also had an uncanny way of strolling the girls when Roger was out with the dogs. It happened more and more, and Roger was believing that Melissa was getting good at knowing his schedule and habits. Her activities appeared a little too coincidental. That was okay. There was a piece of him that was attracted to Melissa. He could no longer ignore the feelings. She was more mature than April and certainly more together. A conformist to April's bohemian. She was focused and reminded him of the way he was when working his T-shirt company. Back then, Alyssa thought he was the free-spirited one, the surfer dude. The winter sandal wearer with long hair. But he was a go-getter, a guy with a growing enterprise. Someone laser focused. April instead lived the life of a young person not sure what the future held, and with little care of what was ahead.

Roger took the dogs out and headed up the street. It was the most joyful time for the dogs. They liked the adventure of being out and Roger would take the dogs on different routes to mix it up and keep it exciting. Sometimes he walked them on the county hill path, through acres of woods. Other times he took them down to the salty docks or on the streets and through the neighborhoods, seeing children at play. That day he found himself looking around for Melissa and not just relying on a chance encounter. Roger wondered about her, keeping eyes peeled in the hope of finding her on the morning walk. He changed the path and walked north toward downtown. There she was, pushing the stroller into Gardella's Grocery Store. He walked the dogs toward the store before detouring down another street and then back again. It was a timing thing. A hope that he would see her again. Roger met people along the way, wanting to say hello or pet the canines. All the while he kept his eye toward the store.

As he looped back, he saw the stroller leave the store with Melissa behind it. The plan worked. The purposeful chance encounter. She walked away not seeing him and the dogs. A bag of groceries filled a back pouch behind the girls.

"Hey, Melissa."

She turned back. A face of uncertainty crossed her face as if unsure who he was. Roger lifted sunglasses onto his head. He squinted the January sun reflecting off patches of snow.

"Oh, its good to see you," said Melissa, with hesitation. "For half a second I was unsure who was calling my name. You know, with the dark glasses and clean-shaven face. Then I noticed the dogs." A sincere smile sparkled her face. Cyrus, Lady and Buddy pulled their leashes towards the girls.

"Yeah, I decided to shave the beard off."

"You look more handsome without it."

Roger felt the compliment. "How are the kids?"

Melissa tilted the stroller back and pivoted it on the rear wheels toward Roger. Sophie and Emma were bundled up in heavy coats, gloves and hats. They shared a blanket in their laps.

"Wow, they look warm." Both girls waved to Roger, their little open hands turning back and forth. "At least the temperatures are a little higher. Things are getting a little slushy and messy. It may get to forty today."

He turned his attention to the two girls. "Hi, girls!" said Roger through a broad smile. "Do you remember me?"

"They remember the dogs," said Melissa through a playful laugh. She turned her head into the front of the stroller. "Sophie, Emma. What do you think? Do you miss the beard or not?"

They both shook heads with serious expressions on their faces.

"What does that mean? Did you like Roger's beard? Do you miss it? Or do you think he looks better now?"

The younger one, Emma, shook her head no. Sophie spoke to her mother in a shy whisper. "No beard."

Melissa looked up to Roger while still bent over. "You heard it, Roger. The girls are down on the beard. Smooth cheeks all the way."

Roger studied the charm in Melissa's face. The gentle tug of attraction for her was still there. Even a greater pull toward her handsome, womanly looks. "I'll keep the beard off. I was tired of it anyway. It became my New Year's resolution. No face whiskers."

"Are you still working at Amazon?"

"Oh ,yeah. No reason to go anywhere else."

"You need to get back to what you used to do. You know, being an entrepreneur. Doing your T-shirt thing or something like that. That warehouse thing is not you."

Roger was amazed at the insight. The intuition that Melissa had. She did not know him, but she somehow did. The way the single mom was able to pick up on his personality and thinking.

"Yeah, I think about it all the time. I've even working a little on my laptop designing some new T-shirts. Even found a contractor I could use, since I do not have the money to buy my own equipment. But I don't know.

Amazon isn't great, but it's a steady paycheck and they are talking about making me an assistant supervisor. I'd make more money and I still get my bennies."

"Bennies?"

"Benefits."

"Oh," Melissa said with an embarrassed laugh. "Okay, if that's what you want. I just don't see you as an Amazon supervisor or whatever. I see you as the creative, self-made type of guy. The surfer guy who knows how to make things and turn it into money. And then there's the freedom. That's you, Roger. That's the real you."

The statement hit Roger like a slap to the face. It was the way he thought. Amazon was safe but owning his own business was an adventure. Melissa's intuition continued to surprise him. Cold gusts pushed through the streets. Chilly pedestrians walked by. Roger pushed hands deep into empty pockets while pressing arms tight to his body, an attempt to stay warm.

"Yeah, I think you're right."

"I know I'm right."

"You better keep going. Your two girls are going to get cold."

Melissa leaned over the girls assuring their hats covered their ears. Sophie and Emma continued taking turns petting the dogs. "Are you two cold?"

Both shook their heads no.

Melissa laughed. "They like the dogs so much, they don't even think of this winter weather."

"Well, in any case, I better let you move on."

Melissa looked at the ground and rocked the stroller back and forth. It appeared she was gathering her thoughts. Not ready to move on. "I'll be done with my two-year degree in May. I'll actually start training at the hospital at the end of February. I'll be a respiratory therapist."

"Wow, congratulations. That's exciting."

"Well, I'm excited. The best part is the hospital will pay for the second half of my education. My goal is to be an RN. And then a nurse practitioner, after that."

"I remember you saying that you wanted to be a nurse practitioner. It pays well. You are going places, Melissa."

"I think so. I did not want to be a welfare mom. I did not want my kids to see me like that." She paused before speaking again. "I did not want to see myself like that."

"You really have picked yourself up by your bootstraps."

"I think so. I also do design work for a publisher. I create book covers for them and even do some independently."

"You do? I did not know that."

"Yeah, it is how I make money from home. I learned some graphic design in high school and took a couple of classes as electives at the community college."

Roger was surprised at what she said. "I had no idea you did that kind of thing. So, you must be quite creative."

"I do all right. The publisher really likes me. They have authors who ask for me specifically."

"I like creative people. If I get the T-shirt company going again, I could probably use someone like you. You could do side work for me."

Melissa smiled sheepishly. "You should get your t-shirt company going again. You are very creative."

"I've been giving it a lot of thought lately. It's a tough decision."

"Don't let having no equipment stop you. Before when you started last time, what did you have? You started at the bottom, right? Then you got equipment. Just figure it out."

"Ever since my incarceration, I've been on my back. I lost everything. It seems so hard to start over."

"You can't change the past, only the future. "

Roger smiled. He knew what was coming.

"That was one of your shirts. Underneath it was a man looking into the clouds," said Melissa.

"Yeah, that one was a good seller."

"Maybe you should take your own advice."

"I have to figure it out. I suppose I have to find my old self."

"You need to find your new self. The old self is gone forever. Adios."

Roger was so enjoying the conversation with Melissa that he forgot about the cold. "I better let you go. Those poor girls will be freezing."

"Yeah, petting the dogs lets them forget the cold." Melissa spoke to the girls. "Sophie, Emma. Ready to go?"

One of the girls spoke. "Yeah, I guess so."

Melissa laughed. "Well, we will go." she said through a bright smile. "See ya, Roger." She turned and started to walk away.

"Good-bye, Melissa. By the way, who do you want in the Super Bowl? Packers or Patriots?"

Melissa turned back. "Who do you want?" she asked.

"I guess I just want a good game."

"That's a cop out."

"Okay, I want the Packers."

"I see. Roger wants Aaron Rodgers. Sort of makes sense."

"And you?"

"Tom Brady."

"Oh, a Patriots fan."

"A Tom Brady fan."

"Really?" Roger was intrigued.

Melissa pushed the stroller few steps closer. "Yeah, that's right. I love Tom Brady. I think he's awesome."

"Well, he is a great quarterback."

"He is great because he has confidence. He is great because he so believes in himself."

"I know what you mean."

"Do you?"

"Well, he has the Super Bowl rings to prove it."

"When the Patriots played Atlanta in Super Bowl LI, they were down twenty-eight to three late in the third quarter. Everyone thought the game was over. Players on the Atlanta bench were congratulating each other. The Falcons' owner gave his granddaughter victory hugs. There was only one person who genuinely believed that the Patriots could come back. That was Tom Brady. He walked the sidelines getting the team psyched up. He was not about to quit."

"That guy is a gamer."

"He is more than that; he's a winner. All because he believes in himself. That is what you need to return to, believing in yourself. You are allowing a mistake to chop you down. Get back in there, Roger. You are not a warehouse guy. You are an entrepreneur. A businessman."

Melissa stopped and stared at Roger. There was sage-like seriousness to her expression. "It's late in the third quarter and your team is down twenty-eight to three. What are you going to do, Roger Wilson?"

Roger absorbed Melissa's learned remark. He responded with a serious smile and gentle nod.

"Thanks, Melissa. I get it."

She turned and started pushing the stroller away. She yelled without turning back. "Big blizzard coming."

"I heard. It'll be here in a few days. They're saying Sunday. Super Bowl Sunday."

"Stock up on supplies. We might be homebound for two or three days."

"I will, Melissa. I will."

Chapter 24

THE ride toward Roger's parents' house was dusky as the winter sun fell behind the horizon. He did not want to get involved with his parents, especially his father. Timing was intentional. He needed a miter saw to cut molding to be added to the corners of the ceiling and around the doors. He could rent one from Home Depot, but money was getting tight, so it was better to use the miter saw stored in his father's tool shed. The plan was to just borrow the saw without his father realizing it was missing, then return it the same way. A stealth operation like that would allow Roger to avoid his father's moodiness.

Roger knew Friday night was date night. Father and mother always went out to dinner then, often bringing neighbor Gerry along. He knew they would be out for about two hours, so there was a window of opportunity to get into the shed, retrieve the miter saw and leave without ever being noticed. He parked the car in front of the home and got out. The Jeep Cherokee his father drove was missing from the driveway and the home was mostly dark. He glanced over at Gerry's home. The smallish Colonial home was dark with a car siding the house. It was almost certain the neighbor was with them. That was a good thing. The fewer curious eyes, the better.

The building was unlocked. Roger switched the light on in the unheated premises. Dusty fire department photos decorated the walls. Multi-sized screwdrivers were organized on a hanging rack. Red wheeled drawer racks filled with more tools sided the space. The shed was neat and orderly in the way a Marine barracks might be. The miter saw was big enough where it should have been easy to find. Roger remembered it normally stationed next to the workbench, but a quick look and it was not there. A grip to the handle of a tall metal cabinet of gray and rust. A twist and pull. The tinny doors shook. Tools, paint cans and supplies, but no miter saw. A look under the bench; it was not there either. He searched beneath the tables by moving some boxes around but did not find it. Roger wondered if his father loaned it to someone or if was using it for a project in the home. Then a voice startled him.

"Need something?"

The words jolted Roger. It was his father. Broad shoulders filled the doorway. Serious expression like the older man caught someone in a restricted place. Gerry, the neighbor, stood outside breathing cloudy breaths.

"Ah, yeah, Dad. The miter saw. Why are you here? How come you are not out to dinner?"

"We went already. Early Bird Special at the Lobster Hut. Half-priced lobster." Roger's father stepped into the workroom and Gerry followed him in. "You can't beat it. Just have to order it between four and six. You should see the line to get in. We get there early."

Roger was still recovering by the unexpectedness of his father. "Wow, sounds like a deal."

"You won't find the miter there. Its over your head." With the condescending facial expression of an unamused school principal, Roger's father stood with a finger pointed toward the loft.

There was a storage loft overhead. It was a place that the father usually kept seasonal items, such as decorations, life jackets for the boat and gardening items. Roger would not have thought to look there. Roger's father removed a ladder hanging on the wall and walked past him with an air of smugness. Roger knew the deal: his father's shed and his father's way of doing things. The ladder was leaned against the loft. Roger took a step forward as an offer to get the miter saw. The father would not have any of it and climbed the rungs. The loft was orderly like the rest of the shed; everything had its place. A movement of a couple of boxes exposed the miter saw. Roger's father pulled the circular saw mounted to a mitering table and lowered it down to Roger. A climb down and the ladder put away.

"You should have let me know you were coming over; I would have gotten it down for you."

"I did not think I would need it. Thought I might just rent one from Home Depot."

"Rent one from Home Depot? Why would you even think of that? Why, when I have one?"

That was the reason. Dealing with his father. His constant hostile, condescending voice. His father always thought that Roger would become a firefighter. The truth was that Roger never wanted to do that. He never wanted the firefighter lifestyle. Mr. Wilson's fellow firemen were good guys and had treated Roger well when he was growing up. However, Roger became put off by their one-dimensionality. The other firefighters would visit the home and the entire conversations were nothing other than firefighting. It was as if it was all they knew.

He liked being an entrepreneur. Working when most everyone else was playing never bothered him. There were the benefits of being your own boss. Of being able to leave work for a few hours to catch some waves when the surf was up. Roger often thought about how weird it was that his arrest saved him from having to join the fire department. One weekend his father took him to the training academy where Roger could test himself. It included running up flights of stairs with seventy-five pounds strapped to his body, hose drag, ladder raise and other endurance challenges. The father with thirty years in the department stood with a stopwatch and timed Roger in the simulated drills. Roger passed them all. He was ready. And then there was the arrest.

Joining the fire department was something that Roger was only doing to please his father. At the time, he convinced himself otherwise. That being a firefighter was more of a real job than running a T-shirt business. But deep down, he knew he could not fool himself. He equated being a firefighter to being like his dad. And that is not how he saw his life.

"I just did not want to bother you about it, Dad."

"So, you just come over here and take it?"

Gerry exhaled a breathy laugh. It bothered Roger like it always did. He could not even have an argument with his father without Gerry in the audience.

"No, Dad, I just decided to come over here and get it. I knew you and Mom were out to dinner. "

"Well, if you told me you were getting it, I would have had it out for you," said his father with derision on his face. Roger was feeling the heavy weight of being in his father's shed and needing his father's miter saw. He regretted being there. The cost of a tool rental felt so much more than tolerating his father's personality. Roger responded to his father by not responding. He did not look at Gerry, but could feel a snarky stare. Roger stood holding the miter saw as he watched his father leave the shed. Once outside Roger's father turned and leered at Roger. He grasped the door with one hand while wiggling two fingers from the other in an invitation to move forward.

"C'mon, don't just stand there. Get out here so I can shut the door and turn the light off."

Roger despised that superior voice. It was demeaning. He kept his mouth shut and moved out of the shed.

"Is that it?" asked Roger's father.

"Yeah, that's it."

Roger's father looked at Gerry and gave a contemptuous shake of the head. Gerry lips spread into a closed smile before huffing half a laugh through his nostrils.

"By the way, your uncle is still bitching about your dogs. Your mother sometimes has to hear it. You should have discussed the dogs with your Uncle Ray first, before putting them in his house. I don't blame him. It's his house, you know."

The comment was an exaggeration. His mother liked to take little things and make them bigger. The remark did not make any sense. Uncle Ray had been recently in the home, praising Roger's progress. He never complained about the dogs. It was all an outcrop of the arrest and incarceration. A way to dig at Roger. It was why he avoided the home. Roger's father was an angry man. He blamed himself for much of it.

"I don't think so. Uncle Ray was over the other day

and never mentioned the dogs. In fact, he is real happy with what I am doing with that old bungalow house." There was annoyance in Roger's voice.

His father walked back and stuck his finger in Roger's face. "Your mother talks to her brother all the time. I am just repeating what she said. You are not calling your mother a liar, are you? You better not," said his father in a voice laced with extra hostility.

Roger did not believe it. His mother liked the drama and would repeat old things said as if they were new things. And his father liked to stoke the fire. Roger was not going to be sucked in. He made an about-face. Roger walked across the icy yard toward the car while lugging the miter saw, feeling shaken by the way he was spoken to, as if he were a little kid. He still had to end it on a positive note. He could not just walk away and not say anything, or he would hear about it later. It was Roger's way of easing the tension.

"Thanks, Dad. See you, Gerry."

Neither man answered. Roger looked over to the lighted house. He saw his mother walking past windows from room to room. He stopped and waited for a response. "Thanks, Dad."

Still nothing. He watched the two men walk toward the back door of the house, their actions illuminated by a night light. A whisper to Gerry. Gerry returned a quiet laugh.

Roger yelled, breaking the night quiet. "Why do you have to be like that? Why can't you just respond to me?"

Roger's father looked at Gerry with a mix of disdain and curiosity. He then swiveled his head toward Roger. "Because you fucked everything. I have friends who have their kids in college, the service. Some are getting ready to take the fire department test. But you, you have to get involved with the drug business. Look what that got you. I thought I raised you better than that. I thought we were better than that."

The remarks landed like a punch to the chest. Hurtful. He knew he let his father down. He let his mother down. Legal bills put the pensioned couple in debt. He did not know how to respond. Maybe there was no way to respond. He turned and walked toward the car gripping the miter saw. A lift to the back hatch. He landed the tool into the rear compartment. The front door of the home flew open.

His mother, unaware the confrontation seconds earlier, stepped out onto the stoop, *sans* coat. "Roger, I made pea soup today. Let me give you a container to take with you."

All that Roger wanted to do was get out of there. "No, Mom. I have plenty of food at home."

"Take some Roger. You can freeze it."

"No, Mom. I have to go."

"Honey?"

Roger got in the car and started it up. He pulled away, leaving his mother standing on the stoop with arms crossed to keep warm, looking bewildered. Roger gave a perfunctory wave and kept going. Heart thumps. Hyperventilating. He wondered if this was his life. To be a failure in his father's eyes. A big disappointment as compared to a younger sister with a scholarship to Duke. All the guilt and sadness from the arrest was in him. Roger hated what he did. Roger was hating himself. The regret, the loss. What he was. What he wasn't.

He gripped the wheel and drove with no direction in mind. A turn here, a turn there. Roger visited neighborhoods he had not driven through in years. At that moment, his only motive was to get away. To get the Subaru to a main road. More lefts and rights. Any way to get away from the childhood home. Roger cruised for fifteen minutes in the wrong direction, ignoring jug handles that would correct his route. He did not care. Mindless driving calmed him. More driving, less anger. Just riding along. Steering and thinking.

Roger neared the vicinity of the street of bungalow homes. He took an exit where he could cut through the downtown area; there he could take a few side roads that would get him closer to the piers and to the house. Coming up on the side was the St. Francis of Assisi

Church. It was the church he grew up in. It was where he was once an altar server. The church where Roger, Sr. and Roger's mother never missed a Sunday Mass or holy day of obligation. Roger grew up to hate the required Mass attendance. Sermons were overlong and boring. Rituals seemed fit for ancient times. He did not get anything out of the services. He usually sat there wishing it were over. When Roger reached high school age, he ceased attending church. He did other things on Sundays. Softball leagues. Surfing. Festivals.

As an inmate, Roger started attending Mass again. A local priest would arrive on Sunday afternoons to say Mass to the convicts and several guards inside the prison chapel. He went because he was looking for something. An attempt to find the Spirit inside him. Sermons were relevant to inmates' circumstances. The homilies were inspiring, not preachy. The priest who came to the prison gave those who attended rosary beads. He said prayers for the inmates. The Virgin Mary always gave forgiveness. *The Mother of Mercy*, as she is known in the Catholic religion. There was grace. He attached his mind to the one thing in the Catholic church that reso-nated with him. The idea that, no matter how bad you messed up, you could be forgiven. If you could admit that what you did was wrong, and even better yet, confess your wrongdoings, you could move on. Not to be judged by one's fellow man, but to be forgiven in the

eyes of God. There was that path to starting over. A way
to salvation.

A kaleidoscope of multi-colored stained glass
glowed through the evening darkness. Roger impul-
sively brought the car into the empty church parking
lot wet with snow melt. He glanced up at the side of
the building. Black roof. White cedar shakes. A steeple
reaching for the night sky. It all looked the same.
Churches rarely changed. He thought of his absence. A
lapsed Catholic. It was more than ten years since he had
entered the heavy red doors of his home parish church.

Roger walked into the whispery insides of the cathe-
dral-like building. Elevated ceilings were painted with
angels and saints. Heavy overhead timbers spanned from
wall to wall. Romanesque statues cornered the insides.
A tall painting of St. Francis of Assisi hung toward the
front. The image depicted the thirteenth century friar
with a bird on his shoulder and lamb at his knee, the
patron saint of animals. Candles flickered at the edges.
A giant crucifix hung above the altar. Religious images
painted in muted hues decorated the backdrop. More
ceramic statues. More flickering candles.

A couple sat in the forward pews. They got up
before quietly exiting out a side door. After their depar-
ture, the church was empty except for an old woman
sitting in contemplation. Roger walked a few steps in
and genuflected before sitting in the pew. He knelt and

said prayers. When Roger was done, he sat, taking in the holiness. There was peacefulness inside the Catholic hall. Roger felt it. It calmed him.

The older woman got up. She hobbled her plump aged frame down the center aisle, passing slowly while looking ahead as if she did not detect someone else's presence. He turned and looked to the altar. Eyes closed. He thought of the things he did and asked the Virgin Mary for forgiveness, for her graceful intercession. He wanted desperately to be lifted from the pain of past actions. He stopped. More silence.

A few moments later a priest walked casually on to the altar from the side sacristy door. He gently bowed to the crucifix before attending to electrical panel box. The click-click of lights switched off. A darkened altar. The priest moved away from the altar and took a long step to the floor below. He went to another switch box, turning off overhead lamps hanging heavily from ceiling chains. Front pews darkened. Hard shoes tapped along smooth linoleum floors. One more panel box. More click-clicks. More darkness. Emergency lights glowed red above exits. Hazy brightness shone in from the corridor. Roger stood up, knowing that the priest was unaware of his presence. He turned to leave. The priest, slightly startled, spoke to him from several feet away. Enough light allowed Roger to recognize the clergyman. It was Father Joseph. He was tall with an Irish ruddy face. The man's hair was white and unusually full for such advanced age.

"Oh, I am sorry. I did not realize anyone was here."

"That's okay, Father. I was about to leave anyway."

"I lock up the church at seven, so you are always welcome to be here and sit but just know when I have to close things up."

"I will remember that for next time."

"Do I know you? Are you a parishioner here?"

Roger hesitated to formulate an answer, too conscious of a poor attendance record. "I am a parishioner here, Father. I was an altar server here and did my first Holy Communion and confirmation here."

"What's your name?"

"Roger, Roger Wilson. You know my mom and dad."

"Oooh," said the priest is a way indicating some special revelation. "You are a parishioner here."

"Technically, I suppose I am. My parents attend Mass here. You may know Roger and Linda Wilson. My dad is a retired firefighter."

"I know who you are," said Father Joseph in a voice telling he was given more than enough information. "Your parents told me about you." A curious change came across the priest's face, as if the knowledge of who he was meant something. He nodded.

Roger hesitated before speaking again. "I was raised in this church. I was an altar boy; I mean altar server here. But lately, my attendance record is spotty. Actually, it's just about nothing."

"Your parents came to me about your situation. Is that all behind you?"

"Yes, I have been out almost six months now. I did attend Mass when I was in prison. Never missed a Sunday or holy day of obligation. But I have not been going since I have been out."

"What brings you here tonight?"

"Prayer. I needed to be in a quiet space."

"Anything in particular that is bothering you?"

"Lots of things, I guess. You go to jail and you get out and everyone looks at you sideways. They think you are some demon or something. Its hard to get back into things. To turn life around. I let a lot of people down. Especially my father."

"He was quite upset. I heard the whole story ... of course, your parents' version of events." said the priest sympathetically. "You let them down, but you let yourself down. Well, you can grow from the experience. You can better yourself. You have knowledge of things that other people don't."

"Are you saying going to prison was a good thing?" said Roger through a tempered laugh.

"No, I probably would never suggest someone go to prison as a way to become a better person," said Father

Joseph, trying to contain a wry smile. "But there have been those who were heading down a path of complete destruction and prison saved them. I am not suggesting that was your situation. But you know what it is like to lose your freedom. I am sure you appreciate your liberties more than most people after having lost them. You probably appreciate little things, like privacy or coming and going, like you never did before. That is what I am saying. Try to take that bad experience and use it for your improvement. That is what I would suggest."

Roger nodded. "I will, I guess."

"Was there one thing that caused you to come here this evening?"

"I had a fight with my father. We fight a lot ever since I was arrested. He wanted me to become a firefighter. I was about to take the training when the cops got me."

"Was that what the fight was about?"

"No, sometimes we fight just to fight."

"The firefighter thing. Is that what you wanted to do?"

"I was never crazy about the idea. It's a good job and it has a pension. But I always wanted to own my own business."

"They told me you were quite successful. That you had a growing business."

"They said that? They never said any good things about my business. Especially, my father. He always thought it was a hobby that I was trying to turn into a living. That I was sort of lazy."

"Your parents were proud of your business successes."

Roger searched the floor before raising eyes to the priest. "They never acted real keen about my business. My dad always said it was something I could do on the side once I became a firefighter."

"They said it was successful. Was it?"

"Yeah, it was called Quotable-Ts. It was doing well. We had some cashflow problems in the off season. That is what led to me getting into trouble."

"I see. Thought you could make some easy money?"

"Yeah."

"So, there are problems with you and your father?"

"Yes, I am a big disappointment to him. He's an ex-Marine and very disciplined guy, and my getting arrested is something he can never get over."

"Well, maybe in time he will."

"I don't think so. He thinks I ruined my life and brought too much shame on the family. He'll never let it go."

"Does that make you feel guilty?"

"All the time."

"Well, stop that. You served your time. Besides, what is the point of worrying about a career that you did not want anyway? Your father's anger is his problem.

Do not make it yours. Learn to live your life and not his."

Roger liked what he was hearing, even if it was a little hard to imagine not feeling bad about what he had done and the humiliation he brought his family. He welcomed someone being on his side.

"I suppose I can work on that. It is not easy, you know."

"Of course it is not easy. Life is not easy. That is why you need God. You can't do it alone. Trust the power of God and you will find your way."

Roger just nodded.

"What else is going on in your life? Do you have a girlfriend?"

"Yes, her name is April."

"Are you intimate with her?"

Roger felt the heat of blush fill his face. He could hear embarrassment in his voice. He responded in a whisper. "Yes, sometimes."

"Remember that the relationship with a woman is a gift from God. Learn to respect her."

Roger did not respond. He only nodded with a tight mouth.

"Anything else? Are you staying out of all trouble?"

"I guess. I am not perfect. I got in a fight with a couple of guys, but they started it."

"Okay, maybe you should learn to stay out of places

where those things happen. If you are confronted in such a situation, be like Jesus and be the peacemaker."

It made sense. Roger did not like big parties, anyway. "I will."

"Good. Is there anything else?"

"Like what?"

"Like anything you need to discuss with me and the Lord?"

"No, not really. That is it. Maybe I need to get to confession one of these days."

"You just did. I absolve you of all your sins in the name of the Father, the Son and the Holy Spirit. Amen," said the priest, making the sign of the cross with a sideways open hand.

"That was my confession?"

"Yes, it was. Go, and have a good evening. Remember that you are Jesus's son. You have been forgiven. Do not wrestle with the past. Move confidently into the future. I pray I see you here on Sundays, Roger."

"You will, Father. I will be here. Goodnight."

Roger stepped away and headed to the rear doors of the church. The priest spoke to his back.

"Goodnight, I am glad you stopped in."

Roger turned his head to the priest. "Me too, Father Joseph."

Roger pushed through one of the oak doors, feeling the cold night air. He stepped down the wet cement stairs to the grinding sound of rock salt under boot soles. There was a lightness in the way he felt, as if some weight of past actions was lifting. Roger walked through the freezing night air, renewing a sense of who he was.

Chapter 25

A NOTHER merciful blast of the factory horn signaled the shift end. It had been a long night. Roger started the evening performing the mundane work of a sorter, pulling boxes off a conveyor belt, scanning them, and putting the boxes on the correct pallet. He carried out the task for more than half the night but was pulled off that duty to work "inbound," which was unloading trucks and getting the boxes onto the conveyor belt where they were pulled to specific areas. Roger liked that job better, finding it less tedious. It was also more physical. There was more lifting and moving helping him stay in shape.

It was Super Bowl Sunday. He headed straight from the warehouse to church for the early 7 a.m. mass. Roger was back to going to church and went to the first service to avoid his mother and father who traditionally attended the 10:30 service. The early mass allowed him to be anonymous and not feel the awkwardness of seeing his parents. Their relationship was getting rockier and he found himself avoiding them. He did not want to have to answer questions or listen to any unsolicited remarks about the dogs. Roger just wanted to feel the holiness of the church.

After the service, Roger went to Gardella's Grocery Store and bought a plate of eggplant parmigiana. He loved the homemade food there. The store was bustling with people buying items in anticipation of the Super Bowl. Tables behind the counter were stacked with silvery aluminum trays of prepared foods waiting to be picked up and served at Super Bowl parties. Carts were full of pillowy bags of chips, dips, cheeses, hot dogs, paperware and the like. People were also buying for the days ahead. A Nor'easter was moving into the area. Weather bureaus were updating the forecasts every hour. Winds of upwards to seventy miles an hour. Two to three feet of snowfall was the latest prediction. Some local flooding in low lying areas.

Thoughts of April. He found himself missing her. She recently took a trip to the West Coast to spend some outdoor time hiking and camping with her brother and sister-in-law. She had asked him to drive her to Newark Airport a week earlier for a twelve-day trip. The visit came as a surprise. She had mentioned the trip only the afternoon before. April said it was a spur of the moment thing. She was bubbly with enthusiasm about spending time out there. Deep down, Roger felt a little pang of rejection that he was not asked to join her. He did not complain. He hardly mentioned the suddenness of the excursion. Roger may not have been able to get the time off, anyway. However, there was a part of Roger who wished he had been asked.

He knew about the friction between April and her mother, with whom she lived. Roger thought maybe she needed to get away from her for a little while. April spoke often of her only sibling, who was a professor at St. Martin's University. There was a ten-year gap in ages, but it appeared to Roger that they were close even if they were a country apart. He was the one in the family with a solid foundation. April's father had run off with another woman when she was only in fifth grade and she hardly had seen the family patriarch since. The mother was a self-centered alcoholic whose concerns were her own activities and lifestyle. Roger figured April decided she needed some time with her brother. Maybe there were familial issues that she wanted to talk out, that the spontaneity of the trip could be attributed to conversations that may be too private even for him to hear.

Roger entered the bungalow home to the anxious dogs, who surrounded him seeking attention. Each dog took turns moving their heads toward a petting hand. Cyrus, the largest of the three dogs, easily muscled to Roger's hip while the shorter Lady and pint-sized Buddy bounced noses into Roger's legs. Cyrus lifted his front paws and laid them on Roger's midsection in an affectionate attempt to get his head closer to Roger's face. Roger smiled and petted the canine's bulky head. Buddy hugged Roger's leg and ankle, while a smiling Lady pivoted half paces back and forth, wooing for attention.

"I know, I know. You guys want to go out. We're going to go to the state park for a long walk. You guys can go looking for stuff."

The state park was a barrier island where Roger often surfed and sometimes brought the dogs when he had the time. It had been a couple of weeks since he had brought the dogs there, as there was a sense of urgency to get as much work as possible completed on the house in case Uncle Ray came by. The dogs loved the all-afternoon adventures and Roger was set on taking them there before the football game started in the evening. Kick-off was not until 6:30 p.m., so there was plenty of time to get the dogs out.

He turned on the television while filling the dogs' food bowls. The news was the typical mix of current events and pre-game hoopla. But the airwaves continued to be dominated by the coming weather patterns. A cyclone created from a low-pressure system one hundred miles out to sea was heading to the area. The approaching storm was a Nor'easter that was going to bring gale-force winds, creating rough seas and flooding. Meteorologists forecast two or more feet of snowfall for the Jersey Shore area. The storm was expected to hit landfall around four in the afternoon. Television personalities sounded the alarm to stay indoors once the cyclone system arrived. It was still early. They had most of the afternoon to do what they wanted.

Roger unpacked a bag of groceries onto the Formica counter. He had followed the masses that stocked up on milk, bread and other items in anticipation of being homebound. The several bags of groceries were way more than he usually came home with. After a shower and two-hour nap, Roger packed a backpack with bottles of water, some apples, a blanket, and a box of dog biscuits. He got the dog coats on each of the three canines. A look on the cell phone to check the weather. Temperatures hovered above freezing. No winds. Clear sky. He dressed up in jeans and a flannel shirt. Feet were pushed into hiking boots. He donned a ski jacket, gloves and knit hat. The dogs were loaded into the back of the Subaru and off they went several miles to the state park.

Chapter 26

ROGER drove the Subaru over the top of the Johns River drawbridge, where steel grates hummed the tires. The vantage point provided a momentary vista of day clearness and ocean calmness. Searching eyes found no evidence of the coming gale-force winds, heavy snow, and rough ocean. A scene full of indigo waters and yellow sunshine.

A few blocks in, Roger turned onto Route 28, a two-lane highway leading into the state park. The long road took the car past a couple of dozen parking lots fronting beaches and ocean. Lots were either empty or contained a parked car or two of hikers, dog walkers or die-hard fishermen looking for a day out.

The phone rang. Roger glanced at the screen. It was April. Roger held one hand on the wheel while picking up the phone, thumbing the answer button. He touched the speaker option and laid the cell phone on the passenger seat.

"Hello, April, how are things in Seattle?"

"Hi, Roger. I'm in Olympia, I told you that. I only flew into Seattle. They're great. I'm having a blast with my brother and his wife. We did some winter camping. The Capitol State Forest is beautiful."

"Was it cold?"

"Yeah, it was, but I was prepared. My brother and Janet are such good campers. They got me a sleeping bag that is so warm. I loved it. I love it here, Roger."

"Maybe you'll move there some day; you never know."

Roger saw a parking lot with only two cars. The call helped him pick the spot. He wanted to stop and speak to April unencumbered by driving. Roger turned absently onto the lined blacktop.

"I might not want to wait that long," said April.

"Hold on one second, April. I'm just getting the car parked."

Roger fit the vehicle between two white lines and turned the engine off. Cyrus gave a woof-woof. It was the Pit Bull's way of saying *we're here*. Each of the dogs moved around excitedly.

"I can hear your furry friends."

"We are at the state park. I am going to walk the dogs two or three miles up the beach. They love it here. I wish you were with us."

"Be careful. I hear that you guys are getting a bad Nor'easter. Lots of snow. Kinda sorry I am going to miss it. I love big snowstorms."

"You would never even know a storm was coming, April. Not a cloud in the sky. Not even real cold today. Above freezing. Feels even warmer with the sun out."

"The storm is coming. You guys are going to get hit. Just the calm before the storm, I suppose."

"I'll have the dogs back by four. It's almost noon here. Plenty of time to walk and get back. Like I said, wish you could be joining us. You could have stayed over and watched the Super Bowl with me. And got stuck over with us for a couple of days," said Roger with a laugh.

There was a pause.

"April?"

"Roger, like I was saying, I might not want to wait that long to come out here to Washington."

"You are in Washington."

Roger heard April give a frustrated exhale.

"I know I'm in Washington. I'm just saying that I might want to come out here. Maybe not wait around."

"What do mean, you might not want to wait around? What are you thinking?"

"I'm thinking I might move out here, Roger. It is beautiful here."

"You could move out there. Heck, maybe I'll move out there with you one day. They have Amazon out there. You know, that's where Bezos started it. I could get a job there, you know?"

"I am thinking about now. The State of Washington is wonderful. I love it here."

Roger was taken aback by the comment. He was

okay about playing around with an idea but, with remodeling the bungalow, could not even consider picking up and moving on. If April even wanted him.

"Just like that, you think you want to move? You are on vacation. Everything is wonderful when you are on a trip. It's all fun and games. You need to think about this."

"I have my brother out here and Janet is great, and they are such outdoorsy people. My brother wants me here. We keep talking about it. I could get used to this real fast."

"Are you thinking of it or are you doing it? I mean you just got out there."

"I think am going to do it, Roger. The three of us were out all day working on this. Janet has a brother with a garage apartment they can rent me sort of cheap. I already spoke to the manager of the PetSmart out here and they would hire me the first day. And the rescue shelter on the west side of Olympia is amazing. They said they would actually give me a part-time job, so money is not going to be a problem. It seems like every-thing is falling into place. This is the break I have been looking for."

The enthusiasm in her voice could not be missed. Roger felt blindsided and curiously hurt. He liked April a lot. Her free-spirited attitude and independence were some of the qualities he found attractive. And now it was those qualities that were going to take her away. Her leaving was like another failure.

He felt his heart sink. "So, this is all happening now?"

"Well, I am coming back to Jersey to get my stuff and finish up some business. Jenny said she will get me at the airport when I return in a couple of days, so, you don't have to do that. But my decision is pretty much made. I have nothing in New Jersey but my mother, and my mother and I don't even get along."

"Well, about your mother… maybe you need to reconcile with your mother. Try to get along better with her," said Roger weakly.

"My mother has her boyfriend. They are two peas in a pod. I don't get along with him, either."

"Well, if that is the way you feel. I just thought that maybe you would eventually move in with me."

"Oh, I know you mentioned that, Roger. And you are a great guy. But we only started going out around Christmas. This has nothing to do with you. I really like you, Roger. It's that I have to try something like this. Something where I am on my own. Not with my mother. Not with a guy. Just something where I am controlling my future. That is what I am doing."

Roger's mouth dried and stomach churned. He liked April. He liked her a lot. Not an infatuation-type thing or close to a love thing. She was right; they only had started going out. It was not like with Alyssa; she was his first and only true love. But April had gotten him out of a funk. She helped him forget about Alyssa, helped him forget about the mistakes he made. Even if it was just for a short while. Not a love thing as much as a deep like. Losing her would be tough. It was the feeling of rejection. The feeling of being alone. But he knew the way April was. She was a loose horse, someone who could take off anywhere. April did not have to stay put. She was not going to stay put. She was going west.

"Well, I do not know what to say, April." Roger felt the emotion rising in his throat. He tried to add strength to his voice. "Its just that this is so sudden. I thought we were going to go camping in the spring."

He regretted what he said. He knew it made him sound weak, even a little petty.

April exhaled a laugh. "Oh, I know, Roger. That would have been good. But there is so much camping here and I need to move on. You need to move on."

"That's it? That's all you have to say? That it's time to move on?"

"Roger, I'm twenty years old. I'm not looking to get married. And if I have something to do or someplace better to go, I am going to go. Don't take things so seriously. Don't take me so seriously. Our relationship is no big deal. At least, it's not for me."

The comment felt like a punch to the gut. "I hope you are not saying that to make me feel better," said Roger with sarcasm lacing his voice.

"Oh come on, Roger. You are great guy. And I enjoy being with you. But you're moody and obsessed with your incarceration and all you lost. Frankly, it gets old, Roger. I'm not your friggin' psychologist. Sometimes I wish you were happier."

"I didn't even know I was unhappy."

"Oh, Roger. You are so naïve. Everyone knows it. You are a sulking type of guy. People who know you say you were not always like that. But jail did you in."

"I know I sometimes talk about my arrest, but I never thought I was that bad. And who said I was a sulking type of guy?"

"It does not matter who. You are what you are. You need to think of the future. You need to look ahead. You have to put the bad behind you and some good out front. You can do it. You can be what you were before and so much more. But let me say that is not why I am going to move. I'm moving to learn what's out there. What's best for me."

"Well, I get it, April. Do what you have to do."

"And you do the same, Roger. Good luck."

The phone went dead before Roger could say another word.

Chapter 27

ROGER picked up Buddy before he climbed out of the Subaru and placed him on the ground. The dogs were excited, Lady and Cyrus paced eagerly inside the small space. Cyrus gave Roger a couple of woof-woofs, as if to signal him to hurry up. He opened the rear hatch. Athletic Cyrus leaped from the back onto the parking lot pavement sprinkled with windblown sand. Roger wrapped arms around Lady's abdomen before pulling her up and setting her down. He did not leash the dogs. Not for a day on the barrier island. The three huddled obediently around his legs. A lean into the back compartment. A stretched arm reached for the backpack. Roger pushed arms through the straps. One step toward the wall of bulldozed sand and the dogs took off running like excited children.

Roger was still shaken by the earlier discussion. The way April was so cavalier in breaking things off. He thought their relationship was more than what she made it out to be. The accusations that caught him off guard. He never thought of himself as moody or downcast. He began to evaluate himself, trying to recall every conversation. Each time together. *Was it true? Was he that bad? Did he really put people off? What were his friends saying?* He didn't even think he had many friends anymore. Maybe there was a reason for that.

The dogs raced between the dune-grass-topped walls of sand onto the open beach. Roger caught up with the trio frolicking beneath the clear sky, each sniffing and searching scattered curiosities. Sun rays passing through windless air, heating Roger's face. A glance at the smoothly flat ocean. A horizon that was no more than a pencil line between two blues. A distant freighter appeared motionless. Lake-like waves gently lapped the sandy shore. February looked like June.

Each dog stepped around the debris line, poking snouts at what washed up. Bleached shells, driftwood, scattered refuse all got their attention. There were a few people on the beach. Some couples walked the water's edge. A father and son knocked a ball back and forth in a paddle ball game. Roger walked to the water and turned toward the north. Still no evidence of a storm that was predicted to hit the area in just a few hours. He walked what he planned would be a three-mile jaunt to where the island fell into the ocean. Cyrus and Buddy stayed closer to the middle of the beach and poked their noses at the line of things the high tide left behind. Lady joined Roger. She stayed far enough away from any water that washed on the shore. Her short legs were aged; she did not run, but rather paced herself like she was pacing life.

Roger sucked the salty air through each nostril. The briny scents were invigorating. He tried to take his mind off April. Another loss. There were other things to think about. He knew a life change was due. He wanted to restart the T-shirt business and pondered what that might take. Thoughts of being back in business brought feelings of exhilaration. He would use quotes he never used before. Wise words penned by Shakespeare, Meister Eckhart, Rumi and Simone Weil. Roger dreamed of a future. Something better than where he was now. He rationalized the loss of April. They were not of the same ilk. That there was not enough between them. An interest in dogs and some sexual excitement. Not much else. She was taking off to Washington. A free spirit that was not held to any one thing or person. A vagabond, of sorts. A nonconformist. Roger sort of admired that quality, that April could just go. There was no point in overthinking her decision. He had no right to hold her back. He couldn't, even if he wanted to.

He hiked, allowing Cyrus and Buddy to find stuff while moving along. Dozens of sand plovers with their toothpick legs moved effortlessly through the wave wash. Several skinny-necked cormorants floated offshore, gently bobbing like cork decoys while taking turns slipping into the sea below. Ahead were three anglers. Fishing poles were held vertical by plastic pipes stabbed in the beach. Taut nylon lines ran into the flat ocean. Two middle-aged men and a twelve-year-old boy watched the rods for signs of a catch. A heavy stomach pushed against one gentleman's blue uniform jacket adorned with a patch identifying the man's employer as Carteret Warehouse & Delivery Corp. He pushed ungloved hands deep into loose pant pockets. The skinnier man wore a thin jacket over a hoodie and Roger suspected he was the father. The boy was dressed in a puffy green coat and blue jeans hemmed an inch above well-worn sneaker. He showed a youthful interest in the approaching dogs.

"Catch anything?" said Roger as he neared the fishermen, a way to initiate a conversation. Fishtails rose out of a bucket. Cyrus went right to the pail to investigate.

"Yeah," said the kid proudly in a Slavic accent. A finger pointed to the bucket. "We caught a few dogfish, and I caught a sea robin." An excited smile crossed between dimpled cheeks.

Roger's head hung over the bucket to inspect the catch. The dogfish were also called sand sharks. He and friends always considered sand sharks and sea robins garbage fish, throw-away fish. He never thought they were worth anything.

"You like keeping those fish?" asked Roger.

"Sure," said the heavier man in a thicker accent

than the boy's. "People throw them back, but they don't know that they are good eating. No sense in throwing away a good fish. Where we come from, we don't throw fish away. We eat them."

"Where do you come from?"

The man smiled a mix of gold caps and shabby bridge work. "Ukraine."

"Ukraine?"

"Yes, we Ukrainian. Americans are choosy. They keep some and throw other fish away." The man explained with hand gestures. "But we eat them. What we don't eat now, we freeze. Then eat later. There are plenty of these fish. In Ukraine sometimes we catch fish and sometimes not. But when we come here, we always catch fish. Never not catch something."

"I get it. You can eat those fish. I am not even sure why I throw them away, but I admit I do. When I fish, I usually just keep bass or blue fish."

The heavier man laughed while the skinnier man grinned an amused smile.

"No bluefish in winter. But maybe a bass. Bass are good. Most bass gone South. Water too cold even for bass. But maybe one or two stay. Right now, just these fish. Not a lot. But enough."

The dogs were liking the attention received from the fishermen. The bigger man gazed out into the ocean as if he were done talking. It was time to move along.

"C'mon, gang," Roger said to the dogs. "Good luck, guys," he said to the two men and boy, as he ducked beneath the fishing lines. The dogs followed.

When Roger was about a hundred yards away, he turned back to see where the dogs were. Lady was following close behind while Cyrus and Buddy were back on higher beach searching the sand for items. Roger looked back at the two men and the boy. The heavier of the two men stood watching the lines while chewing a bite of sandwich. The skinnier man reeled in one of the poles to freshen the bait and the boy studied his phone. Roger knew the type of men they were. They were hardworking immigrant types. The kind of people who appreciated the possibilities of being in the United States. The boy had a future in their new country. Here they could shield the boy from the leftover poverty of the former Soviet Union. In the United States, all of them had the chance for a better life. Roger suspected they came to America with little more than the clothes on their backs. And for the beautiful chance of being in the best democracy in the world, they showed their gratitude by working hard each and every day. It was the only way for them. They enjoyed an appreciation for a country that so many in the United States took for granted. For them, everything was better in America. A better system. Better schools. More opportunities. Guaranteed freedoms. Law and order. To be in the country of George Washington and Thomas Jefferson was better for the child, better for their future. Everything in America was better.

Even the fishing was better.

Chapter 28

ROGER and the three dogs walked all the way to the tip of the barrier island where they watched a Coast Guard cruiser circled the end, leaving in its path a foamy wake. The pilot steered the vessel toward the docking station inside the inlet's protection. The hiking warmed Roger enough to unzip the ski jacket. A wool hat he wore was removed and put inside a coat pocket, as were the gloves. Cold air felt good.

April got into Roger's head and stayed there the entire hike. It was too soon to undo her. The loss hard to process. She was gone. He would make no attempt to change her mind. Not like when Alyssa went away to college and she was meeting new friends. He remembered the change in his high school sweetheart. The increasing gaps between weekend home visits. Vague excuses. There were jaunts to her college for the purpose of keeping the love flame lit. It did not help. Roger felt uncomfortable on the campus, like a non-member at an exclusive club. People talked around him. They were not his classmates. Not his friends. It was Alyssa's world. Not Roger's. He saw the relationship fizzling, and the harder he tried to keep it together, the more painful it was, like stabbing himself with his own knife. When it ended, he promised he would never make the same mistakes again. There would never be an attempt to hold together a doomed relationship. This time he would do things differently. It was better to let April go.

The ocean was still flat even though lake-like waves were replaced by waist high breakers. It was a sign that some of the storm's energy was sneaking up just beneath the surface. Roger viewed the waves with a surfer's eye. Clean, glassblower peels rolled into the beach. Small and just rideable. Beginner waves. Nothing to fear, only to enjoy. Surfers did not come down where he was. Vehicles were not allowed on the state beach and it was too far to lug a board. He imagined that many of the hot spots along the shore were attracting wetsuit-clad board riders. Kids showing up for the chance of an afternoon of negotiating the right type of curls. Winters provided good surfing times when storms manufactured waves. Hot, lazy summers were not the surfer's friend. Autumns and winters provided better surf. Roger studied the waves, admiring their coming perfection.

A slight breeze held broad-winged sea gulls aloft in near stillness, while a couple of others stayed earth-bound. The sea birds trumpeted a ha-ha-ha alarm in response to the approaching canines. The dogs ignored the feathery creatures, preferring to poke snouts at

Roger's legs. Cyrus used a woof to speak for the trio. The dogs were hungry for a snack. Roger reached a hand into the backpack, searching for the box of dog biscuits. He watered the dogs with squeezes to a plastic bottle.

Roger spread the blanket out onto a patch of sand. Another look at the water. It was still hard to believe that a big storm was coming, even though the edges of the northeastern horizon showed the appearance of gray clouds. The ocean surface remained flat. Hollow-coned waves crashed the shore. He looked at the empty beach. No one except the few day trippers in the far distance. Roger's eyes bounced around the endless sand. He thought of the summer crowds, visualizing count-less beach blankets nearly touching each other. Roger daydreamed of people lying under the hot sun, enjoying the rays while others hid beneath umbrellas and tents. Surf splashes. Kids on boogie boards. Lifeguard whis-tles. Coconut oil smells. The notion caused a smile to cross his face.

All three tired dogs found spots on the blanket and rested themselves. The sight made him laugh. Roger squeezed in among the content canines. Surrounded by the three dogs, he reached deep into an unbuttoned pocket and removed his phone. He was thinking of Melissa and the upcoming storm. Although there was more to it than that. He liked her. He liked her a lot.

Roger held back from the across-the-street neighbor because of April. But, in a way, he always knew Melissa was better for him. There was more of a connection. April was going. She was gone. Poof, in the wind. The hurt was still there. He could not ignore it. Roger wanted it to go away.

Thumbs tapped the digital keyboard. *Big storm coming.*

Roger stretched legs and lay in between the dogs; each gave up a little space to accommodate him. He only had a two-hour nap after returning from the night shift and was feeling it. Tired. Heavy eyelids. A yawn. The sun on his face felt good.

A look at the phone. Melissa responded, *Yes, big storm coming. Might be 2.5 ft. Not sure I will get the girls out tomorrow.*

Roger responded, *I will dig you out.*

I reward chivalry. How do you like your eggs?

Scrambled.

I make the best scrambled eggs on our street.

Roger liked Melissa's dry send of humor. *LOL, I bet you do … see you in the morning.*

Where are you?

Three miles up the beach.

Don't stay there too long. Get home safely.

Go Patriots!

Go Tom Brady!

A smile crossed Roger's face. Melissa was smart. She was mischievous in her wisdom. He could not help but find that attractive.

He pushed the phone deep into a pocket before snapping the button. Roger lay back in between the dogs. Cold breezes replaced the former stillness. A zip of the jacket. More sun warming rays. Eyes closed. He thought about Melissa. A heart stir. A fuzzy feel due to a lack of sleep. Roger began to doze off.

Chapter 29

WOOF-WOOF! It was Cyrus. Then the quick yelping barks of Buddy. Roger leaned forward and rested elbows on the beach blanket while looking through bleary eyes. A quick shake of the head to stir a sleepy mind awake. The dogs stopped barking, staring at Roger like wondering children. He surveyed the surroundings. The day changed. It was darker. A gray blanket replaced the blue skies of earlier afternoon. The feel of colder air. Snow flurries swirled through the air like ashes rising above a campfire. Breezes evolved into wind. Polished curls of green water were gone. An angered ocean hit the beach with sloppy, uneven waves.

Roger stood up, turning to the west. Gloomy black and purple clouds bruised a falling tangerine sun. A pocket search for the cell phone. The screen displayed the temperature plummeting to twenty-four degrees. The time was 4:16. A nap exceeding two hours. The dogs circled him. Hunger on the canine faces. No wagging tails. Roger sensed the dogs were worried about the approaching storm. Time to leave.

"We better get going. I overslept. Sorry about that."

It was mealtime. He normally fed them around

that time or had their food out when he was at work.
Roger pulled a bottle from the backpack and watered
the dogs; each lapped at the clear pour with thirsty
tongues. A shake to the biscuit box got the dog's attention. Only three edible dog bones left. One was given
to Lady. Roger broke one in half for Buddy and one and
a half biscuits to Cyrus. It was not much, but all he had.
Roger regretted going so far up the beach. Thoughts of
April and the earlier conversation were mind stinging.
It clouded his thinking and allowed him to forget how
far he was walking on so little sleep. Analyzing thoughts
of the breakup led him to walk a bit aimlessly, much
like some nomad. Three miles between them and the
car. Roger figured that he would move the dogs along
faster. Not the distracting, snaky stroll that got them
there. The sooner they got back to the car, the sooner
they could get warm. The dogs were hungry, so they
would cooperate. Then the thirty-five-minute drive
back to the house.

Roger shook beach sand from the blanket and
folded it before returning it to the backpack. Arms
pushed through the shoulder belts. A body jerk put the
knapsack higher on his back. Straps were pulled tighter.
Skull cap adjusted. Gloves donned.

"C'mon, gang. Let's go."

The dogs did not need any convincing. They
followed close to Roger. Lady got out ahead. Cyrus

dogtrotted alongside. Roger turned his head. Buddy was moving along in the quick, motor-leg Chihuahua walk.

"If you need me to carry you, Buddy, I'll carry you," said Roger. He knew Buddy would start yelping if the distance was too much and he wanted to hitch a ride on an arm.

The beach was completely vacant. Everyone who took advantage of the earlier fair weather had headed home to beat the storm, many readying for the Super Bowl. Roger's stomach growled. He looked forward to being in a nice warm home, feeding the dogs and showering before heating up his eggplant parmigiana. The sleep rejuvenated him. A bit of spring was felt in each step while increasing winds tried pushing him around.

Chapter 30

B UDDY was relieved to be heading back home. It was cold. Mysterious ice flakes rained down. Darkness was near. Buddy had had enough of the outside. The afternoon fun of searching the beach for things ended hours ago. The three-mile afternoon trek to the end of the park was tiring, but the beach nap while snuggled against a sleeping Lady did much to reenergize the Chihuahua. Buddy also knew that if he tired on the way back to the car, all he needed to do was stop and give a few yelps. Roger would then slap a knee side, the signal to be picked up and carried. All that Buddy had to do was walk to Roger's waiting hands.

Lady took the lead, staying thirty feet ahead of Roger and Cyrus. The trek was a little tough on her, even if Pembroke Welsh Corgis were bred for sheep and cattle herding. They were trackers with stronger than normal upper body strength. Even shorter legs could be deceptive. Her breed could run up to twenty-five miles an hour. Up there in age, the old girl was not what she once was. She certainly did not have the energy of a puppy. Roger could not carry Lady the way he could the picayune Buddy. She would have to forge on, no matter what. Buddy did not want to ask for Roger's help. He wanted to try and make it back to the car the way Lady and Cyrus would, on four legs.

Something poked out of the sand. An item that Buddy missed earlier. Something in a colorful orange. Buddy deviated from the procession. He ran up to it. A plastic shovel left behind on a much warmer day. Buddy sniffed the item. Sensitive canine olfactory glands took it all in. The tangy, chemical smell of plastic. A faint perfume fragrance of sunscreen. The faintest hint of sweat from a toddler's hand.

"C'mon, Buddy."

The Chihuahua sprinted back into line, bringing up the rear. He saw Cyrus pacing himself aside Roger while Lady's short legs took quick steps, occasionally breaking into a bouncy dog trot to stay ahead of Roger's long strides. The falling sun balanced on the edge of the western horizon. Daylight continued to fade. Buddy looked curiously to the sea ducks floating just beyond the breakers. Each waterfowl rising and falling with every roll of a wave.

A flock of sandpipers in their dull plumage performed skinny-leg dances back and forth along the shallows of foamy surf. Some of the skittish birds took short flights when Roger and the dogs passed, even though they were ignored by the trio. Others in the standing flock simply Chaplin-walked a wide berth.

Buddy stopped. He studied the prancing shore birds pecking the sand for water bugs and worms each time a receding wave exposed the sand. The waders seemed completely unconcerned by the approaching storm but went about their business as if nothing were amiss. As Roger and the dogs got farther up, the birds returned confidently to concentrating on the meal-getting. Distracted by their eating, the birds did not notice Buddy high on the beach. He knew it. The hunter in him triggered. The ancient impulse to attack and capture was not completely diminished by so many years of domestication. The DNA that the Chihuahua shared with the grey wolf still filled Buddy with an instinct to hunt. He did not look at himself as some pocket-sized pooch or silly little lapdog. He was a real dog with a Mexican ancestry. A breeding that tweaked the gnome to create a canine specialized for clearing out rats and other vermin. A noble heritage. A proud lineage. There was something the Chihuahua wanted to prove to himself. Here was an opportunity to hone inherited hunting skills not provided inside a fenced-in backyard or at the end of a leash. Here was a chance to demonstrate what he could do.

Head lowered; Buddy slowed his gait. Snout pointed. Eyes focused. Astonished by how close he got to the unsuspecting birds. He stopped. Hind legs scuffed the sand, digging in to prepare for the dash.

Wave water slid back into the surf. Ready, set, go.
Buddy darted from the high point of the soft beach down
to the wet sand. A mad rush. A tight surface quickened
the pace. Buddy narrowed in on the unsuspecting flock
of sandpipers like a guided missile. When he was within
ten feet, the birds were spooked. A feathery explosion.
A cloud of sandpipers. Panicked wings lifted each bird
safely into the air. Buddy stopped. He stared at the prey
huddled in the ocean winds, all out of reach.

A sudden push of sneaky water slammed Buddy's
legs. The Chihuahua was flipped onto its side. Coldness
shocked him. A chameleon tongue of seawater pulled
Buddy in, sliding the Chihuahua down the slope
of wet sand into the trough. Ocean jaws of the next
wave closed, swallowing him. Buddy tumbled around
in the frigid washing machine currents. Submerged.
Ambient bubble sounds. Water flooded Buddy's throat.
A desperate need for air. Terror. Was he going to die?
Cold stunned the canine. He needed help. *Where was
the help? Where was Roger, Cyrus and Lady? Where was
the world?*

Four-legged paddles got Buddy to the surface,
poking his head out of the alien place. An aerosol blast
of nostril spray. Breaths of nourishing oxygen filled
starving lungs. The dog's snout barely above the thin
surface skin. Frigid water sapped energy. A need to let
Roger, Cyrus and Lady know where he was. *Were they*

gone? Not coming back? He attempted a bark. A weak yelp. Nothing more than a whimper. Not enough to overcome the sounds of Nor'easter winds and pounding surf. He saw the beach. Nothing. No people. No Roger. No dogs.

Frigid water quickly took its toll. Buddy would not last much longer. This was worse than anything ever experienced. More lonesome than locked-up in a cold puppy mill warehouse. Scarier than the fat man. More intimidating than any big dog housed at the rescue shelter. Thoughts of his mother. She would not want him to die.

Was this it? No one knew where he was. He felt the cold tugging at him. The soaked dog coat weighing him down. Exhaustion. *Was he going to die?* He thought of his mother. Her eyes looking at him just before her demise. She would want him to keep going. To survive. To live. There needed to be a way out of the ocean. He had to give it one more attempt. Buddy pressed lips closed over canine teeth. Saliva and seawater swirled inside a shut mouth. A swallow. A clear throat. Buddy tilted his head back, sucking in the snowy atmosphere while filling lungs with frosty air. With little energy left Buddy barked out a signal. The loudest sound he could muster. A yelp of last hope. A distress signal to the ears he most trusted.

A direct call to Lady.

Chapter 31

NO more a mere snow shower. The weather system was worsening. Increased wind. Snow flurries multiplied several times over into an all-out snowfall. Walls of water took their wrath to the shore. A thin blanket of white coated the beach. Dune grass swayed on mounds of protective sand. Roger regretted sleeping so long. He knew they should be home, not trekking the cold, isolated barrier island. Roger's gloves and ski jacket were good insulation, but the cold was still getting through. He tightened the wool hat over his ears. A beardless face exposed to the elements. Cruel winds nipped defenseless cheeks. Lady continued leading twenty feet ahead. Cyrus trotted alongside. Roger was confident that Buddy continued to bring up the rear.

Lady turned suddenly. She ran toward him. A Lady sprint. Lady rarely ran. Maybe a backyard chase on an unsuspecting butterfly. Even such occasions were unusual. *Did something spook the old girl?* Roger looked back to see what was sending her in return gallop. She was running fast. Fast for Lady. *What was the sudden burst all about?*

There was no fear in Lady's face. No playfulness either, only seriousness. Determined. Eyes down, tongue in. She raced past Roger and Cyrus. A Cyrus woof. The Pit Bull sensed the alarm. Cyrus turned and joined the chase. Roger still unsure what was going on, followed. A focus on the two dogs' sudden strange behavior. Buddy was momentarily forgotten.

"Hey, what's going on? We got to go home." Roger trotted toward the running dogs. "What's going on?"

Roger yelled at the dogs, "Get back here, you two." *Was Lady chasing after some offshore bird? Was this some silly diversion before going home?*

Lady stopped at the water's edge. She paced hurriedly back and forth, barking urgently. Actions that were strangely unlike the old girl. Roger believed she was reacting to some creature distraction.

"What do you see out there?" yelled Roger over howling wind, "I don't see anything, Lady. What do you see? A seal? C'mon, let's go."

Cyrus ran into the frigid wash and ran back, barking just as loudly. *What are these dogs up to? Don't they just want to go home?*

Roger searched through the fog of blizzard snow. Past the rollers was a snout and two eyes breaking the waterline. The animal head turned in a tight circle. *An injured seal?* What was it? What was upsetting the dogs? Roger looked around. Lady and Cyrus.

"Buddy?" exclaimed Roger.

Roger looked up the beach. Then behind him. A desperate search. No Buddy. A turn back to the ocean. Roger's heart dropped. *How did he get out there?* Gloves off. Hat off. Coat off. Roger sprinted to the breakers. The freezing water chilled his lower body as the cold temperatures soaked in. The foreboding curve of a cresting wave. Roger dove in headfirst at its base, resurfacing on the other side. Coldness attacked every inch of flesh. Energy sapped. Sucking breaths. Blood pushed through his heart like an overworked pump. He was fit. A good swimmer. That was fortunate. A person of lesser strength might drown.

Quick and urgent arm paddles. Roger struggled to flutter kick heavy, waterlogged hiking boots. Eyes burned with saltwater. He squinted directly at Buddy. The clean swim circle was gone. Buddy sunk beneath the surface and returned to the top. Time was running out. Buddy was drowning. Roger had to reach the Chihuahua, or the puppy would go down and not return. Urgent swim strokes pulled him closer until he reached out and grabbed the tiny dog from the cloth coat and lifted him onto his shoulder. Buddy was nothing more than a rag doll laying limply between shoulder and head. The Chihuahua choked up sea water, then a weak spray to clear his nostrils. Roger side leaned to attempt an unorthodox breaststroke with Buddy lifted on a shoulder. Heavy hiking boots were like anchors. The frigid water sapped Roger's energy. He was a strong swimmer, having surfed for years. Now there was no board to rely on. No wetsuit to keep him warm. He had to do this. A fight against stormy currents. A struggle to overcome paralyzing frigid water. He had to make it to shore. A need to get out of the cold water, or he and Buddy would die. Surfing was Roger's sport, no stranger to battling cross currents or rolling waves. Roger could get them to the beach. He was a surfer. He was a waterman.

The ripping tide, the icy water and the unnatural swim stroke all took their toll on what energy Roger had left. Roger saw the beach intermittently with the rise and fall of every rolling wave. One hand gripped Buddy. The other paddled to keep their heads above the surface. Time was the enemy. Too much cold. Roger found himself sinking. Progress barely more that treading water. Most energy expended just to stay afloat. He tried again, trying to find the power to keep going. Stronger hand paddles. Stronger bicycle kicks. Sucking breaths. Still so little advancement. Tired arm. Exhausted legs. A head falling beneath the surface. *Were he and Buddy going to drown in the ocean surf?*

Energy-draining rip tides. Paralyzing cold water. Snow-bitten winds. He needed to get out of the violent ocean, or they would perish. Progress was slow to non-existent. Each attempt exhausted Roger to a stop. Soaked hiking boots continued to pull him down. Roger pushed his head above the waterline for desperate inhales. Buddy shivered and cried with the little energy the puppy had left. Roger knew the end was coming. Soon he would go under and not return to the surface.

Roger's head fell below the surface again but managed to lift Buddy so that the pint-sized canine did not go in the water. It was silent, almost peaceful beneath the water where he was not exposed to the roaring wind and sounds of battering surf. Roger's head resurfaced. Panicky gasps of air. He was frantic, barely able to see the shore through blurring eyes. He saw Lady. The old girl paced back and forth. Foamy surf licked the shore. Desperate Lady barks, the old girl's way to coach Roger in. But he did not have it in him. No more strength. The frigid water got the upper hand, disabling him, beating him. Cold took over. Roger became Jonah and the ocean was the whale. No longer did Roger have it in him to make the forty yards back to shore. Barely any energy. Human spirit lifting from within him. The fight was over, the battle lost. Poor Buddy lay limp on a shoulder. Only a matter of moments before Roger went under and would have to surrender to the winter ocean. No chance of saving himself. No chance of saving Buddy. And the two dogs left on the beach to defend themselves against a surging blizzard.

Roger went under once again. No longer was he able to hold Buddy above the surface; instead, the Chihuahua went into the water. The puppy was dying the same death. The natural need for oxygen forced Roger to rise above the water one more time. One more sucking breath. Then the sight of something. It skimmed along the top of the water. A V-shape crease pointing directly at him and Buddy. A head traveling just above the surface.

Cyrus.

Chapter 32

THE sight of Cyrus paddling down the smooth side of a rolling wave awakened hidden reserves of energy. A sudden flicker of hope. Buddy gave a barely audible yelp. The Chihuahua was still alive. Suddenly, there was the possibility that they might both make it.

"C'mon, boy!" yelled Roger. Seawater entered his mouth. A choke. A spit. Roger's head bobbed up and down. Desperate leg kicks to stay afloat. A swirling hand just beneath the surface a way to stay steady until Cyrus reached them. Roger did all he could to hang on.

Just as Cyrus got there, Roger wiggled stiff fingers to lubricate the joints enough to hook a hand into the dog collar. Roger managed to curl four fingers inside the leather loop encircling the Pit Bull's neck. A feel of strong shoulder muscles. A tug. The Pit Bull towed Roger toward the shore. Bicycle kicks to move them along. He held Buddy tight and out of the frigid sea. They rose with the rollers. The threatening sound of crashing waves. Slow, real progress being made.

Buddy whimpered. The Chihuahua was deathly cold. Hypothermia set in. Roger sensed fear in the puppy with the rise of every swell. Ambient sound of howling winds. Waves landing forceful strikes to the shoreline resulted in explosions of seawater, spray, and foam. Roger was scared too. He sized up their situation. Pounding slams of the ocean hitting hard sand pushed a flood of water to the beach until river-like rapids rushed back into the sea. Roger knew there would be only one shot to get to safety. They had to ride the crest of the wave where they would be thrown down to the sandy floor below. Then there would only be a few seconds to get himself upright and make it to dry beach or receding water would muscle them back into the surf.

"Hang in there, Buddy. We are going to make it."

Daylight was dimming. A half sun lay on the western horizon painting clouds purple, black and orange. Thickening snowfall blanketed the sand. Roger saw Lady as she watched the action from the high part of the beach. Anxious paces back and forth. More Lady barks of encouragement.

Cyrus towed Roger and Buddy to right behind the breakers. He had to take the ride. Roger knew the score. One shot at survival. One chance to stay alive. He was too weak for a second try. A body surf with Buddy in a grip. The wave would have no mercy on him. Roger could feel the powerful storm energy raising the walls of water. A racing heart. Fear mixed with experience. A surfer. A wave rider. A waterman. Time to go.

Roger did not bother to look back. No point in waiting for the right wave. They needed to get out of the frigid water. A rolling wall of seawater. Only twenty yards from landfall. Only twenty yards and a halfback rush through the formidable backsplash. First, he had to let Cyrus loose. They would weigh each other down going over the wave. Roger also needed a free hand to negotiate the forces. He let go of Cyrus's collar. With the detaching, the Pit Bull looked back. There was fear in the dog's eyes.

"Go!" yelled Roger, "Go, Cyrus, go!"

Cyrus paddled toward shore, climbing the outside roll of the wave. The Pit Bull was lifted and left to the unforgiving breaker. Cyrus made a whining cry of distress as he disappeared. A death call. Lady barks came from the beach. Cyrus was gone. Lady ran down a cliff of sand marking the erosion line. She ran back and forth through the foamy surf. She barked in the direction of where Cyrus was moments earlier, but the brave dog could not be seen.

Roger yelled out. "Cyrus!"

Nothing but the sounds of howling wind and crashing surf. Roger one-arm paddled. He looked behind at a curling wave of gray capped in boiling white. It was their turn. Time for Roger to take them in. Heavy hiking boots. Muscled legs performed desperate paddle kicks to get ahead of the wave. A near frozen hand slowly tightened onto Buddy's coat. Rising water took Roger from trough to the crest. A panoramic view of the snowy beach and dunes. The land was still, motionless. A yelp of fear from Buddy. The two were shoved forward on a roller-coaster ride. The ocean curl slammed Roger violently down to the sand below. A full body wham. A flesh and bone concussion. Wind was knocked out of him. Then tumbles and flips. He miraculously maintained a grip on Buddy. Roger pushed himself onto two feet. The water slid back into the surf, ready to take victims. The ocean wanted them back. Seawater rushing around legs like bridge supports in a raging river. He leaned forward in a desperate attempt to keep from being pulled back in. The water drained. Another crash of a wave pushed more water onto the shore. High leg lifts used the last bits of energy. Twenty-five feet to shore and he would be safe from the monstrous surf. Another water draining. One step after another going against the leftover backwash. Roger did all he could do to maintain steadiness. A loss of balance meant he and Buddy were going back in. Going back in meant certain death for both.

He held the ground. Lady trotted thirty feet from them in shallow water. She barked searching for Cyrus. There was no sign of the Pit Bull. Each leg lifted heavy hiking boots toward dry sand. A life or death struggle against cold and exhaustion. Winds howled. Snow fell. Roger cradled the Chihuahua tight to his body. Lady was frantic. Eyelids squeezed against dripping saltwater. Knees collapsed onto the beach.

Roger ran a hand over Buddy's head. The dog was limp. No sign of life. A stringless puppet. A little skeleton sack. Unresponsive. Not breathing. Roger ripped off the soaking wet dog coat that was doing the dog no good. He shook him. He gently squeezed the seawater from the dog's lungs. Then Roger looked back, still no Cyrus. Lady continued to pace like a frightened mother worried for her child.

Roger tilted his head back and screamed to the sky. "Cyrus!"

Lady's yapping increased. A rapid blast of barks aimed at the waves. A tight turn of the head. Roger studied the surf through burning eyes. He saw what Lady barked at. Cyrus was in the churning water, ahead of the waves but unable to get any footing. With one hand gripping Buddy, Roger went back into the ocean wash. Up just past his knees, he grabbed Cyrus by the collar. A yank. The ocean did not want to let go. A stronger pull to spring Cyrus from the ocean's grasp. Both trotted against receding water to make it onto land. Roger peeled the Velcro to release Cyrus from the soaked dog coat. Cyrus stood still for a few moments. No flinch or a shake. Just a stunned statue pose. Then Cyrus shook off a shower of seawater from his fur.

Roger went back to work on Buddy. Knees in the sand and back to the storm he massaged the dog's chest before attempting life-saving breaths into Buddy's mouth. He gripped the dog's hind legs. A shake to awaken Buddy. Nothing. More breaths into the canine's mouth. Still nothing. Cyrus stood by the two of them. Cyrus's head just inches from Buddy. He barked at Buddy as if to rouse his friend from a deep sleep.

Lady showed up, a layer of snow built up on her dog coat. Roger's ski coat gripped in her mouth. She had dragged it over from where he dropped it before plunging into the ocean. Roger took the coat and laid the limp Chihuahua into the puffy fabric. Again, he dropped his mouth into Buddy's and exhaled lifesaving breaths into Buddy's lungs. Stormy wind whistled in Roger's ears.

Both Cyrus and Lady continued barking at Buddy. There was that animal instinct, as if the two canines knew there was still a life in the motionless body. They called their dog friend to awaken. A rhythmic bark after bark after bark.

Roger picked Buddy up again. He breathed into Buddy's snout before laying Buddy down again. Light pushes on the dog's chest. Then a miracle. A cough. He wrapped Buddy into the coat with only his head partially exposed. Roger's body shielded the dog from the wind. Roger stuck fingers into the fabric folds massaging the tiny chest.

Roger joined the chorus. "C'mon, Buddy. C'mon."

Then a sneeze. Roger looked for more signs. He

pulled the coat back. Buddy's chest was showing a slight throbbing movement. He was breathing on his own. The Chihuahua was alive.

Roger stood up. The wet clothing was beginning to freeze. Wet hair turned to ice. Misery. Hypothermia. They survived the icy waters and violent waves. Another urgent situation. He needed to get out of the wind and snow if they were to live. Two and a half miles of beach lay between them and the car. It was a matter of life and death. Buddy was still barely breathing. Roger used a bare hand to whip the snow of the backs of Cyrus and Lady. The deep cold was taking its toll. No evidence of the day was left except purplish blackness just above the horizon. Darkness finally setting in. Time to go. He stumbled forward. Lady went ahead and Cyrus walked along side. The soaked hiking books felt like cement blocks to exhausted legs. He pushed forward trying to negotiate to the hardest sand between the sandy beach and the soaked surf.

Lady led Roger to the gloves, wool hat, and back-pack. He checked on Buddy. Eyes were slightly open. Small, short breaths. The coat was like blanket that could shield the Chihuahua from the storm and keep him warm. He laid the bundled Chihuahua on the ground. Roger moved stiff hands in a clawing motion to ease their movement. He retrieved the blanket from the backpack and draped it over Cyrus. He tied the ends to give the Pitbull a makeshift dog coat. Roger pulled the wool hat over his freezing scalp and ears. Hands were now so cold he could hardly move them and struggled to peel gloves over stiff fingers. There was one bottle of water left. Roger took a swallow washing some of the sea salt from his mouth. He gave a thirsty Buddy little splashes on the dog's dry tongue. Then he split the rest between Cyrus and Lady. He picked up Buddy and allowed Lady to continue their trek up the snowy distances. Wet, freezing blue jeans began to stiffen. He placed one foot in front of the other, continuing to walk.

The urgency of their situation was with Roger. The storm was intensifying. Lady was an old girl, years past long youthful walks. Cyrus and he were exhausted from the icy violence of a Nor'easter sea. Buddy was barely hanging onto life. They had to get out of the bitter cold weather. Cruel winds bit exposed cheeks. Body shivers. Winds tried to push him over. He was so cold. Quick body shakes and a lack of balance were signs of advancing hypothermia. Snow collected on the backs of Lady and Cyrus. He knew that their only chance was to keep going. To keep fighting against the cold blasts of air sent by the winter storm.

The beach was now a frozen tundra. Roger continued to shiver. Nearly out of strength, he carried on. Stopping would mean death. Movement pushed life-sustaining blood through veins. One foot in front of the other. Almost two miles of mechanical walking. They continued. One mile. Then another. Lady continued leading the way. Cyrus marched alongside. Roger kept going. A single light in the old light house museum. It meant they were nearing the car. A line of thirty-two parking lots. Each numbered. Each with its own entrance and exit. All looked the same. Dunes made of indistinguishable mounds of sand fronted the lined squares of blacktop. Confusion. Another sign of hypothermia. Despair. Another sign of giving up.

Roger could not remember in what lot the Subaru was parked. He had not been paying attention then. All the focus earlier that afternoon was on April's phone call and the announcement she was breaking things off between her and Roger. Now he and the dogs were lost. Snow-filled blizzard winds camouflaged the landscape. Sandy knoll silhouettes lay in their discouraging sameness. Ice continued building on Cyrus's and Lady's backs. Roger took a gloved hand and knocked it off only to have it build up moments later. The dogs were slowing down. The winter wind becoming too much on all of them. Despondency. Roger was needing to find something in him to continue. The museum light helped. It meant they were closing in. The car was not far away. Where it was, he could not be sure.

"C'mon, Cyrus. Let's keep going," yelled Roger

over the howling storm winds, while walking the beach of frigid wasteland.

Cyrus barked back with the call of his name, plodding along in a lumbering trot. Lady was the oldest but now the strongest, as she had not been submerged and weakened by the frigid sea. She stayed thirty feet ahead pacing the group.

Roger's nose poked Buddy's snout to get a reaction. He sought a body wiggle or head jerk. Any movement was a miracle. A slight shift. The Chihuahua was still alive.

The trio began lagging. Lady became aware of the three falling behind. She stopped and waited. Cyrus approached Lady and signaled her with a woof, as if to say *keep going, Lady.*

They reached the old lighthouse. Just a museum, it was closed and unmanned. The tower was always lit and stood adjacent to the last parking lot. Roger knew he had not parked there. That, he would remember. Roger was too exhausted to check each parking lot. He was too miserable with cold. And he knew each dog had its own issues. Cyrus was cold and tired. So was Lady. Even with Buddy wrapped in the ski jacket, he still needed to get the Chihuahua in a warm spot if the puppy were to survive. Roger was cold in wet clothing. He tried to walk faster. Gale-force winds roared. Darkness set in completely. He watched the dogs.

Squinting eyes searched the dunes. There was nothing to see. Too much darkness. Too much snow. Too much sameness.

Then the dim light of a parking lot lamp. Swirling snow. He followed Lady. He watched the old girl lead the way. He wondered where the car was. He was confused. Where? Then another parking lot and lamp. Then another. Roger questioned himself. *What parking lot did we go to? Did they pass the car?*

Lady kept leading the way. Roger and Cyrus followed the ten-year-old Pembroke Welsh Corgi. They passed another parking lot. Brutal winds blew snow through its lonely light while rattling the pylon. Roger gazed along the darkened beach. No distinguishing features. A moonwalk of similarity. He was lost. No idea what parking lot to go to. Limited vision. A body wanting to give up. He followed Lady but blamed himself. Keep going, he thought, but to where?

Lady turned up the beach. Roger and Cyrus followed. Frozen clothing. Stiff walking. The faint amber glow of another parking lot lamp. Sheets of white passing through its soft light. One foot in front of the other. Roger marched through the more than two inches of snow-cushioned softness of upper beach sand. He followed Lady. She walked with assurance through a cut out in the high dunes. A walking path to the parking lot. Grass patches on sand mounds wind bent into snowy pompadours.

Pembroke Welsh Corgis were smart and known for their tracking ability. Despite the snow and wind, Lady could smell the trail from which they walked. She kept going. Past the leaning fence. A parking sign with a number fourteen. The car had to be there. Roger was unsure if he could continue if they were in the wrong lot. He was feeling the end, not certain if he could go on.

A foot placed on hard pavement. Roger turned to his left. The sight of the car. Lady got them there. She knew where to go. Roger quickened the pace. Heavy steps across the windswept parking lot of low nascent snowdrifts snaking across exposed blacktop. Low boot kicks. Short snowbanks exploded into white powder. Lady and Cyrus went to the back of the vehicle pacing back and forth anxiously. Roger used front teeth to clamp down on a fingertip to slide a glove off. Buddy still wrapped in the ski jacket was balanced beneath an arm. He pushed a hand into a coat pocket to find a ring of keys. He opened the driver's side door sticking his head in. Buddy was left on the passenger seat with the nylon jacket as a bed. Buddy moved around. The Chihuahua rustled beneath the coat. The liveliness was encouraging. He looked as if he may try to stand up.

"Take it easy, Buddy."

Roger put the key in the ignition. The turn of the starter. Motor sounds were a symphony of relief.

Chapter 33

HEADLAMPS on. White flakes churned in cones of light like a shaken snow globe. The engine was warming. Roger opened the rear gate. Lady was too low to the ground and always needed to be lifted in. Cyrus normally jumped in under his own power but was too weakened by all that happened. Cyrus laid paws into the back compartment. Roger lifted him in to join Lady and shut the back. Roger circled the vehicle using a gloved hand to wipe snow off the windows.

Built up snow was cleared. A pull of the driver's side door. Roger pushed the seat back a couple of notches. So cold and stiff he found it difficult to conform his body to the driving position. Waterlogged hiking boots were nearly frozen. Aching feet. Exhaustion. He lay back, shutting his eyes. So tired, a mind going blank. Too worn out to even think. All he could do was breathe. Roger started to doze.

Warm, grateful neck licks. Roger shook his head awake. It was Cyrus. Roger stared at the Pit Bull through the rearview mirror. A right hand up, he pulled Cyrus's big head next to his. He patted and rubbed the dog's cheek. The dog who risked his life to tow him and Buddy toward shore.

"Thank goodness for you, Cyrus."

Roger looked down at Lady, who rested on her favorite spot, chest lying on the console. The Pembroke Welsh Corgi with head turned toward Roger. Her Lady smile was back. Short, quick breaths were happy pants.

"And you too, Lady! You led us to the car. If not for you ... "

Roger rubbed a grateful hand across the top of Lady's head. Buddy was now back on his feet. The Chihuahua moved his face to the front of a heater vent that pushed out the first hints of warm air. Roger placed a hand over a vent moving it back and forth in a clawing motion to loosen stiff hands. As he did, he thought of Melissa. Suddenly he found that such ponderings were a salve to a wounded heart. He looked forward to the morning when he could shovel his way to seeing her again.

The car cabin warmed. Roger opened the glove compartment. Searching fingers located a pen knife stored there. Wet, swollen, leather boots strangled each foot. Roger pushed the sharp blade underneath each stressed shoelace. A snapping sound as each pulled cord was cut. Like a hand washing a hand, he used both feet to push the boots off and peel away the wet socks. He dropped each waterlogged boot over a shoulder in a kerplunk. A bare foot revved the engine. Heated air from the lower ventilator warmed water-wrinkled, pale toes. Digits were wiggled in an effort to allow blood to flow.

Roger thought of them getting home. He planned it in his head. The dogs would be brought into the bungalow where each would receive a warm bath to remove the salt and sand. He would then fill up their bowls of food and water, allowing them to have their dinner. Then a short walk downstairs to the cellar where he would strip off all clothes and put them in the washer. After that, a hot shower would warm away any remains of the winter chill.

After getting dressed in some sweats, he would heat up the eggplant parmigiana and have his dinner before going into the bedroom to watch the game. By the time he lay down, the game would have started. He would bring Buddy into bed with him. Then he planned to do something he never did before. He would allow both Cyrus and Lady to join them on the queen-sized bed. That evening there would be no rules, only togetherness.

He pulled off the wool hat and tossed it to the seat where Buddy was. Leaning over, he looked in the mirror, flopping fingers through damp, thinning hair. Then he ran a hand over Lady's head. "You are such a good girl."

Cyrus laid a heavy head into the crick of Roger's neck. Roger rubbed the side of his face into the dog's cheek while running a palm over his head and ears. As Roger did that, Buddy enjoyed warm blasts of air streaming from the heating vent.

"And you, Cyrus. Buddy and I would still be in the ocean if not for you."

Roger held the dog's cheek affectionately to his. When Roger released the hold, Cyrus stepped back. The Pit Bull gave a woof-woof. Buddy responded with a couple of yelps. Lady's starry eyes peered up to Roger. Even she gave a little bark. He could tell what they were saying. It was dog talk. Roger knew the language. The translations were words of love, loyalty, and security. They were family.

Roger backed the car up before turning the wheel to head to the far corner of the parking lot exit. They crossed the windblown hardtop of low-lying snow waves. There was an incline to the empty highway. They needed momentum. Roger hit the accelerator, anticipating the ramp's icy conditions.

The road was dark. No other headlights. Even the park rangers were inside. Roger got to the road, turning onto the southbound lane when the Subaru fishtailed, nearly going off the road. Cyrus lost balance with the centrifugal force that pushed him sideways. A quick recovery. Cyrus returned to all fours. Buddy fell onto the floor of the passenger side, but quickly leaped back to the seat. Lady was little affected as she stayed snug on the center console. Knowing the dogs were okay, he spoke to them after a short chuckle. "Hang in there, pups. We'll be back at the house in half an hour."

A look over at Buddy, who stood on hind legs with front paws planted on the dashboard, a long stare through the windshield. It was the young Chihuahua's favorite way to ride in the car. Eyes peeled to the outside, watching everything. A Chihuahua enjoying the rush of oncoming scenery. That closed mouth expression of intensity. A co-pilot, of sorts.

Roger sometimes wondered what went on inside their heads. Even if he could not unlock that door and walk around, he was certain that each had a zest for their very existence. Dogs were smarter and more thoughtful than given credit for. He saw it in the trio. In their individual personalities. In their mannerisms. A tail wag. A head lay. Happy barks. Concern for one another. Protectors of property. Looks of pure kindness. And they were so forgiving, able to let go of most grievances. That was what amazed Roger the most. Dogs were better at surrendering the past. A Zen-likeness of living in the now.

Dogs were special animals that not only had a joy for life but delighted in loving their caretakers even more than loving themselves. They acted as beholden creatures. If you showed them love, they returned love a square root sum back. Roger experienced that

unconditional love in dogs so rarely found in humans.
A truthfulness. A loyalty. An authenticity. A true friend-
ship. Roger knew that if you wanted to see a dog's soul,
all you had to do was look in his eyes.

A hand tightly held the steering wheel as a shoeless foot pushed down the gas pedal. Wheels spun until
rubber treads reached the course road. A slight jerk
forward. The Subaru moved slow and steadily through
the storm. Buddy stayed in the standing pose, peering
into the night. No smile. Just a tail swinging side to
side.

Roger searched the darkness lying beyond the
headlight beams. In that deep blackness was something
for him. Not just a collection of countless moments or
string of connected days. Even more than single years,
but an entire lifetime. Decades that were his, a future
belonging to him and no one else. There were wants
to satisfy, adventures to trek and events to experience.
He only needed to step out to where they were, then
take them as if they were his own. A rustling tickled his
core. Doubt was pushed away, fear cast aside. Roger was
ready. A new beginning.

The blizzard raged on. Sheets of snow raced
sideways through high beams as a gusty hand of the
Nor'easter shook the car. A couple of quick yelps. A
glance at Buddy. Canine eyes fixed straight ahead.
More yelps as if warning of oncoming turbulence. A

smile spread Roger's tightened cheeks. "A tough storm, Buddy. It's a big one."

A frosty roadblock of foot-high snowdrift crossed Route 28. Roger motored the Subaru through the curling wave of white powder, causing a fun, puffy cloud to pass over the hood. Some quick Buddy yelps. A slight head tilt toward Roger. Buddy's deep pink tongue hung cheerfully from the corner of his mouth. A Chihuahua face of happiness. A canine grin proclaiming that he was the luckiest dog in the world.

"We are on our way, Buddy," said Roger through a blissful smile, "We are on our way."